THROUGH THE HAZE

KELLY KIERAN SAMPSON

ISBN: 978-1-0688013-1-0

DEDICATION

To the twelve-year-old me who didn't think it was possible,
and to Kim for reminding me it was.

And to those who are celebrating with me in spirit:
Mom, Dad, Andrew & Brian.

CHAPTER 1

He knew better than to ignore the crawling sensation. The spiders under his skin. It started with an itch, restlessness, then crept along beside him to wake him at night. If he ignored it, he'd get the shakes—sometimes just his fingers, sometimes hands and arms, other times knees giving out beneath him. Those were the subtle hints.

The first time he felt the crawling, he just climbed back into bed and waited for it to pass. For a while, that seemed to work. At least for a few days, maybe a week.

Eventually, as the feeling drove him from his bed, he'd pace his room, pace the house and, when the space became too confining, he'd pace the neighborhood. Moving seemed to work. Again, at least for a few days.

Today, it doesn't. He starts down the street, unsure of what he wants to do as his thoughts bounce back and forth.

It will pass.

But it hasn't.

Keep walking.

What if it's more? What if I'm like her?

His mother had tried to get clean, so many times. His childhood was potholed with her highs and crashes, trips to emergency, visits to clinics and halfway houses, leaving him with his uncle until she had her feet under her again. She'd come for him. She'd try to make it up to him, and the last time she had managed to do it for almost ten years before falling into the last

1

pothole. This one she wouldn't be getting out of, the small stone with last year's date engraved in it made that clear. He had vowed never to be like her, to touch drugs.

He keeps walking.

What is wrong with me?

Nothing is wrong with you.

Then why do I feel like this? Am I going crazy? Was she crazy? Is that why she did drugs: to make this stop?

You are not crazy. And you know it.

He spots a bird about six feet ahead. It hops back and forth, flies up about four feet, then drops to the ground. He watches it do this several times before he notices the cat. A calico statue, coiled. Its only movement is the tiniest twitch of the tail, while its eyes follow the bird to its four-foot mark in the air.

He looks back at the bird and wonders why it won't fly away.

The bird grows more frantic, swooping over the cat's head, closing the gap between them, careful of the cat's reach. The explosion of the cat's coiled springs and explosive jump could catch her full flight, but instead, the cat stands its ground.

He notices a small lump on the ground. He steps closer. The bird now turns on him. The cat remains stone.

He steps closer yet. The bird swoops nearer to his head. He realizes the lump is a baby bird. Half pink skin, half pinfeathers, its eyes giant grey orbs in its tiny head.

Its movements are subtle, mouth opening and closing. Its tiny chest bumps with every heartbeat. He bends and leans over the chick. The mother cries and swoops, making small gusts against his ballcap. He looks at the cat, its giant pupils now set on him, the intruder threatening to steal his meal.

"Can't say it looks that tasty," he says to the cat. It stares. A small growl in reply.

He reaches down and touches the bird, the pad of his pointing finger almost the same size as the baby bird's head. It is soft and smooth. He can feel the heat of its body and wonders how that can be since it is half-naked.

"But you are supposed to be tucked in under your mother, aren't you?"

That's when he tilts his head towards the adult bird and its gallant effort to save its young.

"How will you get it back to your nest?" he asks the tiny bomber, knowing that she can't. She is not like a dog that can lift with its mouth. It will lie here while its mother tries to protect it, until her baby's last breath. But then how long will the mother stay? How long until she believes her baby is gone for good? Then the cat can come and claim its prize. Will the cat eat it? Or will it lose desire once the fight is gone?

He looks at the cat still watching its potential meal. He has the power right now: let the cat get it, chase the cat away, leave the two to nature again, or scoop up the little one and find its nest.

He places his hands on his knees, slowly uncurling his spine until he is straight. The cat's head moves as it watches.

"Eenie. Meenie. Miney. Mo," he says, as he points from one to the next of the trio, then drops his hands and steps forward to crush tiny bones beneath his foot.

He lifts his foot, pivots, and heads for home. His shakes are gone.

CHAPTER 2

As soon as Tilly opened the door, she knew something was wrong.

"Mom, I'm home," she called from the front door, closing it slowly behind her. She waited for her mother's reply, which was always followed by a barrage of questions about her day at school or volleyball practice. Instead, the click of the door closing echoed in her ears.

The house was dark.

"Mom?"

Silence.

"Mom?"

The empty house sent a chill down her spine. She shuddered.

"Dad?"

More silence.

"Where is everyone, and why the hell is it so dark in here? It's only five o'clock,"

Maybe they've gone to pick up Nathan, she thought to herself, afraid to break the eerie silence. Her father always picked her brother up at his after-school program on his way home from work. Nathan had entered the program last summer to help him prepare for junior high. Their parents worried about his social skills. "A twelve-year-old needs friends," her mother would say. "Real ones," added under her breath.

Had her mother decided to go too? Maybe Nathan had a baseball game after school. He didn't play on a team, but he had

4

watched the games so often the team had adopted him as their bat boy. He was an unofficial Eastman Badger. Although it had irritated Tilly to have to babysit her brother while he helped during the games, the Badgers' pitcher, Bisson, was pretty cute. His eyes were so dark she was sure they were black, but her best friend Angela had insisted that people couldn't have black eyes. Now that Nathan had a job as batboy with the team, her parents went to all the games to cheer the team on, not needing her anymore.

Standing in the silence of the house, she felt a little annoyed, frustrated that no one had bothered to let her know where they were. She reached into her back pocket, to check her phone for any text messages. Her fingers found her pocket empty. Her heart skipped a beat. Had she lost it? She forced herself to stay calm, at least until she checked her school bag. She looked around for her bag. It was not on the bench beside the closet door, where she usually dropped it right after coming home. Tilly began to question everything, starting from the minute she'd arrived at home. Had she lost track of time?

She checked her watch.

Her wrist was bare.

"My watch?" Her voice rebounded off the walls as if accusing her of something. Her right hand instinctively touched where her watch should have been.

She felt her heart skip again.

"I know I put it on this morning. Oh my God, did I lose it? Did I forget it in the gym?" Her parents had given it to her on her last birthday, and she'd worn it every day since. It was more like a bracelet, with its band of three braided strips of leather, each with a charm. Love. Dream. Believe. The back had her family's names engraved on it.

"No, it has to be in my room. It has to be." She started for the stairs.

As Tilly's hand grabbed the banister, however, she forgot all about her watch. For a split second, she smelled dirt or grease. Her mouth went dry. Her flight response was overwhelming, but flight from what? Then, she thought she heard her mother crying.

5

"Mom?" she called to the dark landing above. Nothing.

"Nathan?" Tilly heard the pitch in her voice rise.

Tilly was not afraid of the dark, yet she hesitated.

"Guys?" she whispered.

She knew she had to go upstairs. She took a deep breath and slowly let it out, shaking her arms and shoulders as she did.

"Ok, stop being so stupid, Tilly!"

She took her first step. As her weight shifted onto her foot, the stair seemed to creak louder than its usual protest. The sound made Tilly stop. She felt exposed, like a thief about to be caught; but when the creak didn't bring anyone running, she took the next step.

The next stair made the same noisy complaint as the first. She stopped. She realized her heart was racing. She stood frozen on the step. The scenes of every scary movie she'd ever watched flashed in her head.

"Just stop it, Tilly," she scolded herself. "You are being ridiculous." She wiped her hands on her jeans.

Her words did not completely remove her creepy feeling, but she forced herself up the rest of the stairs, the squeak of each one building in her ears like a drum roll. Standing on the landing, Tilly looked down the staircase—she had never heard the stairs make so much noise.

"Everything's exaggerated when you're scared," she told herself with another set of movie scenes running through her head as proof. She pushed the thought aside as she turned on the landing.

"Anyone home?"

She slowly walked down the hall, the runner feeling extra soft under her feet, closing around them, absorbing the sound of her footsteps.

Reaching Nathan's room first, she turned and peeked in the door. His room was empty. Even in the darkening room, she could see that it was as meticulously tidy as always, except for a shirt folded over his footboard and a pair of dress shoes by the base of the bed.

Weird, Tilly thought.

Nathan hated anything on his bed, and he would never put his shoes on the floor. Shoes always went on the mat inside his closet—only his slippers were allowed in his room, always placed at the edge, never on, the mat beside his bed.

She turned her attention back to the hall. At the end, across from each other were two doors. On the left, her room. On the right, her parents'. She decided to bypass hers and went to her parents' room.

Standing at the doorway she was suddenly overwhelmed with sadness. All at once, she missed her parents and wanted to see them more than anything.

"They're just picking Nathan up," she reassured herself, trying to shake the feeling. Trying to convince herself that was where they were.

She looked around their room but didn't go in.

The bed was made, but obviously her father had made it—you could always tell by the way he flipped the blankets over and gave them a quick iron with his hand to get rid of lumps. When Tilly's mom made a bed, it was perfect. And they wondered where Nathan got his neatness from.

Her mother's bedside table had a photo of Nathan, her father, and her holding a birthday cake; beside that, a box of tissues and a pile of used ones scattered over it.

"Yuk."

Her father's table looked like it usually did: a tall stack of books and magazines, half a glass of water, and his alarm clock. The numbers made Tilly stop.

7:50.

"What?"

She blinked.

7:50.

She spun and ran to her own room, to her own nightstand.

7:51.

She sank to her bed, grabbed the clock and pulled it to her lap.

But I just got home from school. Did the power go out?

She scanned her room looking for her watch. With no sign of it, she put the clock back, then she headed for the kitchen, racing down the stairs, not caring what noise they made this time.

In the kitchen she looked over at the microwave.

7:55.

"What the hell? Where is everyone?"

Tilly's thoughts swirled around in her head, making her dizzy. She sat on a stool.

Maybe they had an appointment. Yeah, they must have told me, and I forgot. Maybe they're seeing a new doctor for Nathan. They'll be home soon.

At night? It's almost Nathan's bedtime.

Maybe they left a note.

She flipped the light switch by the door, flooding the kitchen with light, and was a little surprised to see dishes in the sink and a box of Nathan's favorite cereal sitting on the counter. She picked up the cereal box, put it away, then loaded the dirty dishes into the dishwasher.

With the sink empty and the counter cleared, out of habit she scanned the room for any other dirty dishes. She spotted her father's mug on the computer desk next to the patio doors. The shelf above it held a framed photo of her, ziplining. She had been so scared that she planned never to do that again. Another frame held an image of Nathan posing in his bat boy uniform, King Arthur, their old cat sitting tall behind him, looking like he was trying to say "cheese." The grey tabby had died six months later. Cancer.

"Oh, Dad," she said as she reached for the mug. "Mom would kick your ass for not putting this away. You so owe me."

When she lifted it, the sheet of paper that it was sitting on came with it.

"Coasters, Dad," Tilly grumbled and pulled the paper off the mug and set it back on the desk. A perfect brown circle smudged her father's notes. She knew the notes were his handwriting because he seemed to be the only one able to understand it; he liked to call it his personal shorthand.

It looked like it said Dr. Dubé with a bunch of numbers scribbled below his or her name.

"I knew it," Tilly said aloud, as if she had just proven her point to someone. "They've taken Nathan to a new doctor."

But this late at night?

Her stomach tightened as she tried to read the rest of the note. It looked like Medical Examiners…Questions…Anytime. That was all she could make out.

A scene flashed in Tilly's mind. Chairs knocked over, a broken red bowl, green apples scattered all over the floor, a phone receiver lying among them.

She blinked and looked at the island's counter, looking for the bowl of fruit her mother kept there, always encouraging healthy snacks.

There was no bowl.

She looked at the kitchen floor again. It was spotless.

Panic hit.

Grandma! Something must have happened to Grandma!

CHAPTER 3

Tilly almost dropped to the floor when the phone rang. She turned to the island and reached for it, but the cradle was empty. She spun around looking for the receiver, knocking her father's note off the table. With her heart slamming against her ribs, she scrambled to find the phone, then raced into the living room for the other receiver, trying to get to it before voicemail kicked in.

"Hello?"

The other end was silent.

"Hello!"

Static answered Tilly at first, followed by the 'beep' to begin voicemail, then her grandmother spoke.

"I tried your cell phone, but you must have it turned off."

Tilly's body melted at the sound of her grandmother's voice.

"No Gram, I think it's in my bag. I didn't hear it ring." Her breathing was slowly returning to normal. "Grandma, are you ok?" She heard her voice crack.

"I guess your appointment is running late. I'll call you in the morning."

"Gram, it's me, Tilly. Mom and Dad haven't come home yet but—" before Tilly could finish her sentence, her grandmother hung up.

"Gram?" Surprised at being cut off, Tilly hung up. Her grandmother was slowly losing touch— *old timers.* Well, at least now she knew where her family was. They'd be home after Nathan's doctor's appointment. Everything was all right after all.

10

Tilly walked slowly back to the kitchen, pulling the elastic out of her hair, and let the hair fall around her shoulders. She slipped the elastic around her wrist.

8:03.

"Well, I might as well make something to eat," she said. Her head hurt, and her body felt strange. Her limbs felt light, like when she was floating in the swimming pool, yet heavy at the same time, forcing her to pay attention to every movement. Her swimming coach called it *ungrounded*. Food might ground her.

Too impatient to cook anything, Tilly pulled out a package of chocolate cupcakes.

Don't ruin your supper, she heard her mother's voice inside her head; but being home alone had its advantages.

"This would really get mom fired up," she said, putting the cupcake into a bowl. She went to a different cupboard. Grabbing a bag of chocolate bar bits, she sprinkled a generous handful over the cupcake.

Retrieving ice cream from the freezer she spooned out two giant scoops, which then meant two more handfuls of chocolate bar bits were needed.

"Perfect." And she took a soup spoon from the drawer.

She stuffed a heaping spoonful into her mouth.

But Tilly couldn't eat her work of art. Right after she swallowed, her throat tightened, and her stomach flipped. She ran to the bathroom.

Bent over the toilet, hair gathered in her hand, she heaved. But nothing came up. Her stomach lurched again. She hated throwing up more than anything in the world. Once more, nothing. Body shaking, she sat quietly on the cold, tiled floor waiting for everything to settle, trying to remember what she'd had for lunch.

Thinking didn't help.

"Well, this sucks," she mumbled slumped against the bathroom wall. "Get the house to myself and I'm partying with the toilet. Big whoop."

When she felt it was safe, she stood up slowly. Still shaky, but at least her stomach didn't protest.

She left the bathroom and returned to the kitchen to clean up her mess, to remove the evidence of her food crimes and avoid a lecture from her mother. She put the chocolate bar bits away then picked up her bowl and carried it to the garbage can. Stepping on the pedal, the lid lifted. She bent to scrape the cupcake mixture into the garbage. Her body stiffened at the sight of something red sticking out from under tinfoil and Styrofoam containers.

Like a spectator, she watched her own hand stretch into the bin, reaching for the chunk of red—the image of the bowl falling to the ground, shattering, spilling apples across the floor filled her head. Her heart felt as if it had been pierced with the tiny shards. Yanking her hand back, instinctively grabbing it and clutching it to her chest, she stepped back. The lid slamming down.

She looked around the kitchen that now felt abandoned, dangerous. The spinning in her head started again, blood rushing behind her ears making shushing sounds, like an old-fashioned steam engine from her father's Western movies. She stepped on the pedal of the waste bin again. The red was gone. As she scraped the cupcake into the bin, the spoon caught the edge of the bowl, flipping it from her hand, sending it to the floor where it broke into three large chunks.

"Shit!"

She gathered the pieces and dumped them in the can. Tossing the spoon in the dishwasher, she rushed across the kitchen to the stairs, ignoring their loud creaking.

By the time Tilly reached her room, her head throbbed. She dropped onto her bed and picked up her favorite teddy-bear.

"Where is everyone, Simon?" she asked her furry friend. "What's going on?" But Simon just stared at her with blank eyes, always interested in what she had to say, never replying. She absent-mindedly bounced him on her lap. "Maybe they texted me." But then she remembered that she couldn't find her phone. Too tired to look for it, she lay back on the bed. She hugged Simon close to her chest as she curled into a ball.

"Tilly, where are you? You need to come home," Tilly's mother cried. Her voice was full of fear. "Tilly, please," she begged.

"I'm right here, Mom," Tilly answered.

"I told you not to go anywhere alone! Why didn't you listen to me?"

"But I'm right here," Tilly yelled to her mother. "Mom, please!"

She felt lost. Alone. Scared. She couldn't move.

"Tilly!"

"Mom," she cried, as tears streamed down her face.

"NO!" her mother howled.

Tilly woke with a jolt. She sat up, gaze darting around the room. Her body was stiff. Her chest hurt. It felt as if her heart had been replaced with a boulder. Then she remembered. Her mother. She had heard her mother calling her.

"Mom," she yelled, leaping off the bed and sprinting across the hall, rushing into her parents' room. When she saw her parents, she felt relief wash over her. She wasn't alone anymore.

They were asleep in the dark room lit only with quick flashes of light from the television, its sound turned down low.

"Mom?" Tilly whispered.

She took a few steps closer.

"Mom," she whispered a little louder. Hadn't her mother just called her? Had she dreamt it? She walked up to the side of the bed.

"Where were you?" she asked her mother. Her heart ached but she was so happy to see her.

Tilly reached out to touch her mother, to make sure she was really there. Her mother looked like she was in pain, like she was having a bad dream. Just before Tilly touched her, her mother groaned.

Tilly pulled her hand back.

"Mom?"

"Tilly."

It was muffled but she was sure she had heard it.

"Yes, Mom. It's me." She was surprised at the excitement in her voice.

"Oh, Tilly! I miss you!" her mother said again.

"Mom, why didn't you come in and say goodnight when you got home?" A sudden loneliness began to override Tilly's excitement. Tilly was surprised at how she felt like a five-year-old who wanted to crawl into bed with her parents after a bad dream.

Her mother didn't answer. If she had been awake, she wasn't now.

Tilly knelt at the side of the bed.

"Mom?" She reached and placed her hand on her mother's arm, needing to touch her. She felt a sharp prick at the ends of her fingers, which pulsed through her body like the snap of an electric shock. It stabbed at her temples.

Her mother groaned, whimpered, then mumbled something before rolling over, settling back into sleep. Tilly had a rush of emotions… feeling abandoned, rejected.

She stood, fighting back tears, watching her parents sleep, listening to their breathing, her father snoring slightly.

She looked around the room, catching quick glimpses through the flashes from the television. Used tissues still covered her mother's nightstand; and on her father's, the TV remote sat on a stack of books. Her dad's outdoor jacket was draped on a chair just outside the closet. She looked at the television and thought she saw herself on the screen; but whatever she had seen, it was now gone. She walked closer to the TV, but with only a few steps to go, it turned itself off.

She spun around to look at her parents, both still asleep. They had set the TV's sleep timer. Tilly felt loneliness returning, seeping in through her skin and into her bones, into her soul. It was a chill she felt she might never be able to warm. The cold made her feel more than just lonely: she felt like the only person on the planet. Lost.

Now, Tilly became aware of how heavy her body felt. She struggled to stand as the weight of her limbs and her chest dragged her toward the floor. Perhaps her cries as she dropped would wake her parents so they could scoop her up like they did when she was little. She fought the urge to fall. She was no longer that child. Instead, she shifted her body, dragging her feet as she left her parent's room.

She felt a pull, a lifeline. She turned right down the hall and headed to Nathan's room.

From his door, Tilly could hear the soothing sounds of waves coming from his amazing bedside lamp as it sent colorful star silhouettes floating across his walls.

Tilly fought the urge to wake him. She knew he could cheer her up; but knowing how hard it was for him to fall asleep, she didn't dare. You didn't mess with Nathan's routines. Instead, she stood by Nathan's bed and looked around his room.

The room had been set up exactly as he wanted it, how he needed it. It was his sanctuary. Unlike her parent's room, Nathan's room made her feel peaceful, contented, at rest. She stood quietly and watched the stars glide across the walls, dance over his drawings. She listened to the waves, imagining them washing over her. Feeling calmer, she turned to head back to her own room. That's when she noticed a new drawing on the bulletin board beside Nathan's bed. She leaned in to get a better look as stars flickered across the drawing.

It was of her parents. Her father had his arm around her mother and her mother looked very sad, while Nathan stood off to the side, waving.

But then she couldn't help lifting her hand to her mouth when she noticed who Nathan was waving at. Was that supposed to be her? He had drawn her up in the right-hand corner, all on her own. She was drawn in muted tones, softer outlines. She was waving back.

She moved her hand to the paper and ran her fingers over her watercolor self. She felt her heart skip.

"Wings?"

She jumped at the sound of Nathan shifting in his bed and watched to see if she had woken him, hoping she had. She wanted to ask him about his drawing.

"Nathan." His name barely audible to her ears, she regretted calling to him as soon as she had done it. She knew she was being selfish. When he didn't respond, she quietly slipped out into the hall.

Back in her room, Tilly changed into pajamas, wanting to feel normal again. The same questions kept playing in her head: why didn't anyone wake her when they came home? Where had they been and why hadn't they said goodnight? For an instant, Tilly thought about going back to her parents' bedroom and asking her mother these exact questions and telling her how angry she was that nobody had said anything to her. But in Tilly's house, anger wasn't allowed.

Tilly thought about how even though she had been alone all evening, her mother always seemed to be inside her head. This half-comforted, half-annoyed the hell out of her. She climbed into bed and promised herself that she was going to give her mother a piece of her mind in the morning.

CHAPTER 4

It takes weeks for him to earn the squirrels' trust: sitting in the grass, bag full of peanuts, tossing them a few feet away. Slowly they grow accustomed to him sitting there, at first grabbing the nuts and dashing away to eat them; but eventually, they sit near him and eat their prize, keeping a watchful eye on him. Two feet become one; twelve inches shrink to six. The squirrels stretch their slender bodies, extending tiny arms to grab the nut, still in the shell, in time, feeling safe, they hop up in front of him to pluck the nut from his fingers. Their tiny digits curl, tickling his finger as they wrap around the peanut, their nails gently scraping across his.

These weeks of waiting make him ache. The itch pushes to rush the process, the spiders under his skin now a swarm of fire ants, stinging.

He tosses a nut to get their attention, and they start to gather. Another nut draws them closer. He feels for the knife tucked under his thigh to ground him while hairs on his arms stand to attention. He pulls out another nut. With the nut pinched between his fingers, he rests his arm across his knee, letting his hand hang.

The first squirrel takes the nut and hops to the side.

He straightens slightly; replaces the nut.

A second squirrel hesitates inches from him. It looks around, stretches, then sits. A third hops past it without pause and reaches for the nut.

It screams as his knife plunges into its slim body, piercing heart and lungs.

The other squirrels scatter as the itch goes away.

CHAPTER 5

Tilly woke to sunlight streaming through the blinds on her window. She felt drained but was anxious to see her family. She had missed talking to them last night. Ever since school yesterday, all she wanted was to feel at home again.

She jumped out of bed and rushed downstairs ready to hug everyone. She knew her mother would wonder what had gotten into her, but she didn't care.

The kitchen was empty.

She looked around and saw traces of life, proof that someone had been here. There were new dirty dishes in the sink.

When did that become acceptable around here?

An empty cup sat on the counter with a note:

> Try to eat something.
> I will call you later.
> I love you.
> Wil

Her mother's cup. Tilly had given it to her last year for Mother's Day. Ordered through the photo counter, it had a picture of Nathan and her making faces. The caption said, *Just like Mom.*

The cup was empty. Still clean.

She turned and bolted up the stairs to her parents' room. The blinds were drawn and the room dark.

The sight of her mother in bed stopped her in her tracks.

"Mom?" she called from the door, voice shaky.

When her mother didn't answer, she went to the side of her bed.

"Mom. Are you, all right?"

She wanted to reach out and shake her, but memories of the needle feeling in her fingers last night kept her hands at her side. Had her mother moved since last night? She looked around the room and saw her mother's clothes piled on the chair in the corner. She stood beside her mother's bed, listening to her breathe.

"Mom. Are you sick?" Hoping the sound of her voice would wake her. "Would you like me to get you something?" She looked at the nightstand, and among the pile of tissues, she saw a glass of water and a bottle of pills lying on its side.

She lifted the bottle and tried to read the label.

She squinted, but it was too dark to read. She walked the few steps to the window, lifting the corner of the blind before she could make out any of it.

Cenersys 1 mg
Lorazepam
Take as needed. Do not exceed five pills daily.

Tilly opened the bottle and saw half a dozen round pills, with Cs on them. She snapped the lid back on and looked at the label again.

Quantity: 20

She looked at her mother. "What are these for?" expecting an answer from the sleeping woman. She didn't remember seeing the pills on her stand last night.

"Mom, when did you get these?" she snapped at her. "When did you start taking these? They're almost gone!" She touched her mother's shoulder, shaking it, wanting to wake her. She ignored the needles biting her fingertips.

Her mother groaned and tried to shrug her off.

Tilly grabbed her shoulder and shook harder. Tilly's fingers no longer tingled, her hand was now numb, her arm getting heavy, like it had fallen asleep.

"Why are you still in bed?" Her temples started to burn. "Why won't you answer me?"

Her mother made a gagging sound. Tilly broke her grip. "Can't you just leave me alone for a minute, I feel like I'm going to be sick!" her mother said as she rolled over, turning her back to Tilly. She heard her mother say, "leave me alone," while the rest of her words slowly fell off to a mumble.

Tilly could feel her jaw tensing, her face getting hot. Her temper rose.

"What's your problem anyway?"

"Tilly?" Her mother's back was still to her.

"Forget it, Mom!" She felt her temper getting the best of her. She left the room, trying to push her anger down—nothing good ever happened when she lost her temper. Losing her temper was swift and impulsive and usually meant a lot of apologizing afterward.

As she walked across the hall, she heard her mother call again, "Tilly?"

Tilly bit her tongue, something she had become very good at in the last couple of years, thanks to Nathan.

How many times had he run to his room crying because she had snapped at him for constantly chattering with his imaginary friends while she tried to watch TV, or embarrassing her when she had friends over?

Back in her room, she checked the time. 10:30.

"Great. I'm late," she growled. "And where is my goddamn watch?" She rifled through her jewelry box, then her underwear drawer. Still no watch. She slammed the drawer hard enough to make the necklaces on the mirror rattle. "And I forgot to charge my phone," she growled, letting her irritation grow, looking for reasons to let it, like how she must have tossed it in her school bag at some point yesterday instead of charging it.

She started grabbing socks and underwear from her dresser, her jeans off the chair, throwing them all onto the bed. She dug in the closet for a clean shirt. Finding one, she settled on her bed and started to put on her socks. She would at least be able to make it to her afternoon classes.

"Tilly," the sound of her mother's voice snapped her attention to the doorway. Mom was standing there in a nightgown, one hand on the door jamb.

"Mom." Her anger quickly forgotten.

"Oh, Tilly," her mother said, still standing in the doorway.

"Man! Am I happy to see you!" Tilly felt her shoulders dropping as her entire body relaxed at the sight and sound of her mother.

"You need something to wear," her mother mumbled as she walked into Tilly's room and headed for the closet.

"What?" Tilly stood up. "I'm wearing this." Her hand hovered over the pile of clothes on the bed. A sock in her hand.

Her mother didn't respond. She walked past Tilly to the closet and started pushing hangers back and forth.

"Mom, what are you doing?" Her frustration was starting to return; she bit it back. "Did I do something wrong?" It was changing to concern. "Why won't you talk to me?"

"You need something pretty. Maybe that prom dress we were looking at in Stedman's last week. Oh, I knew we should have bought it."

"Mom, what are you talking about?" Tilly started towards the closet. "Prom's weeks away."

"No, this is nice," she said and pulled out a hanger with a black and white sundress hanging on it. "More like you."

"What's that supposed to mean?"

"And a nice sweater, that black one you have." She turned back to the closet.

"I'm not wearing that! I don't know what you think I'll be doing today." Tilly sat on her bed, tugging on her sock. She muttered, "I don't know what your problem is today," half wanting her mother to hear.

Her mother dug deeper into her closet; Tilly watched her for a moment longer.

"Do I have an appointment or something?" She sorted through her memory. She didn't remember seeing anything for today in her phone's calendar. Annoyed again to be without it, she'd find it and check it once she was dressed.

"Found it." Her mother pulled the sweater off the hanger and wrapped it around the one holding the dress. "Perfect," she said. She pulled it to her chest, protectively wrapping her arms around it.

"What the heck, Mom?" Tilly felt her frustration returning.

Her mother stopped. She looked at Tilly. She saw her mother's eyes start to fill with tears.

"Mom?" Tilly softened her voice, regretting everything she'd said. Her mother had a way of making her feel ungrateful. Insensitive.

"Oh, Tilly!" Her mother walked towards her, stopping at the foot of the bed. She picked up the t-shirt Tilly had dropped on the bed a moment ago.

"Oh, Tilly," quieter this time. Her mother dropped the t-shirt and threw the dress on Tilly's bed, then left the room. Tilly heard the door to her mother's room slam as she went after her.

"Mom," reaching for the doorknob, "I'm sorry?" But her body collided with the door. "What the . . . ?"

Tilly looked down at her hand. For a moment she thought she saw her hand go through the doorknob. She felt lightheaded, limbs heavy again. She realized she wasn't breathing and took in a big gulp of air. She tried to let it out slowly but only managed half before inhaling another large gulp. The door seemed to blur in front of her.

"*Stop it, Tilly. You are being ridiculous. Breathe.*" She took a deep breath and slowly released it this time. "*In through your nose,*" she took another breath, *and out through your mouth.* She released it. "*Just like Nathan does.*" She put her hand on the doorknob, turning it as the phone rang.

Tilly heard her mother answer.

She slowly opened the door, poked her head in.

"Yes, I'm up," she informed the caller.

"Is that Dad?" Tilly asked, stepping into the room.

"No. No, you don't need to come home," she said as she sat on the edge of her bed, her back to Tilly.

"Mom."

Her mother shifted but wouldn't look at her.

"No, I'm all right."

"Mom. Can I talk to him?"

"You need to stop telling me what to do, Wil. I'll deal with this my way," her mother snapped.

Tilly watched her mother pick up the bottle of pills.

"Don't worry. I know... I know."

Her mother cradled the receiver between shoulder and ear as she lined up the arrows on the bottle and popped the top off. "I know, I know," she said as she continued to cradle the phone on her shoulder. She dumped the contents of the bottle into her palm then slowly let the pills slide back into it while her thumb held back two. She then returned the bottle to the nightstand and put the pills into her mouth.

"Yes, Wil," she answered, with the pills still in her mouth. "I'm sorry too," she said through clenched teeth.

"Mom."

She lifted the glass of water that was on the bedside table, took a sip and swallowed the pills. "I'm going back to bed for a bit. I promise I'll eat something when I get up."

Tilly was about to leave the room to get the receiver from her room when the sound of her name made her stop.

"I was looking for something for Tilly to wear." Another pause. "Yes. I promise. I love you too." She hung up, pulling her feet up onto the bed and lying back.

"Mom, what's wrong with you?" Tilly walked to the side of the bed.

The phone rang again. Tilly looked at it, reading the caller ID. Mrs. Patterson, a neighbor five houses down. Tilly watched as her mother read the name.

"Just leave me alone!" she barked at the phone. "Everyone, just leave me alone."

"Mom!"

The phone kept ringing.

"I can't take much more of this! I just need everyone to leave me alone. Please. Stop."

"Fine, Mom. Stay in bed then." Tilly could feel her body start to shake in frustration. "You think you're the only one pissed off right now? I am so mad at you, I could scream." As much as she wanted answers, she knew she needed to leave. "Don't think I'm not going to talk to Dad about this," she said as she walked towards the doorway. Her father let her feel her emotions rather than stuffing them away, even anger. Especially anger.

"I'm going to school," she announced as she left the room, the door slamming behind her. "And thanks for making me late."

She heard her mother drop the phone, but Tilly kept walking.

CHAPTER 6

Tilly arrived at school just in time to hear the bell and watch the halls clear out. She put her jacket in her locker, grabbed her books for class, and slipped into the classroom.

"You're late," her English teacher said without looking up.

When Tilly opened her mouth to speak, someone else's voice answered.

"Sorry, Ms. Gardner," the voice said.

Tilly turned to see James standing in the doorway. She watched him cross the room and slide into his seat. She snapped her mouth shut and found her desk.

"Take out your novels," Ms. Gardner said as she picked up her battered copy of *Lord of the Flies*. "I'd like you to read the last two chapters today as silent reading, because tomorrow you'll be discussing it in groups in preparation for your test." Then she returned to her desk, sat, and began to mark a stack of papers.

Last two chapters? But we only started the book a week ago.

Tilly looked around at her classmates. They all seemed to be comfortable with the assignment. She considered putting her hand up but quickly dismissed the idea at the thought of everyone laughing at her. Instead, she picked up her copy and opened it to her bookmark. And she had thought she was ahead of everyone.

She started the first line, but the words just couldn't seem to penetrate. After realizing she had read the same line three times, she gave up. It was only hurting her head. Feeling left behind was not a feeling she was used to.

"Psst, Sanjay," she whispered to the boy in the seat in front of her.

He didn't respond.

"Sanjay," she whispered a little louder.

Nothing.

This time she kicked his chair.

Sanjay looked down at his chair legs. He looked around, then pulled the chair closer to his desk, quietly returning to his book.

"Great. You ignoring me, too?" she mumbled under her breath. "Jerk."

Tilly shifted in her seat.

"Alexis," she quietly called to the girl on her left.

Alexis ran her thumb over her lower lip with her other hand spreading her book between her thumb and little finger.

"Alexis, what chapter are you on?"

Alexis looked up from her book, licked the tip of her index and turned the page. The book settled between her thumb and finger again, and she went back to rubbing her lip.

As each second passed, Tilly felt further behind. She was starting to panic. She had never failed at anything before in her life and she wasn't about to now.

Digging in her pencil case, she pulled out a little pink eraser and tossed it at her.

It bounced off her classmate's arm and landed in the aisle between them. Alexis glanced at her arm, brushed her hand down it, then returned to her book.

Tilly stood up, walked up the aisle and picked up the eraser. When she turned, she saw a red-headed boy sitting in her seat. "Matthew?" They had been friends through elementary school until he skipped ahead a grade. He went to junior high while she stayed behind and started grade six. It hadn't ended their friendship, but it was enough to set them in different circles. And then the worst had happened a few weeks ago. In this moment, she realized how much she had missed him.

He smiled at her.

"Hey, Tilly."

"Matthew?" She felt a quiver run down her legs; she tightened her muscles to stay standing. "But... aren't you—"

"—Dead?" The red-headed boy sat smiling at her.

She glanced around the room, looking to see if anyone else had noticed him. Or her. No one was paying attention. She felt not just light-headed, but as if her whole body was a helium balloon no longer tethered.

"Am I going crazy?" She knew it was a ridiculous question. If he answered her, no matter what he said, it would mean yes, she was definitely crazy. She couldn't help herself. "But you're ...supposed to be dead?"

The bell sounded.

Everyone was up and out of the classroom within seconds, heading to their next class. Tilly followed instinctively. Needing to put a little space between her and the boy who couldn't possibly have been sitting in her desk, talking to her.

In the hall, Tilly spotted her best friend heading down the hall.

"Angela!" She yelled over the clamor of the other students.

Angela kept walking.

"Angela, wait up!"

"She can't hear you."

Tilly spun around to see Matthew close behind her.

"I'm sorry, Tilly."

When Tilly turned back, Angela was gone.

Everyone seemed too busy for her today. Everything kept moving too fast. She needed everyone to stop so she could catch up to them. The sound of the lockers slamming, feet shuffling, so many voices vibrating in her head all overwhelmed her. And now she was looking at a dead boy. She needed to get away, fast.

Tilly ran down the hall and burst through the front doors out into the deserted schoolyard. She rushed through the gates, and as she rounded the corner, she almost collided with a woman and her dog. The spotted terrier lunged for her, barking, and baring its teeth. Tilly jumped to the side to avoid it.

"Francis," the woman yelled and tugged on the little dog's leash. "Bad boy," she said in a voice reserved for toddlers and small animals.

Francis protested his shortened leash but then gave up and trotted beside his owner as they continued their journey. The dog looked back at Tilly one more time, sneezed, then let out a final yap.

Looking into the little dog's eyes, Tilly felt whole.

"Stop being so silly," the dog's owner scolded in a playful voice. "There's nothing there."

Tilly's heart sank.

Nothing. What did the woman mean, *nothing*?

Tilly turned into the park just before her house instead of continuing home. She made her way across the grass towards the swings. Settling on the middle one, she slowly pushed with her toes to get it moving. As she picked up momentum, she closed her eyes and let the gentle wind of her movement blow on her face. She pumped the air with her legs, going higher, releasing the last few days.

"So?"

Tilly almost fell off.

Opening her eyes, she saw Matthew standing in front of her.

She closed her eyes again, pumping her legs harder.

"You're not crazy."

She hummed as loud as she could, leaning back, letting momentum move her struggle to block the memory of her parents telling her about Matthew's death.

"You know I'm dead." He leaned back on one foot, his hands in his back pockets.

She concentrated on hanging on.

"I've got all day," he said.

"If I can hear you, I must be crazy." She kept her eyes closed and let gravity slow her. "Cause if I'm not crazy then…." She started to hum again until it turned into mumbling.

"Or you can stop so we can talk about this."

"I'm definitely crazy," she said, dropping her feet, letting them drag, slowing her to a stop. She didn't have the strength to fight anymore; she barely had the strength to hold herself up.

They sat silently, Tilly digging her shoes in the dirt.

She dropped her shoulders and let out a sigh. "Sorry," her shoulders dropped a little further. "I shouldn't say crazy." She paused, fighting the thoughts in her head, "But she's right," scarcely above a whisper.

"Who's right?"

"The lady with the dog." She let go of the swing's chains and let her hands drop to her lap. "I'm nothing."

"You are *not* nothing."

Tilly couldn't focus on his words. There were too many thoughts bursting inside her head. What if she was imagining Matthew? What if she wasn't? What if she was dead, like him? She wanted to squeeze her skull, to crush every *what if* scenario playing out, every denial, and let truth claw its way to the top of it all. This cyclone threatened to pick her up and carry her away. And she was so tired, she was almost willing to let it.

It was several minutes before Matthew spoke again.

"Come with me?"

"Where?" She wasn't sure she could handle much more.

"Just over there." He pointed to a woman and her infant son.

"Why?"

He put out his hand. Was she supposed to take it?

Refusing his hand, she wrapped her arms around herself.

Matthew led her over to the woman and boy. The woman lifted her son up on the slide, as high as she could reach, and slid him down, never taking her hands off him.

"Matthew," Tilly said suspiciously. They didn't belong here.

Matthew walked up to the boy's mother and waved his hand in front of her face.

"Matthew," Tilly whispered.

The little boy smiled a single tooth smile at Matthew.

"Watch this," Matthew said. As the little boy slid down Matthew jumped in front of the bottom of the slide and did his impression of a peek-a-boo. The boy laughed.

Matthew looked at Tilly.

"So." She had no idea what he was trying to prove.

Matthew put up his finger signaling her to wait. He then put his hands over the boy's mother's eyes, Tilly noticed he didn't touch her. The little boy looked worried; but when Matthew dropped his hands and yelled peek-a-boo, the little boy screeched in delight, clapping his hands.

"Try it, Tilly." Matthew stepped back.

Tilly shook her head.

"Aw, come on, it's fun."

Matthew played peek-a-boo again and the little boy squealed once more.

"You really like the slide today," the boy's mother said.

Matthew gently pinched a small tuft of the mother's hair between his thumb and finger and lifted it. The woman shook her head as if shooing off a fly. The boy giggled.

Matthew did it again. This time he dodged her arm as she lifted it and waved it over her head.

"You think that's funny, do you?" the woman said and waved her arm again, but the boy looked at Matthew.

Lifting her hair again, the boy's body jiggled as he laughed.

"You need to try it," he said to Tilly.

Tilly couldn't resist this time, captivated by the little boy's happiness, the sound of his laughter filling her heart. She attempted a half-hearted peek-a-boo, afraid to look silly in front of Matthew. The boy smiled.

"You gotta do better than that!" Matthew said.

The boy looked from Tilly to Matthew and back to Tilly.

Tilly squatted then placed her hands over her eyes. "Ummm," then yanked them away. "Peek-a-boo!" Smiling as large as she could.

The boy squealed this time.

"There you go," Matthew said proudly. "See? You're *not* nothing."

Lost in the silly game, for the moment Tilly forgot about everything but the child's laughter.

Until the little boy reached up for Tilly's hand.

"NO!" Matthew yelled.

Too late to stop her hand reaching out, Tilly took the little boy's hand.

The boy froze. His face went blank. His little body twitched, then he threw up all over himself and started to cry.

Tilly stumbled backward, releasing the tiny hand. Her arm pulsed. There was a dull hum inside her head that blurred her sight.

"What happened?" Her vision started to clear. "Is he okay?"

She went to touch him again, wanting to soothe him, but Matthew grabbed her wrist, sending tiny sparks up her arm, like mini fireworks under her skin. It wasn't unpleasant.

"Don't."

Letting go of her, he stepped in between Tilly and the boy. "He's all right. He'll be fine." He drew her away, leaving the mother cleaning the mess from her son's shirt and sorting out his tears.

"He can see me." Tilly looked over her shoulder as she spoke. "I can see you." She turned to Matthew. "Are they dead too?" Her words caught her by surprise.

Matthew shook his head as he walked towards a grassy patch in the park, away from everyone and settled onto the lawn.

"I'm dead?" She said the words, but they didn't make sense to her. She raised her hands in front of her, looking at them as if it was the first time she had ever seen them. Matthew stifled a chuckle. She dropped them. She felt her face grow warm.

I'm a ghost? She felt her heart shrink; it felt as if it had been sucked through a tiny hole at the bottom of her stomach. Gone. Empty. Her energy drained, she just sat. Feeling alone. Lost.

They watched the mother soothe her child, kissing him and hugging him, and no doubt telling him it would be all right. Tilly was surprised when she felt herself become envious of the little boy. How she wanted to be scooped up by her parents and be told that everything is OK—it's all just a bad dream. But what was happening to Tilly was all too real to be a bad dream. Dreams were never this clear or tangible. Dreams always had a hint of strange to them. But then, she thought: *This isn't strange?* Her body was starting to feel like a sack of stones again. Could she pretend anymore?

"I don't want to be dead, Matthew." She felt guilty for saying that to him, and she wished she had said it differently. "I'm sorry."

He touched her arm. She felt a snap of electricity where his fingers touched her skin. She pulled away. "I think it's a mistake." She rubbed her arm. She wanted to take it all back. "Maybe this is a bad dream." She looked at her arm where he had touched her. She glanced up at him; he was softly shaking his head. "Okay, maybe I'm laying in a hospital bed, hurt but I can just decide to wake up. I'm in limbo, like in the movies." He continued to shake his head.

"But how can I be dead?" Her voice was starting to rise in pitch. "I woke up in my own bed this morning. I went to English class." Matthew continued to shake his head. "Stop it," Tilly snapped at him.

Matthew wrapped his arms around her. At first, she stiffened, unsure if she'd receive the jolt she got from touching her mother, the pulsing hum from touching the boy, or the fireworks from Matthew earlier. Her body relaxed when that question was answered with tiny nips of energy that slowly released and caressed her, like stepping into a warm shower on a winter day. At last, she released her tears as she buried her face in his chest. He gently squeezed her while she melted into him and wept and wept.

CHAPTER 7

He sits in the beat-up recliner chair watching television. Each night, while he eats supper, he watches a nineteenth century police officer solve a different mystery. Tonight's supper is a ham and cheese sandwich. Tonight's mystery is a body washed up on the shore of a lake, a bite taken out of it.

With his mouth full of sandwich, he lifts his beer to help wash the dry bread down, then replaces the can on the wet semi-circle it left on the side table.

The day started simply enough. He got up. Went to work. Ate lunch alone. Finished work — and now eats his dinner alone. Except for work, the day was just the way he likes it. Alone. He might go out later or might not — it will depend on how the second beer tastes.

He cracks it open as the detective catches the killer with his latest invention: 'finger marks'; then he drinks half the beer and lets out a belch. Seems like there might even be a third beer in the very near future.

The opening credits of the news roll as he downs the last of the can then heads to the kitchen, tosses the plate in the sink and grabs two more cans from the fridge. Decision made.

He returns to his chair, sets his beers on the side table, and grabs the remote; but a story on the news catches his eye.

A reporter stands in front of an outdoor riding arena. There are horses and riders behind her, trotting in tight circles, then changing direction and circling again. He has had a soft spot for horses; when he was a kid, his mother would take him to the exhibition grounds at the edge of the city, and they'd spend the day eating corndogs and watching the horses. It never mattered who the rider was, you always rooted for the horse, for a clear round.

The news scene cuts to a teenage girl who stands next to her horse, the top of her head reaching its shoulder. Someone places a medal around her neck. He watches the rider's face. Her eyes. Where was her excitement? After all, she's just won a major competition, so the reporter says.

The same someone then clips a rosette to the horse's bridle as it shakes its head, tugs on the reins. The horse looks into the camera, its round eyes making contact with his. He sees himself in the animal: never being asked what it would be like, but always expected to serve someone else.

"We bought him last year; he has an impeccable pedigree," the girl says. "We knew he could take me to the next level. I may keep him for next year's circuit, but I'll have to see how he finishes up this season." Her name scrolls along the bottom of the screen. It seems familiar.

"The season has just begun," the reporter says. "I'm sure he will make you proud."

"The season is so short." The girl starts to walk away from the reporter. "We don't have time to waste."

"We," he says. He downs the beer. "As if!" he says to the TV. "Your parents bought you the horse. The horse got you the trophy." He opens his third beer. "And if he doesn't, you'll get Daddy to buy you another one. Spoiled bitch!"

He feels his chest tighten with a small jerk. Here we go again. The rich getting everything they want. Never having to work for it; just buying shit. Why don't you just save yourself the time and buy the trophy?

He can feel his upper lip begin to curl, and he knows exactly what that means.

It means that soon he will feel the itch coming.

The reporter thanks her, and the camera follows the pair as they approach a man just at the edge of the screen, likely the other part of the we: the rich daddy. Rich Daddy looks familiar as well.

Taking his beer, he moves to the desk and turns on a big old desktop computer. As it loads, he chugs the first half of his beer. When the screen is ready, using only two fingers on the keyboard, he pecks out a search on her name.

Her name isn't on the first page of hits. Instead, he clicks on the word 'Images.' They fill the screen.

"I knew I knew that name!" he tells the screen, remembering some of the facts he'd once researched.

Captain Winston Williams — Astronaut. Retired Engineer. Co-designed and monitored the construction of an optical non-destructive evaluation facility. Now travels across the country, discussing space exploration with teachers and students, and promoting STEM subjects: science, technology, engineering, and mathematics. Visits community centers in poorer parts of the country, showing young people how much fun science can be, encouraging them to stay in school. Has received multiple awards and honorary keys to cities —where he volunteers or helps in fundraisers.

He'd done a ninth-grade school project on Captain Williams. He never did know what 'non-destructive evaluation' meant and had little interest in science, but his mark had been decent.

Today, though, all he sees is a spoiled rich girl.

It takes him five days to track down the stable at which she boards her horse; and on each one of those days, the itch grows a little stronger. He tries to block it out. He walks more, trying to burn it off. He drinks more, trying to dull it. He sleeps more, hoping it will be gone when he wakes; but it is now at the point where it wakes him during the night. It is no longer just an itch under his skin; at times it burns. First, it feels like the tight, hot skin of a sunburn, but then it seems to work its way into his muscles. They twitch, jerk, cramp. His ears start to ring. His stomach clenches at the thought of food.

He has to show her. He isn't sure what he will do when he finds her horse. He has an idea, but there are so many variables out of his control. He is dealing with a huge animal this time; and while horses are flight animals, any animal cornered will fight — eight hundred pounds of fight!

CHAPTER 8

"Tilly." Matthew's voice was so faint she could have mistaken it for the wind. She hesitated to pull away from his arms, to leave this cocoon. The headaches were gone, there was no dizziness, no limbs made of stone. "We have to get going," he said.

"Where?"

He pulled away, just enough to make her move. "Your wake." He stood and put out his hand; she stood, and this time she took it. "Take a deep breath and, well, you might want to close your eyes."

She did.

Everything blurred. She felt blood pulse in her ears, her head throb. She fought an urge to vomit. Then she sat with a thump. When she opened her eyes, she realized she was no longer in the park.

"Matthew?" Her head started to spin again. "How did you do that?"

"Take slow breaths," he said, lowering himself to sit beside her. "Closing your eyes helps."

Impatient for the dizziness to pass, she closed her eyes, took in a deep breath and let it go.

"Slower," he told her. "Put your head between your knees."

With eyes closed, she just focused on breathing.

"It gets easier," he said.

Slow breathing helped. She could feel the tension loosen a little, lighten even. She rubbed her temples then slid her fingertips back and forth across her forehead, up to her hairline, making her eyebrows raise as she did.

She opened her eyes just a little, afraid the awful feeling might come back. When it didn't, she opened them completely and looked around slowly. She saw a large parking lot, a sign set at its entrance. It was black with white letters:

CARSON & SON
Funeral Home
(Since 1957)

She twisted to see a red brick building and realized she was sitting on the front steps of the funeral home that she had passed many times — and always with a little shudder.

"Matt!" It came out more like a squeak.

He looked at her. She started to shake.

"I don't remember dying!" It was as if a rock had been placed on her chest, its weight sitting on her heart. When she tried to take a deep breath, the rock dug in and wouldn't let her lungs expand. "I really am dead," she said with a wail. Tears started to build in the corners of her eyes. She felt so small. She felt like a child, like when her mother could kiss her boo-boo and make it all better. She wished her mother could do that right now. Make her all better.

Matthew shifted closer to her but didn't touch her. He didn't speak.

She stared at a flock of birds searching the lawn for lunch.

"When did I die?" asking herself rather than Matthew. "*How* did I die? And if I'm dead, why do I feel like crap all the time?"

Matthew's hands dangled between his legs. He rubbed the palms together.

"I am still figuring it all out myself," he said, looking away. Then he shifted on the step so that he could look straight at her. "Tilly. You died five days ago."

She didn't think she could be shocked about anything after realizing she was dead, but she was wrong. Matthew's statement sent her brain into a flurry, searching her memory.

"Five days! How is that possible?" She reviewed the mental slideshow of her last few days. "I was at school yesterday, and today."

He said nothing.

"How did I die?" She shifted closer to him, craving the safe spot she'd felt in his arms, but she allowed herself only to lean against him.

"I can't tell you that, Tilly. I don't know how you died; but somehow I know that it is you who needs to remember it." He let his head lean on hers. "I know that when I remembered mine, I started to feel … better. Different"

"Feeling better!" She pulled away from him. "How am I supposed to feel better when I'm dead?"

The birds in the parking lot near the steps exploded into the air.

She could feel her face heating with anger. She shifted on the step, turning farther away from him, placing her head between her hands, her elbows on her knees. Her fingertips dug into her scalp. This time it wasn't nausea; her head felt like a balloon filled with too much air and threatening to pop.

She could feel Matthew waiting. She knew she wasn't mad at him, but it was so hard not to take these awful feelings out on him. She wanted to lash out, and he was the only one around.

"Sorry." She turned back to Matthew and forced herself to make eye contact with him. He didn't deserve this. He had come here to help her, support her.

"It's okay, Tilly."

She tried to interpret his look.

He took a breath. "Let's back this up a bit and start over. What day is it today?"

"It's Wednesday."

"Actually, it's Monday."

"Monday?" Tilly's head started to spin; her stomach rolled. She leaned over to throw up, which ended up being a dry heave.

"When was the last time you ate?"

Tilly stopped to think. Last night? Had she eaten at all today?

"I had a cupcake last night for supper, well, kinda."

39

"Kind of?"

"I threw it up."

Matthew gave a small laugh. "Sorry. All of that will eventually stop. Once you accept you're dead, you start to let go of your body, and it stops trying to react to everything around you. Throwing up and being dizzy are just memories you have. You only think you're supposed to respond that way."

"And why is that so funny?"

"'Cause I threw up all over everything after I died. I was a little slow catching on, as well."

"Are you calling me slow?" She tried to look angry, but couldn't. Her laugh came out as a snort.

They sat on the step, laughing. Because it felt good.

"Matthew, Why are we here?"

He looked at her, and his smile slowly faded.

"You know why we're here. Funerals, wakes and memorial services are places to say goodbye—and now so will you."

Tilly understood his look now. It was compassion. He knew what she was going through because he was going through it too.

Tilly thought about the years they had gone to school together. How they had hung out all the time. She'd had a small crush on him, but would never have admitted it to him. When the school and his parents had decided to advance him a year, putting him in high school, Tilly lost touch with him and busied herself with other friends, and playing volleyball.

Now, here he was, the only one she could talk to, the only one here for her. She looked at him, really looked at him.

"I'm sorry," she finally said.

"For what?"

"For everything. This can't be easy for you either."

They sat quietly on the step as Tilly scanned the building: its large white columns, carved wooden doors, windows with black shutters.

She watched as cars pulled in and parked. She watched the occupants, some her neighbors, friends, get out and come towards her, then disappear into the building.

"Matt, I'm afraid to go in there."

"I know. I'll be with you." His eyes were filled with the same kind of compassion he had shown her earlier. He had such sweet eyes, she noticed—vibrant, green. This thought brought her back to reality.

"What if I don't go?"

"There's no rule saying you have to, at least not that I know of." He attempted a smile. "But one thing I do know is that it will help you."

"I guess."

"Being there will help you come to terms with your death. Remember what I said before about how it will help you and your body finish the transfer."

Transfer? Transfer to where, to what? She wanted to point out he was still here. Instead, she took a deep breath and slowly released it.

She stood.

"Okay. Let's do it!"

CHAPTER 9

Tilly turned and stepped through giant wooden doors and into a room that was a feeble attempt at impersonating a living room. It was bland: brown furniture, dusty rose carpet, walls a lighter shade of rose. On the left, there was a gas fireplace with an electrified oil lamp on its mantel with a large mirror hanging above it all. Plaid chairs were set on either side. Further along the wall were two sets of open double doors, an easel between them.

The wall directly across from Tilly had two deep-rose couches along it with a small wooden end-table between them. To the right, Tilly saw bifold doors open to a wide closet with hangars, a hallway next to it with a small sign pointing to washrooms, and a door with a small gold and black sign saying PRIVATE. A competing scent of flowers and perfume hung in the air, but there was another smell hidden beneath, and she could taste it.

People stood talking quietly in small groups, hung their coats in the closet, and walked from the hall with the washrooms to the double doors leading to the large hall she assumed was used for the service.

"Ready?" Matthew asked, his voice gentle and patient.

Although Tilly wished she could see more without having to go inside, she nodded to Matthew and followed him towards the closest set of double doors. As she drew closer, she saw that the photo on the easel was of her. Last summer her mother had dragged them all to the park by the waterfront to have a family portrait taken. The photographer who met them there immediately started taking photos. She said she preferred candid shots. Tilly remembered how every time she turned around the woman was there, clicking away. The photo on the board was her mother's favorite. It was of Tilly sitting on stone steps with her chin resting in her hands, a hint of a smile on her face.

Tilly unconsciously sucked in her breath, spun around and stepped away from the board. Matthew placed his hands on her shoulders. She felt the now-familiar thread of electricity run through her.

"I need a minute." She closed her eyes and concentrated on her breathing. "I just need a minute." Patting her chest as she tried to breathe, she walked back to the main entrance. She paced from the front door to the door marked PRIVATE, back again, rubbing her chest the whole time.

"Take your time."

On her third turn, it suddenly struck her that if she was a ghost, why would she need to breathe? But it didn't matter, because right now all she wanted to *do* was breathe.

She forced all thoughts out of her head and just concentrated on her breath. She could feel her heart slow, her chest ease. Tried to prepare herself for what she'd see next.

She turned and looked at Matthew. His gentle smile encouraged her, telling her he had faith in her, that she could do this.

Afraid to speak and trigger her panic again, she nodded instead. They stepped through the open doors by the easel with Tilly's picture.

The first thing she encountered was two rows of chairs covered in a velvet-like material — more dusty-rose. They all faced the front of the room. A carpet of a darker shade of the same pink color covered the floor, but the windows were draped with white sheer curtains with heavy floral-patterned drapes pulled to the sides. Spaced wall sconces gave off a measured amount of light. As she turned, she could see tables with flowers and lamps, but nothing particularly memorable. The room's attempt to look comfortable and inviting fell short somehow. Who were they trying to kid: everyone knew why they were here.

Dozens of people shifted around in their seats, talking quietly to each other. She saw Auntie Joan rubbing Auntie Hilda's arm, offering her some tissues. A small group of cousins huddled in the corner, whispering and giggling.

What's so funny? Tilly thought, wanting to go over to find out, until she noticed her best friend, Angela, walking towards her with her parents. After everything that had happened since this morning, she wished desperately that she could talk to her. The realization that she was losing her best friend pierced her heart like a needle. That thought was interrupted when she heard Angela speak to her mother.

"What will I do without her? We were supposed to graduate together and go to college together."

Tilly could feel the needle of despair push deeper.

Angela wiped away fresh tears with the back of her hand. Her eyes were puffy, her nose red.

Angela's nose always gives her away, even before she cries.

"We had even planned that when we had families of our own, our kids were going to be best friends."

Angela's mother wrapped her arm around her daughter's shoulder, pulling her close.

"I could have sworn I heard her call my name yesterday at school."

"I knew I shouldn't have let you go to school," her mother said, fighting tears of her own.

Tilly wanted to shout at Angela, *You did, you did! You did hear me call your name!*

"How will I manage without her?" Angela was barely able to finish her sentence before her sobs overwhelmed her. She turned into her mother's chest. Her mother guided her to a grouping of chairs off to the side.

Tilly started towards Angela, tears running down her cheeks.

"You can't help her, Tilly," he said softly, bringing her attention back to him.

"So, this morning was yesterday?"

He nodded.

"But you heard her. She said she heard me at school today when I called her — I mean yesterday — whenever the hell it was!"

"It doesn't change anything." He nodded toward the front of the room. "Come on, Tilly, keep going."

Tilly wiped her eyes, gave Angela another glance, then reluctantly turned her attention back to the room.

She wove around the rows of chairs to where an arc of them were set up at the front. No one was using these; people just stood in front of them. Tilly became excited when she spotted the back of her mother's head. Then she noticed her father beside her, and, if she was not mistaken, her grandparents.

She snaked through the crowd and in front of the arc of chairs.

"Mom. Dad."

Tilly ran to her mother and wrapped her arms around her. But instead of giving Tilly a loving hug in return, her mother made a gagging sound, fell to her seat, and started to cry. Tilly backed away. Her whole body felt numb, then she felt the sensation of the pins and needles that happens when your arm has fallen asleep.

"You can do this, Maggie," her father whispered to Tilly's mother, his forehead resting just above her ear. Then he kissed her.

"Wil, I think I'm going to be sick!" her mother said, holding her hand to her mouth.

Tilly watched her father help her mother up, wrap his arm around her shoulder, and lead her out of the room.

Matthew put an arm around Tilly's shoulder exactly as her father had just done to her mother, and she allowed herself to lean on him. She wasn't sure she could hold herself up.

"I forgot," she said as she fought her tears. "I forgot that I mustn't touch her. I just wanted to make her feel better, I just wanted to help."

"I know," he said softly. "She will be all right in a minute. It fades quickly," he said, trying to reassure her.

45

"But it's not just that, Matthew. Even when I don't touch people, I'm hurting them." The weight of that realization made her want to crash to the floor, but Matthew held her. "I'm the cause of all this. All of this is my fault!"

"It's not your fault, Tilly." He tightened his arms around her. "None of this is your fault."

What would she do without Matthew? She felt so grateful he was here, but then realized guiltily that his death was the price of his being able to comfort her.

"Thank you," she said.

He gave her a quick squeeze. And that gave her enough strength to turn her head and look around again. She saw her family, all of them. Her grandmother and grandfather, Aunt Joan and Uncle John, Aunt Hilda, her cousins Tammy, Andrew, Bruce, Debbie, and Colleen. Her body started to lighten as she saw her parents returning, her mother looking stronger.

"Where's Nathan?" she said, breaking from Matthew, looking around the room.

"He's in the back room," Matthew said.

"I need to see him."

"You can see him in a minute, Tilly." Matthew's voice took a new, firmer tone. "He's fine, and he isn't going anywhere. And you have something you need to do first." He tilted his head towards the front of the room.

She turned hers — and found herself looking at her coffin.

"Matthew?" Tilly whispered forgetting that no one could hear her.

He didn't answer.

She slowly walked to the casket and, one small step at a time, leaned forward to look inside.

Her hand at her mouth, a foreign sound escaped her. Every muscle in her body liquified. She wanted to step back, to walk away as far as it took to erase sight of herself in that coffin, but her muscles had now frozen in place.

Tilly could feel Matthew touch her arm. It was soft and quick but it enough to bring her back, to keep her from fainting.

Tilly looked at the girl in the box. She looked like she was sleeping. This girl had makeup on, something Tilly's mother never allowed her to use. Her mother said she had enough time for that later on and that she was too beautiful to cover herself with cosmetics. Although she had been secretly wearing it despite her mother's ban, she suddenly realized that now she would never be old enough to wear makeup. She'd never win the high-school volleyball championships. Never graduate.

"It's me," she said to no one.

And following that statement was the thought of all the things she'd taken for granted. Things that she expected in her future but also things from her past. There would be no more family vacations or movie night. No more backyard ring-toss games while her dad barbequed burgers, and no more family bike rides by the lake. No more sleepovers at Angela's where they would giggle all night.

She hadn't expected the girl inside the coffin to look so much like her. She realized she had only been to a few funerals, and they were for elderly or sick people. They had a sunken-in look; their skin seemed fake, like a shell. This girl looked exactly like her, and yet so different. Missing something.

"I mean, I know you told me. But now it's so real!" She couldn't take her eyes off the girl.

Her mother was right, Tilly thought, looking closer. The makeup did make her look strange, maybe a little sick.

"The dress."

"What?" asked Matthew.

"That's the dress she took out of my closet," Tilly told him. "I watched her."

She had to sit down. She found herself sitting at the end of the crescent of chairs, questions cascading through her head.

If I am dead, then why am I sitting here? When I was little Mom and Dad told me Grandma Sadie went to heaven when she died, but is she a ghost too? Where am I supposed to go now? What am I supposed to do now?

She looked to Matthew, but he was gone. What was she supposed to do now?

CHAPTER 10

Sitting all alone, Tilly watched people as they paid homage at the casket, her casket. Some whispered, some just stared. While some paused for only a moment, others seemed as if they were never going to leave. She tried to imagine what they were thinking as they stood quietly, what they were saying to her.

She was surprised by how many people she didn't know. She could overhear some of their hushed words when they stopped to speak with each of her family members at the other end of the crescent.

"I'm sorry for your loss," a tall man said to her father as the man's wife hugged her mother. She recognized them from her neighborhood. They lived down the street, the house with the mean German shepherd.

"She was such a polite young lady," the woman who worked at the corner store said. Tilly couldn't remember her name, despite being sent to the store at least once a week for something her mother forgot to pick up. Angie? Annie?

Tilly shifted her attention to the people entering the room, stepping from a line that had formed the length of the lobby. She watched their expressions as they stepped up to her coffin, and then tried to figure out who they were before they reached her parents. Were they truly upset or was this all just a formality to them? After all, if she didn't know who they were, how could they be that upset? She remembered when she went to Grandma Sadie's wake. She was only five and didn't know what to say or do when her mother took her to the casket, so she just stood beside her mother, until her mother took her hand and stepped away. Shortly after that, someone took Tilly and her brother downstairs to Auntie Joan while her parents stayed upstairs.

As she sat watching, she tried to guess what each person was thinking, then strained to see if she could hear their whispers.

Nothing.

She squeezed her eyes tightly as she concentrated and leaned forward in her seat.

Nothing.

She gave up. Settling back in her chair she relaxed and kept her eyes closed.

What am I supposed to do now?

She let her head fall back. She realized it was the first time, in she didn't know how long, that her head didn't hurt.

She listened to shuffling feet, muffled by the rose carpet. The sound of the friction of arms rubbing arms, hands rubbing pant legs.

The poor girl, what a horrible way to die.

Tilly snapped up straight, eyes wide open.

She scanned the room trying to find the speaker. She spotted Mrs. Saunders, her neighbor, standing at the coffin, wiping her eyes.

She rushed to her side. "What happened to me? Tell me! Say it, please!"

Her whole life ahead of her, gone just like that.

Tilly realized Mrs. Saunders's lips never moved. She felt her body tingle. Goosebumps. She felt the hairs on her arms lift, like from the static from a balloon rubbed in your hair then held close to your arm.

But Mrs. Saunders turned to leave.

"No, please don't go!"

The Parkers were behind Mrs. Saunders, and they stepped in front of the coffin. Their daughter Betty-Ann used to babysit Tilly; she was now in her second year at Yale. Mrs. Parker's words were in Tilly's head before she knew it.

Knowing what could happen, why would they let her go home alone?

49

The thoughts of the guests, quiet before, rushed at her now.

What a shame! She should have known better.

Poor Tilly's mom.

She was such a talented athlete.

I knew I shouldn't have let Angela go to school.

For her body to be dumped like that.

Tilly put her hands over her ears, not wanting to hear anymore. She looked at the line of people. Mrs. Silver, her school librarian, a tissue under her nose, was next.

Poor Nathan, what is going to happen to him without his sister? He worships her.

Nathan! How could she have forgotten him?

She had to find him; she had to make sure he was all right. She got up, ran out of the room past her photo on the tripod, into the lobby and down the hall. The first two doors were washrooms, but she found someone in the third room, and she felt relief until she realized it wasn't Nathan. This young man was taller. He was thin, his dark hair in a ponytail. He was pouring water into a coffee maker as he turned towards her. He looked vaguely familiar.

When she looked at his eyes, she felt the snap of an electric shock. Her heart flipped, skipping a beat. She couldn't move. Her vision seemed to blur, losing the outline of him. But it also seemed to double, as if he was standing in front of another person.

Ice filled her veins. She backed into the hall. She couldn't look away. She took another step back. A door slamming somewhere startled her and broke her eye contact for a moment. He started towards her but the sound of something smashing made him turn down the hall toward the washrooms, the way she had come. Shaking herself free, she returned to her search for Nathan, more desperate to find him now than ever.

She found a half-closed door labeled FAMILY ROOM. Inside, she discovered Nathan watching TV. She was surprised to also find Matthew, in the corner, sitting in a chair, his legs draped over the arm. Ignoring Matthew, she rushed over to sit beside Nathan on the couch.

"Your parents thought he needed a break from everything. He was getting agitated."

"How do you know that?" She shot Matthew a questioning look. How did he know Nathan had been upset? How did he know what her parents were thinking?

"I listened," Matthew said. "But you already know that. You just don't pay attention."

"Sorry." Matthew's gaze lowered, hovering on the couch cushions for a moment then slowly rose to meet Tilly's. "I didn't mean to sound so—"

"No, Matthew. You're right." She turned toward Nathan, watching his eyes follow the activity on the screen, lost in the made-up world of television. He seemed to be all right. She tried to see if she could hear his thoughts. Nothing.

Being next to Nathan, she began to feel a sense of calm. This room, unlike the others, had plush couches and armchairs instead of just stackable chairs. As well as the television, it had books and toys in the far corner.

She wanted more than anything to hug her brother, to tell him she was sorry and that he'd be all right, and that she'd watch over him. She fought the urge to reach out and touch him, remembering what had happened with the small child at the park. She looked at Matthew. He gave her a small smile.

When their mother opened the door of the family room Tilly jumped.

"Nathan, we're going home now," her mother said.

Nathan didn't move. Tilly's mother walked over to the couch.

Tilly realized she had lost track of time again. It felt like she'd just sat down.

"Would you like to say goodbye to Tilly?" Their mother said softly. She touched his head. He pulled away. "This is your last chance before she goes to heaven?"

"I don't need to say goodbye," he said, never taking his gaze off the television.

Their mother knelt in front of him, blocking his view. "Nathan, we talked about this before, remember? Tilly has to go to heaven so that she can be an angel with Grandma Sadie." She kept her voice soft. She placed her hand on the cushion beside his knee. "So, let's go say goodbye."

"Tilly's not going to Heaven and she's not with Grandma Sadie — she's right here."

Something passed over Nathan's face that Tilly had never seen before. Was it regret? Frustration? Was he shutting down? Maybe he was just tired from everything that had been going on.

Their mother exhaled. Tilly knew the meaning of that action; her mother used it when she wanted to yell. And in a moment of revelation, Tilly realized she had felt that many times herself. Raising your voice with Nathan got you nothing; and if anything it made matters worse. He would dig in his heels, and it could take hours to get him to change his mind. Or he'd just shut down completely.

"Ready to go?" Their dad asked, walking into the family room.

Her mother shook her head, not saying a word.

"What's wrong, Buddy? Not ready to say goodbye?" he asked, settling beside his wife.

"I don't need to say goodbye," Nathan said, picking up the remote and turning off the television.

"He says Tilly isn't going to heaven. That's she's here," their mother whispered. Their dad rubbed his palm across his forehead then over the top of his head.

They looked at each other but said nothing, and then looked back at Nathan.

As Nathan set the remote back on the table, his dad sat on the couch beside him. He put his hands on his thighs, took a deep breath, then slowly let it out.

"I know you don't want Tilly to leave, but she has to go, Nathan. She's going to be an angel, remember? Your mother and I told you all about what happens when a person dies." He shifted a little closer; not touching him. "Remember the drawing you made for her?"

"Oh my God!" Tilly's hand covered her mouth. She remembered that drawing.

"What?" Matthew looked at her. She had forgotten he was there.

She was grateful when he didn't push her for an answer, instead, he stood next to her. She felt herself calm as he did.

"She's not; she's right here. And Matthew is here with her, too." Nathan said. He crossed his arms on his chest. Tilly had never seen him so defiant.

Their dad twisted, leaned in towards Nathan, his elbows resting on his knees. "OK, Nathan. You need to listen to me." He was obviously trying his very best to be patient and understanding. "We are all going to miss Tilly, but she is going to Heaven. If you want to have her as one of your imaginary friends for a while that will be all right — but only for a while. OK?"

"Nathan?" Tilly whispered.

Nathan turned his head slightly towards Tilly. She wasn't sure if he was reacting to her or not, but she knew Nathan's distress was all her fault.

"Nathan, if you can hear me, don't say a word, just look at me." She waited to see what would happen next.

Nathan turned towards her and looked straight at her.

Can he actually see *me?* She looked at Matthew then back at Nathan.

"OK, Buddy. We need to get you home. We can talk more about this tomorrow, but now it's bedtime. So, what do you say?" He was trying so hard; Tilly's heart went out to him.

She knew she had to do something. She was the reason for all this. If Nathan slid into one of his episodes, it could take days for him to recover from it. She couldn't let that happen.

"Nathan, I need you to go home, OK? I'll see you there later, so don't worry." It was worth a try.

Nathan stood abruptly. "Bye, Tilly."

Tilly felt her body vibrate. Was he hearing her? Was he actually answering her? This couldn't be real.

Tilly heard her mother's sigh of relief at what she thought was Nathan's farewell to his sister.

"Way to go, Champ," Their dad said.

Before her parents got up to leave the room, Tilly went to Nathan. She was still shaking. "How about Matthew and I be a little secret for now?" Tilly said. "Like Superman's real name. OK?"

"OK," Nathan replied and turned to his parents. "Let's go then."

CHAPTER 11

Tilly quietly sat in a chair in the corner of Nathan's room. She knew better than to upset his bedtime routine: if she did that, it would leave him agitated and awake most of the night. She watched as he pulled the covers up to his chest, waiting for their parents to come and say good night. She was surprised at how normal he looked; how he didn't seem upset with her death at all.

"Stop staring at me, Tilly."

The sound of him saying her name made her go warm inside.

"I'm sorry Nathan. I didn't mean to bother you." She paused. "I still can't believe you can see me. I was just getting used to being invisible." Tilly immediately regretted saying that. How many times had she made fun of him and his invisible friends? It had been worse when she was younger and referred to them as imaginary. Her parents chastised her so many times. It was only when she was older that she realized how her words hurt Nathan.

He stared at the ceiling, watching the gliding stars from the little projector lamp by his bed.

She had so many questions for him.

"Tilly, I need to go to sleep now. I can't keep talking to you. Go to your own room." He closed his eyes as if to reinforce his statement.

His words stung a little.

"I know you are still here." His eyebrows shifted in her direction, but he didn't open his eyes. "Go, Tilly."

"But Nathan, you can see me. And hear me." Her voice was filling with excitement, then dropped. "Why don't you want to talk to me?"

"Of course, I can see you." He said it so casually.

"And you can see Matthew?"

He nodded his head, eyes still closed.

"Why won't you talk to me?" She couldn't stop herself, she was terrified he'd stop and she'd be cut off again.

"I am not supposed to talk about it, you know that, Tilly." He opened his eyes and looked straight into hers. She sat on the side of his bed, careful not to touch him.

"And at night, before I go to sleep, I have to protect myself."

"Protect yourself?" She was taken aback. "From what? From me? From how I died?"

"No. From *them*." He closed his eyes and let out a puff of air. "I shouldn't have said anything in front of Mom and Dad. Now they're going to start worrying again."

Tilly's stomach clenched. *Them?* "Your imaginary friends? When did it start again? When did you start seeing your…friends again?"

"Tilly! I am not supposed to talk about it, remember!"

She was starting to feel like he didn't want to talk, rather than shouldn't. Maybe she should give him some time. She leaned in closer to him like she did when they pretended to tell secrets in front of their parents.

"It's OK, Nathan. I won't tell them." She softened her voice. "Besides, they can't hear me anyway." She winked, trying to lighten everything.

He looked at the ceiling. She wasn't sure if he was shutting down, waiting for her to leave, or trying to decide if he wanted to talk to her. She stayed quiet.

"I never stopped." His voice was barely audible. "And they're *not* imaginary." His left eye started to twitch just a little. "Just like you're not imaginary."

Tilly imagined this was what a gunshot felt like: a sharp pierce to the body, but so quick you didn't see it coming and couldn't believe it had happened. She worked to pull herself together, to not break down in front of Nathan. She needed him to keep talking.

"It's okay," she tried. She could see how hard this was on him as well.

"I only said they had gone to make Mom and Dad happy. I just stopped talking about them, and then Mom and Dad stopped worrying about me so much."

That made Tilly's chest feel like her heart was being pulled through her ribs and ripped out of her chest.

"Oh, Nathan. I'm so sorry we didn't believe you. That *I* didn't believe you." Tilly reached out for him but stopped just before she touched him. "Can I see your friends?"

Nathan shook his head. He stopped when he heard their parents coming down the hall.

"I love you, Nathan," Tilly said.

"Good night, Tilly," he whispered.

In her room she sat cross-legged on her bed, rubbing Simon's furry bear-ears. Her head hurt trying to make sense of everything that had happened. She was dead. No one could see or hear her, except for Nathan. Who else could he see? And other than Nathan, her only friend was a dead boy.

"Been a rough few days, eh?"

She looked up to see Matthew standing in the doorway. She thought about sliding Simon behind her back but instead, she twisted around and propped the bear against her pillow.

"Hello, Simon," Matthew said from the doorway.

She had forgotten that Matthew would know Simon from when they were kids; she had dragged the bear everywhere for a while. She was impressed Matthew remembered the bear's name.

"Yeah, it's been rough." She wasn't sure if she had the energy to keep searching for answers. Who would have thought being dead was so exhausting?

He sat beside her on her bed.

Tilly told Matthew about her conversation with Nathan. What was Nathan afraid of? He was definitely afraid of something! Was it of her? Where were his friends? *Who* were his friends?

And the question remained: how had she died?

"I don't remember dying, Matthew," she said. "How did I die?" She wanted him to tell her.

"I don't know, Tilly." His voice was soft. Comforting. Like a soft blanket wrapped around her. "I wish I could tell you."

She looked at him. She wasn't sure if there were tears in his eyes. She wanted to comfort him this time, tell him it would all be okay, but she couldn't.

"I can help you try to remember."

CHAPTER 12

Tilly knew better than to walk alone: her parents had lectured her after Matthew had been found dead. But Matthew had been cutting through the woods, but she wasn't going anywhere near the woods, and everyone knew not to accept rides from strangers or fall for that old lost dog trick. But when a second kid was found dead—Joel, the cute ball player from Nathan's team—although no one could say his death was connected to Matthew's—her parents had lectured her again.

After Matthew's death, parents teamed up and started to carpool kids to school. Tilly's group consisted of Anna and Alex, fourteen-year-old twins from six houses down the street, and Stewart, who'd just turned fourteen. Another neighbor, a Mrs. Sanchez, was today's driver.

Tilly felt like it took longer to drive the eight blocks to the school then it did to walk. During the car ride Anna and Alex constantly picked at each other, and Stewart was so slow getting into the car because he was always playing video games and would try to climb in without taking his eyes off the screen.

Trying to ignore the twins, Tilly heard her phone ding with a text.

Did you finish your report? Her best friend Angela asked.

Tilly realized she had forgotten her English paper.

She kept quiet in the passenger seat as she replied. *I forgot. Thanks for reminding me.*

As Mrs. Sanchez pulled up to the school, everyone climbed out of the car with Stewart still staring at his phone.

"Thank you for the drive," Tilly said and started towards the front door of the school. She took a few steps, gaging the time it would take for Mrs. Sanchez to pull away, then quickly looked over her shoulder to be sure she was gone.

She was.

Tilly turned and started towards the street.

"Where are you going?" Stewart asked. Tilly was surprized he had looked away from his phone long enough to notice her.

"I gotta go back."

"You're not supposed to be alone, Tilly," Stewart said.

"I know, but I'll just be a minute. And I have a free period, first period." She walked backward while saying this, looking directly at him, wanting to reinforce her authority.

"What if your mom finds out you went alone?"

"She won't find out." Tilly was practically bouncing on her feet. She had to get *going*.

"I'll be back in no time!" She yelled back as she turned and broke into a jog, then rounded the corner and ran down the street. She was particularly thankful that her mother had taken Nathan to the dentist this morning, so she'd be home and gone without her mother ever knowing.

As she came towards the twins' house, in case their grandmother was at the window, she darted across the street and ran alongside a cable van coasting in the same direction.

Perfect cover.

Once she felt she was safely past their house she sprinted ahead of the van, crossed back to her side of the street, and ran up her walkway. She slid her key into the front door, unlocked it and slipped in.

Without breaking stride, she was across the foyer and up the stairs. In her room, she checked her watch and saw that she still had time to get to school before the next period. She grabbed her paper. Unzipping her backpack as she left her room, heading for the stairs, she shoved in her essay as she ran down to the foyer. She stopped at the bottom to zip up the bag.

That's when she noticed a man in the front entrance closing the door behind him.

She might have said, "Oh," but mostly it sounded like a squeak.

He was wearing some sort of tan uniform, his cap pulled so low she could barely see his face.

"I'm not sure who you are looking for, but I think you have the wrong house." She tried to sound confident, grown up.

The man didn't move. He just stared at her from under the brim of his cap. Tilly felt her body stiffen as he took a slow step toward her.

She looked to her left. Scanned the living room. Had her mother come home and let him in? Part of her knew that hadn't happened; and the same part, deep inside, told her she was in trouble.

Her gaze returned to the man in front of the door, blocking any chance of her escaping. She looked right, towards the kitchen, trying to gauge how far she was from the back patio doors and how fast she could get out that way. She knew she had only seconds to decide. She looked back at the man. She had to take the chance.

With both hands, she threw her bag at him as hard as she could and bolted for the back door.

Dodging the dining room table, she spotted a cordless phone on the kitchen island. She thought of knocking down the dining room chairs but focused on the phone instead.

Grab the phone and keep running.

The rug beneath the table and chairs gave her traction, allowing her to hurl herself toward the island, grabbing for the phone. She misjudged her speed. She overshot her target, missed the phone and cleared everything off the island.

Dad's phone.

Her last chance was the phone on her dad's desk, by the doors. It wouldn't be easy to grab the phone and open the door, but what else could she do? *What if the door's locked? Can I slide it open in time? How close is that guy?* She was aware she'd started to cry. *This can't be happening!*

Making it to her father's desk gave her hope, but hope was short-lived. The man grabbed her ponytail. Tilly felt the vertebrae in the back of her neck crush together, sending sharp pain down her spine. The front of her neck bowed forward threatening to rip through her skin. Pulled backwards, she heard the sound of her head hitting the floor.

Dazed, she lay on the floor, trying to focus. She rolled onto her side and tried to get her arms and legs under her. But before she could, he flipped her onto her back and straddled her. She kicked as hard as she could. Her legs and feet banged on the floor, unable to shift him, unseat him. She twisted, turned, trying to get him off, to slide out from under him. She tried to scratch at him, but only managed to knock his hat lower. He shifted, then pinned her arms to her sides as he sat on her.

With nothing left, Tilly screamed.

Her scream never made it out of her mouth. His large hand covered it and stifled any noise, prevented any air from getting in. Her heart thumped in her chest, beating against her ribs, faster and faster. Her lungs fighting to expand under the weight of the intruder and their hand. Tears pooled around her eyes blurred the image of the person on top of her, there was buzzing in her ears, and her arms and legs became too heavy to lift or kick. She thought she saw a shadow of someone coming to help, but then realized it was the room around her closing in. She tried to keep fighting, but the room grew smaller, and her limbs were lead, and then it went gray and stopped.

Tilly lay still as she slowly became aware of the cold ground beneath her. She could smell dirt, and underneath that gasoline, and grease. She opened her eyes, Light from a dirty window formed a pool just beyond where she lay on her side.

Jolts of pain rippled across the back of her head as she tired to look around the room. She attempted to lift her hand to rub her head, but her hand couldn't move. Instead, she felt cutting pain in her wrists as her shoulders strained. When she tried again, she realized her hands were bound behind her back. Confused and finding it hard to breathe, she tried to open her mouth to get more air, but it wouldn't open. She could feel tears in her eyes but couldn't feel them running onto her cheeks. Her nose leaked, and what gathered just beneath it stuck to whatever covered her mouth. She felt like she was going to drown.

Trying to open her mouth pulled the skin under her nose and cheeks. She tried to push her tongue past her lips, but they wouldn't open. She could feel her heart beating faster, a bird trying to flap its way out of her chest. She tucked her chin closer to her chest, her cheek dragging in the dirt, and tried to see what was wrong with her body, but she was only able to see as far as her knees. Straightening her legs, she tried to roll onto her back, but only succeeded in pinning her arm beneath her as her shoulder screamed with pain.

Breathe through your nose. Slow down. You can still breathe through your nose.

Tied. I'm tied up.

She screamed for help, but it only came out as a throaty rumble. She screamed again. This time her throat constricted and made her gag.

I'm going to die.

She couldn't get enough air. Air gurgled as it worked its way through the snot building in her nostrils.

No. Get a hold of your breathing. Breathe slowly or you'll pass out.

She curled her feet to her backside. Tightening her stomach, she lifted her head and, ignoring the pain of it, slid up on her shoulder, then let her weight drop. She could hear her shoulder joint grind beneath her weight as she shifted, and the slightest move only intensified the agony. She bit the inside of her cheek to keep from throwing up. Her body demanded more air before it would move again. She forced exaggerated, slow, exhalations in the hope that it would slow her heart rate. It worked.

Get up Tilly; you are not going to die.

Tightening her stomach again, she held her breath and rolled over on top of her hands, making her want to scream with the pain. Arching her back, she straightened her shoulders, and the pain dulled a little.

She could hear her own breathing. Her chest was tight. Lying still, trying to focus, she finally felt tears rolling down the side of her face. Her ears only heard swooshing of blood with each heartbeat.

Slow breaths. Sloooow.

Twisting and shifting her legs, she put her feet flat on the floor. She gave herself another moment to rest. She knew she had to keep moving, but it was so hard to breathe.

With her knees bent and feet on the floor, she used all her core strength to pull herself into a sitting position, fingers straining to support her weight and keep herself from falling back. She looked around in the dim light of the room, not sure what to do next. There was a workbench with tools hanging on a peg board behind it. Hoses were piled on the workbench, and what looked like car parts and tires were stacked beside it.

A shed? A garage? Tilly's brain grabbed at anything to make sense of what was happening.

That's long enough. You need to get out of here. A voice now screamed in her head.

Using her legs, she inched herself over to the wall beside the workbench. Her jeans scraped the filth on the floor. At the wall, she pivoted until her back was flat against it, allowing it to support her weight. Her lungs screamed for air; her legs and stomach muscles twitched.

One...two...three.... She visualized her heart, watching it slow. *Four...Five.*

She let her knees fall to the side. Using her knuckles, she lifted herself slightly, just enough to slide some of her ankle underneath her. Now using her knuckles to lift higher, she slid her feet underneath. She realized that although she could straighten up so that she was on her knees, there was no way that she could get to her feet.

From a kneeling position she looked around the room, looking for something to cut her bindings. Realizing that she was unable to reach anything from the workbench, she scanned the pile of car parts for anything sharp enough to cut herself free.

She dropped to her bum and inched her way closer to the automotive parts under the workbench, ignoring her lungs and the steady stream of sweat running into her eyes.

You can do it. Everything is going to be fine.

By the time she reached the bench, every part of her was in pain. She just wanted to lie down and give up.

Please.

Fighting back tears, she stared at the ground in front of her, dark soil stained with oil and grease. Under the workbench, there were chrome pipes spotted with rust, Next to the workbench was a discarded muffler, a car door. Tilly looked at the car door, trying to see if there was something she could rub her feet against to cut the tape around them. She spotted taillights. Her heart quickened—but this time with hope.

She inched her way closer. Raising her feet as high as she could, she brought them down hard to smash the taillight assembly. She had no idea if she had cut herself and didn't care. That would have to wait. Shifting again so she could use her hands, she searched for a piece of broken plastic. She whimpered when she found a sharp edge, moved her hands and then sawed at her bonds in earnest.

I just need to get a rip started, just a rip.

She was aware of sweat sliding down her face, slicking her palms. For every pick at the tape she inflicted a cut on her arm; but despite that, with a yank of her wrists, the tape broke and her hands were free.

She tore the tape off her mouth, wincing, and gulped in air. She wiped away tears, sweat and snot, took in another gulp of air. The smell of the garage was now overwhelming, and beneath all that something else she didn't recognize. Using a piece of the broken taillight, she made short work of the bonds around her legs, and once free, she bolted for the door.

It was locked.

"Fuck!"

She rubbed dirt from the window and looked out. She could see the back of a house. She was in someone's backyard. On the right was a driveway, and she could see straight out the driveway onto the street. Then she saw a person just disappearing behind a hedge that ran the length of the driveway, a little dog behind them.

Should I scream? Is it too late? What if the person in the house hears me instead? Did they hear me already?

She spun back to the workbench, looking for something but not sure what.

The window? The door? A hammer? She wanted to smash out the window but was afraid of making more noise.

Something heavy. And solid. A weapon!

Tilly spotted a shovel. She grabbed it and started to ram its pointed blade into the door jamb. Wood splintered but the door stayed solid. She spun the shovel around and slammed the handle against the door just under the knob, but the door still didn't move.

Back at the workbench, Tilly frantically ran her hands over bottles of glue, rolls of tape, picking up a glass jar filled with screws. It was the only way to get her hands to stop shaking. A hammer. There must be a hammer here somewhere.

Tilly looked towards the window. She knew she would have to break it. Maybe the noise would bring someone to help her. *Why hadn't it already?* she wondered. She grabbed a pipe wrench off the back wall, surprised at its heaviness. Suddenly, the room lit up as the door opened behind her, and she spun around.

A figure was standing in the doorway, the sun behind him making a silhouette. She froze.

"You are a feisty one." There was a hint of pleasure in his voice.

Tilly saw the street behind him. She saw freedom, but she couldn't get her feet to move.

Tilly's eyes constricted when he flipped the light switch.

"How about you and I get to know each other a little better?" he said.

Squinting, Tilly raised the wrench, threatening to swing it if he came closer.

He laughed.

Furious and terrified, she raised the wrench higher. Her exhausted arms shook with the weight of her weapon. He reached towards her, and she swung the heavy wrench down towards his arms — and realized she had fallen for his bait. Momentum slammed the tip of the heavy metal pipe wrench into the floor where it hit the dirt and sent a shock wave through her. She tried to pick it back up, but he was quicker and yanked it out of her hands.

"Nice try. A for effort."

He stepped towards her. She stepped back. He stepped again…. She watched the door get further away each time. The sudden feel of the wall against her back almost dropped her to her knees. He tossed the wrench aside, pulled some zip ties from behind him, and with his other hand, set a knife on the workbench.

Then, he rushed at her.

—and in her bedroom. "No!" she screamed both in her memory—and in her bedroom where Matthew held her as she sobbed, crushed by memory and the reality of where she was now.

She was dead and there was no denying it. Wishes and childhood fantasies were over, shattered by the truth of what had happened.

CHAPTER 13

A tiny bit of meat, a gentle voice, is great comfort for an animal tied in a yard and left alone day after day. After two weeks, the dog has come to know the friendly visitor and now anticipates his visits.

And when his new friend enters the yard, the black Labrador retriever greets him with a slight bow and wagging tail. Brown eyes look into his, begging for continued love and attention.

The dog's friendly visitor walks towards the doghouse and, once behind it, sits with his back braced against it, legs spread to allow the dog to lean against his chest as he rubs its neck, ears, and chest. The dog licks his face as it continually shifts, trying to get closer to him, as if to be part of him.

He digs in his pocket and pulls out bits of chicken. As the dog takes the meat from his flat palm, licking at the grease once it's gone, his visitor runs his free hand down its ribcage. It isn't hard to find each rib.

He finds his target.

He pulls out another chunk of meat, and as the dog buries his muzzle in his hand, he shoves his blade between its ribs. The dog starts to move; he pushes harder and wraps his other hand around its neck. As the dog twists in his arms, he holds the knife in place.

The dog growls and whimpers, but he tightens his grip, wishing he could see its face, wanting to see those brown eyes.

It takes longer for the dog to die than he thought, and his arms are getting tired. He won't let go. His heart pumps so fast it threatens to leave his chest; his skin tingles. He is getting so tired.

He hears: Feel it! Remember it!

The dog eventually stops moving; but he is afraid to let go. He isn't sure his muscles will let him.

He waits.

The itch is gone.

CHAPTER 14

Tilly slowly pulled away from Matthew and sat up, trying to make sense of the sensations running through her body. The stone that had set up residence in her chest was gone. The space containing her heart and lungs felt light, a hot air balloon ready to drift up and float away. Her head no longer pounded with every thought. Her limbs tingled with electricity.

"Matthew, are we going to Heaven now?"

"No. Why would you say that?"

Tilly felt her face turn red; her cheeks were warm. "I just thought that was why you were still here…. You're an angel to help me get to Heaven."

Matthew laughed. Tilly felt her ears burning.

"I don't even know if there is a heaven," Matthew said, his smile slowly slipping from his face.

Tilly stared at her feet. "Neither do I." She tapped the sides of her shoes together. They made a thumping sound. She felt like she had just admitted to believing in talking purple dinosaurs. "I hear that's what's supposed to happen." She slid her feet closer towards her. She looked at him. "Do you believe in any kind of heaven?"

She saw him shrug.

Tilly watched as he started to pick at the skin around his nails.

"What is it?" she asked. "Did I say something wrong? I'm sorry."

"No. You didn't." He picked at his skin again. "There are some people I'd like you to meet."

Angels? She was surprised she felt a little excited about possibly meeting angels. *What would they look like? Would they give her wings?* A minute ago, she wasn't sure she even believed in heaven and now she was expecting to see angels. She knew she was being silly, but she couldn't help imagining what she would look like. She thought of Nathan's drawing again. She couldn't help herself. "Angels?"

"No." Matthew stood and walked to her bedroom door. He stopped just inside the doorway, waiting. The look on his face reminded her that this was not a game, or a bad dream, or pages from the fantasy novel sitting on her desk—this was her new life, her new reality.

Two teenagers walked into her room.

"This is Suzie Williams." Matthew pointed to a tall, thin girl who looked about sixteen.

Tilly immediately noticed Suzie's long, thick lashes and perfect eyebrows that drew you to green eyes that seemed to hypnotize you instantly. Her black hair was elaborately braided with purple highlights, tied into a low ponytail.

"She was killed two weeks ago. She was the one who tried to explain everything to me."

"Yeah, I've been dead the longest."

Tilly was stunned by her statement. It was so matter of fact, it almost sounded like pride.

Matthew indicated the other person. "And this is Joel Bisson. He died about ten days ago."

She knew him. Nathan's baseball teammate, the one with the dark eyes. Tilly felt her legs wobble beneath her to see Joel's smile close-up, seeing those dimples. At first, she felt her face heat up as she finally stood in front of him. She had watched him pitch; she'd even found herself writing his name in her school scribblers a few times—so childish. Now, to have him standing in front of her …then remembering he was dead. No. He *is* dead. Such a mixture of emotions.

"Hey," Joel said. He turned to Matthew. "I know Tilly."

We know each other? I didn't think he even noticed me.

Tilly nodded her head, then felt ridiculous for doing it. She looked at Matthew, his hands now tucked in his front pockets, then back to the newcomers. It struck her how they had been introduced by name, but also by how many days they'd been dead instead of what grade they were in or what school they went to. Although she knew Joel, she had never seen Suzie.

Her chest began to constrict. Once again, she could feel the weight of her limbs fixing her to the earth. Three dead people were standing in her room. No, four, *four* dead people in her room. Tilly realized that although she thought she had come to terms with her death, she had no idea what that meant.

"How do you guys know each other?" Suzie asked, over her shoulder as she walked around the room, sliding a finger along Tilly's dresser.

Tilly couldn't find words. She stood, watching the scene play out in front of her.

Joel said, "I'm on the swim team and I play ball—,"

"He's pretty good," Matthew said. "Last year's baseball champs, right, Joel?"

"Yeah, it gets me out of the house, and the coach doesn't yell as much as my mother." Joel's gaze turned back to Tilly. "Nathan's our batboy. You used to come with him."

The sound of Nathan's name planted her back in her room. She remembered the day her parents told Nathan he could no longer go to the park. Her parents had told her very little about Joel's death; but that no matter what, she was not to take Nathan to the ball field or to tell him about Joel.

Then Nathan spent the next two days organizing his room and refusing to do anything else until it was complete. Tilly had taken her brother a brand-new set of pre-sharpened colored pencils and a sketch pad to try to soothe him. She wondered now if those were what he used to create his drawing of her with her wings.

"Why are you all here?" The words were out of her mouth before they had even registered in her brain. The thought chilled her that it could have been Nathan instead of Joel.

"I thought you might want some friends with you," Matthew said.

Friends? Why would I need friends?

"They helped me." Joel took a few steps closer to her dresser, pretending he wasn't looking at her stuff.

"With what?" Tilly watched the two newcomers check out her room, feeling more and more exposed as they did.

"There is somewhere we have to be," Matthew said.

"Are you kidding me? What? Another funeral home?" Tilly was getting confused with the bits and pieces of information Matthew was handing out. But did she want to know it all?

CHAPTER 15

It's a strange thing to attend your own funeral, Tilly thought when she entered at the back of the church.

When she remembered that no one could see her, she slowly made her way up to the front. She noticed that most of the people in the pews had been present at yesterday's viewing, and that most were relatives, some she'd only ever seen once a year or even less. She saw her grandparents, cousins, aunts and uncles. There were friends from school, sitting next to their parents. She saw Angela crying.

Nathan sat with their parents in the front row. Her father was rigid and straight, trying like always to be the strongest. Her mother's face was pale, her nose red and eyes bloodshot. She seemed a little… dull, was the only word Tilly could think of. She watched her mother periodically bring tissues to her face.

Nathan sat next to Mom, staring off to the side like he was looking for something. Tilly looked but couldn't see what he was looking at. She walked a little closer and he turned to her. He started to wave, but gave her a half smile instead.

Tilly stopped in front of him.

"Hi." She didn't know what else to say.

Nathan gave a slight nod.

When his father looked at him, he pretended to cough. His mother gave no sign of noticing.

Not knowing what else to do, Tilly sat in the pew next to Nathan. It almost felt normal to be sitting with her family—if it wasn't for it being her funeral.

She couldn't help feeling like an intruder. She felt like she was trespassing on their grief. But it also felt, illogically, like they had betrayed her by just sitting there to listen. It was as if they weren't fighting for her and that they had just given up on her.

She knew these thoughts were ridiculous: how were they supposed to fight for her? She was dead. That was the end. That was how life went. A person dies, and the living move on as best they can.

It was also odd to feel guilt slowly building within her. She didn't die on purpose. She hadn't meant to hurt anyone, and she hadn't done anything wrong. It wasn't her fault. But wasn't it? She had run off alone. As the feelings of having caused this grief increased, the guilt building inside her hurt so much she had to try to shut everything down.

She focused on the pastor, the rise and fall of his voice. She listened to the flattering and sometimes amusing things he said about her and how she was with God and his angels now. He also commented on how everyone here would keep her living within them.

But what did he know? She was sitting here, right in front of him.

Do they just say this stuff to make everyone feel better, so you'll be less scared of dying? It was beginning to feel like a bunch of garbage to her. There was no angel to greet her at her death and guide her to Heaven. There was no peace or happily ever after. If this was eternal life, she didn't like it.

Tilly watched her family. Her father's gaze was locked onto the minister. Nathan's moved from their father to the pastor, to Tilly, with only the slightest movement of his head. Her mother looked ahead, just above the floor line of the stage, in front of the pulpit. Her gaze never left that spot even as she wiped away tears.

Tilly tried to focus on the pastor's words, to hear what he was saying about her, to maybe give her a hint of why she was still here, or when she would go to the heaven he was describing.

"…He that believeth in me, though he were dead, yet shall he live; and whosoever liveth and believeth in me, shall never die…."

But someone sniffling behind her brought her back from her thoughts.

She tried once more, watching the pastor's lips move as he spoke.

"He shall feed his flock like a shepherd; he shall gather the lambs with his arms and carry them in his bosom."

"That's such—"Tilly stopped at the sound of someone's sobs coming from behind her. She turned to see Angela, her hands over her face, her mother pulling her in and covering her with her arms. Tilly twisted further, her knee coming up on the pew, almost touching Nathan.

As she started to get up, Nathan turned to look at her. She could see tears in his eyes. She wanted to go to Angela. She saw Angela and her mother leave their seats and walk down the aisle towards the doors, where Suzie, Matthew, and Joel now stood. Matthew smiled, motioned her to stay where she was, then followed Angela out through the carved wooden doors.

Tilly remained watching the back of the church, looking at the people sitting in the pews. The rows were full. Most seemed lost in their thoughts or the pastor's words. A few whispered to each other. Her gaze shifted around the church, and she noticed the light shining through the stained-glass windows, coloring some of the mourners.

She noticed the spiral staircase to the balcony in the back corner. She had forgotten it was there. She remembered running up and down it when she was younger, when she went to Bible study. Some Sundays, Pastor Marques would let them have Sunday school up there. Tilly looked up to the balcony, and saw the angels carved into the posts of its railing.

Pastor Marques had left the church a few years ago and Tilly had never gotten to know Pastor Nickson who was conducting her funeral. After she received a spot on the high school volleyball team, her father convinced her mother to let her have Sundays to practice and keep up with her homework. Her mother had put up a fight, but settled on allowing Tilly to attend the church's special services. When Tilly secured the captain's position on the team the next year, her mother eventually gave up on that requirement as well.

Tilly looked around the church for more forgotten treasures. She started to stand, and Nathan looked at her. She smiled at him. He seemed to be doing better. She knew it was a silly thought, but she wanted to walk around the church: it suddenly felt like it was welcoming her. She wanted to feel the multi-colored light streaming in through the stained-glass windows. She wanted to touch the wooden angels around the perimeter of the room. Nathan gave her a quick nod.

She moved to an outside aisle and reached out to touch one of the many carved angels that graced the church. She was surprised by the coolness of the wood.

"Bless us and keep us, O Lord!" the congregation chanted.

Tilly snapped her hand back and froze.

"You welcomed children, promising them Your kingdom. To You we pray. Bless us and keep us, O Lord!"

As the pastor and the people continued the litany, Tilly walked around, running hands along smooth wooden banisters, sculptures, the faux-marble columns.

"You comforted those who mourned the loss of children and friends. To You we pray. Bless us and keep us, O Lord!"

Tilly found the service comforting now. She continued to walk, losing herself into the music of the voices. Finally, she wandered to the front of the church.

"Bless us and keep us, O Lord!"

She walked towards the pulpit. Stopped in front of it. Forbidden territory.

"…Give us confidence that she is safe, and her life is complete with You, and bring us together at the last to the wholeness and fullness of Your presence in Heaven, where Your saints and angels enjoy You forever and ever. Amen!"

Tilly walked to the edge of the communion rail and then followed it to an opening at the opposite side of the church. She slipped in behind it, feeling strangely mischievous and playful.

She looked at Nathan. He looked worried at first, but as she settled into a chair, he smiled. She sat, legs swinging, looking at everything from this different view. She smiled. It was her funeral after all, right? Why shouldn't she be upfront and onstage?

She looked at her casket. The wood was the same color as her bedroom furniture, honey brown. It was so smooth you could see the lights reflect from it. Brass bars ran around its perimeter. She wondered if her dad had picked it out; if he knew it matched her bedroom; if that's why he had picked it. It seemed so surreal. She was in that box? With the lid of the casket closed you could no longer see the girl who looked like her. So as far as she was concerned, the casket was just another ornament in the church.

". . . a glimpse of the kingdom of heaven. Spare them the torment of guilt and despair."

She checked on Nathan. He smiled again.

She wanted to keep him smiling.

The pastor lifted his hand. ". . . that they may not be overwhelmed by their loss, but have confidence in Your love."

And impishly, Tilly lifted hers to match. Nathan covered the smile on his face. She looked at the nave of the church and saw Matthew, Suzie, and Joel waiting there for her. They were smiling as well.

As Pastor Nickson stepped out from behind his lectern to walk as he spoke, Tilly followed behind him, first just following, but then exaggerating his movements. She watched her new, and old, friends at the back of the church break up in laughter nobody else could hear but Nathan. And he giggled aloud.

When she saw her father scowl at Nathan, she stopped. Getting Nathan into trouble was the last thing she wanted to do.

She looked at Nathan and gave him an apologetic smile. He put his head down, to please his father, but peeked up at Tilly to let her know it was okay.

Tilly returned to her seat and behaved for the rest of the service.

Funerals are so boring, Tilly thought to herself, and her own, apparently, was no different.

CHAPTER 16

With Tilly's casket loaded, the hearse slowly pulled away from the church and disappeared around the corner. Mourners shuffled around, some unsure what to do, others broke into small groups, talking, hugging, while others took advantage of the opportunity to use the washroom.

They waited for the cue to head to the cemetery, and Tilly was thankful when it came.

At the graveyard, everyone gathered around the casket. Off to the side sat a pile of dirt covered with fake grass, a bad attempt at the real thing. Chairs covered with linen slips were lined up for the family just off to the side of the grave. Tilly figured they were metal folding chairs hidden beneath the light brown cloth. Tilly saw her family seated there—grandparents, and her parents with Nathan between them.

As the minister started to speak, Tilly scanned the faces of those who had come to the cemetery and found herself getting lost in the moments she had shared with them. There were Antoinette and Nicole from her volleyball team, the year they had won the championships. D'Andre who worked the counter at her favorite coffee shop. She was surprised to see him here. Tracey who lived next door and made the best pulled pork that she'd bring to all the neighborhood parties, always giving Tilly a wink when she took off the lid.

The sound of a cell phone cleared her memories. She looked around and saw her cousin Andrew turn red as he dug into his pocket. There was a ripple of laughter. "That was like Tilly," she heard her father say. "Never went anywhere without her phone." This brought on another ripple of laughter.

Tilly looked at Matthew beside her, then shifted her gaze to Joel and Suzie who were a few feet away, but she couldn't hear what they were chatting about. For a minute she thought she might try to listen in, see if she could hear them like she had been able to hear some of the people at her viewing. Would Matthew think that was wrong? She didn't have time to find out; instead, she watched Pastor Nickson walk up behind them, turn, and stop at the foot of the grave.

Her casket now sat above the grave on straps, their ends wrapped around brass poles that ran the length of it. Tilly wondered how the straps could hold its weight and how they were going to lower it.

It was hard to imagine her body lying in that box. She knew it was in there—she had seen it yesterday, at the viewing—but now that she stood beside the coffin with the lid closed, it was difficult to believe that her body was right there inside it. If she was dead, then why could she still *see* her body? Feel it. Why did she see Matthew? Susie? Joel? Why did they look like everyone else here?

When she looked at her friends again, it occurred to her they had probably done this too.

"Did you go to each other's funerals?" Tilly asked.

Matthew started to speak, but Suzie was quicker.

"I was the first, so none of you came to my funeral."

"I guess I hadn't thought of that," Tilly said. She realized she hadn't thought much about them at all.

"We would have, though," Joel said. "I mean, if we knew you, you know, when you were alive, we would have gone." He cleared his throat. "Or if I had died first, then I would have gone."

"Of course, we would have," Matthew added. Joel looked happy for the backup.

"So, did you guys go to Joel's then? And Matthew's?" Tilly asked.

"I went to Joel's," Suzie said. "At the time, I wasn't sure why I ended up there. I didn't know him. I didn't even know where I was. I'd never even been to this part of the city, but then he sat down beside me. I was sitting at the back of the church, and I was just happy to have someone to talk to, someone who could see me."

"I know that feeling," Tilly said.

"They came to mine." Matthew shook his head. Tilly was puzzled by this.

Suzie and Joel laughed. "He kept moving every time we got near him," Joel said. "At one point he was sitting at the back of the church"

"Hiding," Suzie said.

"I wasn't hiding," Matthew said defensively. "I was sitting, watching."

"So, while Matthew was watching," Joel made a quick quotation motion with his fingers when he said *watching*, "Suzie sat on one side of him while I sat on the other. He wouldn't move, he just kept trying to see us without moving his head, only his eyes."

"If they were people, but couldn't see you, then why were you afraid to move your head?" she asked Matthew.

"I wasn't afraid." Matthew's chest puffed out a bit. "But I could feel something wasn't right."

Suzie and Joel giggled.

"Fine. You guys were creepy."

The three of them started to laugh. Tilly felt herself joining in.

The sound of sniffling rippling through the group of mourners around her brought Tilly back to her surroundings. The mourners had moved around her casket and her family. It made her heart ache to imagine the pain they were feeling, what *she'd* be feeling if she were standing there grieving for her mother or father. She couldn't even imagine it being Nathan. Was this the point of being here? Is this why Matthew had brought her here? Did she need to see any more? She thought of leaving.

She was about to tell Matthew and the others that she was going to go when she noticed a haze at the far end of the cemetery. It was just enough to put the trees out of focus, like a wave in the air coming off hot pavement, or the shimmer of heat above a burning candle. As she tried to focus on it, she noticed that it was slowly moving towards them.

"Do you see that?" she whispered to Matthew.

As the haze grew closer, it grew more opaque. The trees became harder to see.

"Matthew, what the hell is that?" She could feel her hands shaking. "Matt!"

"I…I…don't know."

The fear in Matthew's voice made her shake harder. She realized she had started to depend on him.

"Suzie? Joel?" With all her strength, she broke her gaze from the blur and looked at her new friends.

But they also were staring at the blur in shock. And that sent a shiver down her spine.

The blur moved closer to the cemetery.

"What is it?" Tilly said.

"This doesn't feel good," Matthew said, not taking his eyes off it.

"Matt," Suzie cried. "You need to make it go away!"

"I don't even know what the hell it is—how can I make it go away?"

Tilly could hear panic sneaking into his voice.

"Just do it!" Suzie snapped. "Please," she added more quietly.

The blur moved toward a group of mourners. Tilly felt the air grow heavier. The sky seemed to sink a little lower, pressure building.

"What the…?" Joel stepped in front of Suzie, beside Matthew.

Tilly looked at them, waiting for them to do something. Tilly watched the haze darken as it drew closer to the small group.

"Do you guys see that?" Tilly could see strands of color seep from the mourners, floating toward the blurry haze. "Did you see that?" Tilly grabbed Matthew's arm, pulling on it, ignoring the electric snaps in her fingers.

He nodded slowly.

"What is it doing?" Joel asked.

"I don't know. I don't even know what it *is*!" Mathew said.

Tilly looked around for Nathan. He was wide-eyed and tugging on his father's arm.

"Dad! Dad!" Nathan was whispering urgently.

"Not now, Nathan," his father said, still focused on the burial and oblivious to the haze that his son could see.

"Dad! There's something wrong!"

"What is it, Nathan?" Tilly asked him, forgetting he couldn't answer.

Threads of pale yellows and greens wove their way toward the haze from an older woman in the group. Tilly recognized her from the neighborhood. Her son had died in a motorcycle accident a few years ago. The threads leaving her entered and disappeared into the haze. Tilly forced herself to blink, not believing her eyes. As the haze darkened, the woman herself seemed to blur around the edges.

"Dad, I need to go to the car."

"What is it? Are you feeling sick?"

"There are too many people, I just need to be by myself for a minute."

Tilly watched her father struggle with letting Nathan go but needing to stay with her mother.

"You can see the car from here." Nathan pointed to their vehicle.

"Keep the door open, so I can see you." But Nathan bolted before his father had finished speaking. Tilly and her friends followed him. He opened the back door and climbed in, sinking in his seat, leaving the door open.

"Do you know what that thing is, Nathan?" Tilly asked, as the others gathered around the car.

Tilly looked back and saw the woman begin to collapse. She was caught before she fell and helped to one of the folding chairs.

"Nathan?" Tilly asked again.

"I don't know what it is, Tilly, but it's bad!"

"Bad? How? Do you know what's happening?" Matthew asked.

"It's feeding," Nathan said, and sank lower in the seat.

"Feeding?" Matthew and Tilly said at the same time.

Nathan nodded his head.

Joel and Suzie stood behind Matthew, listening as Matthew added, "Yeah. That's what I *thought* it looked like!"

"Feeding on what?" Tilly asked. She knew she shouldn't push her brother, but she couldn't stop herself and Nathan seemed to be the only one who knew what was happening.

"Them." He pointed to the crowd.

"How do you know?" Joel asked, not taking his gaze off the darkening haze.

"I can feel it. It's intensifying. It's getting louder—"

"Louder? I can't hear it," Suzie pushed past Joel, getting closer to the car.

"In my head. I can hear it in my head!" Nathan stayed pressed to the seat. "And that woman is getting weaker, softer, quiet." He was fighting back tears. "Like a whisper." Tilly wanted to grab him and pull him close.

"She's gone quiet, but the thing has gotten so loud!" He pressed his hands over his ears. "There are too many of them."

"Too many?" Tilly put her hands on the seat next to him. "Who, Nathan? Too many who?"

"I don't know." He looked at her, leaving his hands over his ears. "Voices." His eyes squinted as he spoke.

"From the cemetery?" Tilly heard her words, but she didn't know what she meant. "From the mourners? Or from people *buried* in the cemetery?"

"Yes." He shook his head. "No. I don't know. So many at once!"

"It's leaving!" Joel yelled. "It's leaving!"

Nathan bolted up in his seat. Matthew and Tilly turned to see the haze gradually float back toward the trees, dissolving as it went.

Tilly watched two young men help the woman who had collapsed.

"Did the haze do that? To her?" Joel asked Nathan.

"Joel. Don't. Let's give him some space," Tilly tried. They were pushing him too hard.

"I'm all right, Tilly." Nathan shifted. He rubbed his temples. "It's easing."

"Nathan. Did the haze do that to her?" Joel was pointing to the woman being helped back to the church. "Is that what you meant by feeding?"

"Joel!"

"Tilly. I said I'm all right!" Tilly thought she heard an edge to Nathan's voice. She had never heard him sound like this. Was he scared? Angry?

"Yes, Joel." Nathan looked past his sister. "The haze did that to her."

Tilly tried to concentrate on the remainder of the service, but she kept replaying what had happened. What was the haze? What did it want? Was it feeding? What did that mean, *feeding*?

The minister cast dirt on her casket, mourners placed their flowers, and people slowly turned and walked back to the church. She watched as her father helped her mother across the cemetery, back to the car, Nathan still in it.

Finally, with everyone gone, she watched as a funeral attendant bent over and pushed a small lever on one of the posts of the device holding her casket above the open grave, and the straps unrolled slowly, lowering the casket into the ground.

Tilly was still unable to believe that she was in it.

CHAPTER 17

Tilly hitched a ride with her family after the burial, sitting beside Nathan in the back seat. Tilly's mother hadn't spoken a word. It was as if she hadn't heard any of the conversation on the way home. Tilly wasn't even sure if her mother knew anyone was around her at all. She just stared blankly and walked around like a zombie. As soon as they arrived home, followed by a very concerned Tilly, her mother went straight to her room and climbed into bed, only stopping to push off her shoes.

Tilly had no idea what to do. After a while she went back downstairs to find Nathan.

She heard her father's voice as she came down the stairs: "You need to stop this, Nathan, please."

Both he and Nathan were playing with the macaroni and cheese on their plates. She looked at Nathan. He didn't smile at her, but his eyes seemed to send her a comforting vibe, then his gaze turned to their father.

Tilly sat on the stool at the end of the island and looked at her father. She realized how tired he looked, his shoulders rounded and his eyes sunken with dark crescents beneath. When he spoke it seemed to take great effort. He looked deflated.

"But she's here, right here!" Nathan pointed to Tilly.

"Nathan, don't," Tilly said, waving her hands.

"She hasn't gone to heaven, and she isn't an angel—she's here!"

Their dad dropped his fork onto the plate of macaroni and cheese, rubbing his forehead. The neighbors kept dropping off casseroles and lasagnas, but Tilly's father had made Nathan's favorite meal.

"Nathan," he took a moment to breathe. "I don't know how much more of this I can take, Buddy." Another moment, another breath. "Tilly is not here. Dr. Sito has talked to you about real friends and imaginary friends. You don't need imaginary friends anymore, and this isn't good for any of us. You need to let Tilly go."

"It's all right, Nathan. He can't see me, so he doesn't understand." *How could he? I don't understand, myself.* "I know he loves me." She stood beside Nathan, careful to keep her hands to herself.

"But you are here, Tilly. And you're not imaginary." Nathan crossed his arms over his chest. "I'm tired of hiding."

"That's enough." Dad picked up his plate and grabbed Nathan's. "I can't hear any more of this. You can go and find something to do in your room." He turned, walked to the counter, and put the dishes in the sink. He stood staring out the window, running his hand through his hair.

"She says she knows you love her."

"NATHAN!" Tilly and her father both said.

Nathan slid off his stool. He walked to the sink. His father did not turn from the window. Nathan dropped his fork in the sink, returned to the island, picked up his glass and headed for the stairs.

Tilly waited, not sure what to do. She couldn't console either of them. When her father finally turned, she saw tears running down his face. He lifted his arm, and with the back of his hand, wiped them away.

"Oh, Tilly!"

The despair in his voice made her head spin. Her vision blurred. She had to get out of the room. She headed for the stairs, headed for her room.

At the doorway to her room, Tilly stopped, then turned and went to her parents' instead. She was not surprised by its darkness this time, although their ensuite bath light was on. The door was half-closed, allowing only a little light into the room. Tilly's mother lay curled up on her side on the bed. Tilly walked over and sat on the floor, leaning against her mother's nightstand.

"I'm sorry, Mom," Tilly said. "I messed everything up. It's all my fault. I've hurt everyone." She wished her mother could see her, talk to her one more time. Tilly pulled her knees up to her chest and wrapped her arms around her legs. She closed her eyes and dropped her forehead on to her knees.

"I'm so sorry," she whispered. "Why—why—why didn't I listen? Why me? I'm so stupid!" She wiped her nose across her knees. "I'm so stupid!" She dug her hands into her hair, pulling it. "Idiot. Idiot!" She thumped her clenched hands against her head.

"Tilly."

She stopped.

"Tilly, I miss you,"

"Mom?" Tilly wiped her face with the front of her shirt, running her nose along the sleeve.

"I'm sorry I failed you, Tilly. I'm so sorry. It was my job to protect you, and I didn't." Her mother started to cry.

Tilly pulled herself up to her knees.

"Mom, it's not your fault, it's mine." She moved as close to her mother as she dared, making sure not to touch her. "It's my fault, I didn't listen. I didn't take any of it seriously."

"I'm tired," her mother said. Tilly felt a sudden wave of nausea. "I'm so tired. I wish I could just go to sleep and sleep forever."

The pills.

"No, Mom."

Tilly jumped up, searching the nightstand. There was no sign of the bottle or its contents. She raced to her mother's dresser. No bottle. *Dad's.* Turning, something caught the corner of her eye. The corner of the room blurred as a haze began to form.

Tilly stiffened. Her arms started to tingle. She lifted them, watched as their hair stood up.

But.

The tingling changed, replaced with the sense of tiny feet of hundreds of bugs crawling all over her, making her itch. She swiped her arms and legs, wiping the feet away.

Her mother moaned. Tilly forgot the bugs as she saw the haze thicken.

"Why?" her mother moaned from her bed.

"Mom!" Tilly yelled, now seeing the same threads that she'd seen at the cemetery come from her mother. She watched them rise-up like steam and enter the blurry haze that had moved near the bed from the corner of the room. As the threads entered the haze, it seemed to pulsate, grow darker, thicker. Its pulsing was hypnotizing, gripping Tilly until her head throbbed in sync with it.

She took a step towards the haze which was now thickly threaded to her mother.

The sound of her mother's moan broke the spell. She rushed to the bed.

"Mom, get up," she yelled. She grabbed her.

Her mother's shriek filled the room and felt like an explosion inside her head. Tilly wanted to let go, cover her ears—instead, she pulled at her mother.

"Get up!" she screamed at her. "Nathan!"

Tilly couldn't hold on to her any longer. She let her go.

"What do you want?" She yelled, getting between her mother and the haze that occupied the corner of her mother's room. The bathroom light flickered, then went out, shifting her attention for a second.

Her mother moaned.

"Leave her alone!"

"Maggie," her father shouted from behind her, out in the hall.

"Dad. Stay back!"

"Maggie, what's wrong?" He was moving towards the bed.

The last of the threads dried up. The blur shifted and pulsed—but it slowly withdrew and left the same way it came.

Tilly was torn between following it and staying with her parents.

Why did it leave? Was it me? What did it want? How can I stop it?

"Dad!" Nathan's said.

"Maggie, are you okay?" Her father sat down on the bed beside her mother.

She watched her father shake his wife awake.

Nathan came to Tilly. "What's wrong, Tilly?" His eyes were wide with fear.

Tilly didn't want to tell him, but she knew she had to. She realized the best way to protect Nathan was to make sure he knew everything that was happening. He needed to know it was serious, or he'd end up like she had.

"It was the haze from the cemetery," she said. "It was here, in Mom's room. It was doing it to her."

"What is it, Wil?" Mom asked, her voice heavy with sleep.

"You were screaming." Tilly could hear his fear.

"It was Tilly." She ran her hand along her forehead.

Her father slid over to sit closer to his wife. He wrapped his arms around her shoulders and pulled her in. He looked up to see Nathan at the foot of the bed.

"Nathan, Buddy. It's all right. It was just a bad dream," he told him. "Are you okay?" He patted the bed beside him, inviting Nathan to join them. "Do you want to sit with us for a bit?" Nathan did not find relief in personal contact, but Tilly knew her dad's gesture would comfort him.

Nathan sat at the foot of the bed instead.

"I felt like I was falling into an old well. The deeper I fell, the darker and tighter it got." Her mother's voice was muffled by her father's sweater. 'I could hear Tilly shouting. I...I...I don't know if she was in the well." Her father started to rock her as she cried. He ran his hand along her hair, kissing the top of her head. "I was angry, frantic. Then sad. And heartbroken. The walls were closing in and squeezing me. I couldn't breathe."

"It was just a dream."

"It hurt, Wil. It hurt so much."

Nathan looked at his parents. Then Tilly. "It hurt Mom?"

Tilly nodded. "I think so."

It confused her when Nathan made a strange face.

"What is it? What's wrong?" She came to him.

"I didn't say anything."

"What do you mean? You asked if—"

"It's all right, Nathan." Their father said, plainly thinking Nathan had been talking to him.

An unexpected voice came from the door to the hallway. It was Joel.

"Tilly. There's another girl." He beckoned to them to come with him.

Nathan quietly slipped off the bed and left his parent's room, Tilly right behind him. In the hall, they found Joel and Suzie.

"Is everything okay in there?" Joel asked when he saw Tilly.

"I don't know. That haze we saw at the burial was here, but now it's gone and Dad's with my mom." Tilly wished she knew how to help her mother. "It was that same haze again. It was in my mother's room. It was feeding off her!" Tilly's breath was rushed. "It's gone. But what if it comes back?" She looked at Nathan. She turned and crossed the landing to Nathan's room.

"We need to figure out what it wants," Joel said as they all moved into Nathan's room where Matthew was standing.

"It's feeding. We already figured that part out." Suzie's arms were across her chest, her head slightly tilted to the side.

"I know, Suzie, but what is it? And why is it doing that?"

"Duh, *people!*" Her hands flapped as if to demonstrate the stupidity of common folk. "Does it matter?"

"Yes." Joel had started to pace the room. "We need to figure out what it wants. Maybe that can help us stop it."

"Joel's right," Matthew said. "The more we know about it, the more we might understand it. That could help us find a weakness."

"This isn't some superhero movie." Suzie's arms were still folded across her chest. "And what can we do? We're dead. We can't even go to the police."

Joel looked at her coldly. "Maybe you could help with a solution instead of looking for problems."

"And how could we tell anyone, anyway? In case you didn't hear me, we're dead. Nobody can hear us."

"Stop it." Tilly snapped, her hands out like a traffic cop. "You said there was another girl?"

91

CHAPTER 18

"I forgot!" Matthew said as he ducked out Nathan's door. "She was waiting in your room, Tilly." When he returned to Nathan's room, a petite girl followed behind him. The makeup around her eyes and lipstick was as black as her hair. She looked about thirteen.

All Tilly could think of was how another future had been stolen. Another family broken.

"Kaylin, this is Suzie, Joel, and Tilly," Matthew said, pointing to the trio. "That's Nathan," he pointed to Nathan sitting on Tilly's bed. "He isn't... like us, but he can see and hear us."

"Hi, Nathan," Kaylin said, giving him a small wave. Tilly got the impression they already knew each other. "Joel."

"Do you guys know each other?" Suzie asked, echoing Tilly's own thoughts.

"She plays ball at my field," Joel said. "They usually have practice before us."

"Yeh. And I've seen Kaylin at the pool too," Nathan said, smiling at the girl.

Now that Tilly thought about it, the girl did look a little familiar, but it was hard to tell under all that black eye makeup. As she looked around at her group of new friends, Tilly tried to sort out their connections. She had gone to school with Matthew. Matthew knew Joel. Joel knew Nathan, and both Joel and Nathan knew Kaylin, but what about Suzie? Suzie seemed to be a stranger to all of them. Where did she fit in? Where was she from?

Tilly watched as Kaylin settled on the bed next to Nathan. She seemed to be extremely accepting of what was happening around her. When did she die? They had found out about her today, but it took days before Matthew came to Tilly. Did this mean Kaylin had accepted her death quicker? Did she even realize that she *was* dead? That thought brought Tilly back to the moment.

"We have to figure out how to stop the haze," Tilly said, remembering her mother. "Nathan can explain that to you later, Kaylin. We also have to find out exactly what's happened to us."

"To *us*?" Suzie asked.

"How we died. Why we're still here—"

"And we need to stop this from happening to anyone else," Matthew added with a small nod toward Kaylin.

"How can we do that?" Suzie said. "We're dead, remember?"

"I don't know; but there are now five of us, and whoever killed us is going to just keep killing," Matthew said.

"You think it's the same guy?" Tilly asked.

"Or killers," Suzie said.

Killers? "Why do you say that? Do you know who killed you?"

"No."

"Then why did you say that?"

"But she's right. What do we know about our killer?" Joel said.

"I'm just saying that you don't know if we were all killed by the same person."

"The police will know," Kaylin said. "They will get him." Her voice carried that tone of someone who still believes in the Tooth Fairy and happily-ever-afters.

"Well, they haven't yet," Suzie said, looking right at Kaylin.

"SUZIE!" which came out as a group shout.

"Well, it's true," she mumbled, crossing her arms defiantly.

"I think we should talk about this in my room," Tilly started towards the door. "You should stay here," she said to Nathan.

"I'm fine," Nathan said.

"I just don't think you need to be part of this."

"I'm not a baby, Tilly."

"He sees us," Joel said.

"It would just make me feel better if you didn't hear any of this, Nathan." She gave Joel a withering look. "We can fill you in later, Nathan, but I just don't think you need to hear all the details." She wondered if Joel had got the message.

"Maybe she's right, Nate," Joel said. "Some of what we need to say maybe pretty rough."

"Fine," Nathan said. He picked up his sketchbook and started to draw.

"Thanks, Buddy," Tilly said. She smiled at him, but Nathan didn't look up.

Once they were all settled in Tilly's room, she said, "Don't the cops even know who the killer is?"

There were general shrugs all around.

"Well, since they don't, it's up to us! *We* know who he is."

"You just said you didn't know who he was, but now suddenly you do?' Suzie said. "You know his name?"

"No. But I'm sure if we pool our information, we could figure it out."

She looked at her small group. Each one of them had been killed, murdered by the same person, probably. Why not use this information? Gather it and see where it took them.

CHAPTER 19

"It was a guy who took me. He wore a uniform and he wasn't very old." Tilly returned to a memory she thought she'd never go to again. She closed her eyes. "He wore a blue ball cap; his hair was long, I think it was brown, and he had it in a ponytail." She could feel her body stiffen, that fight or flight reaction. She tried to tell herself it wasn't real this time; but if she wanted to remember anything, she'd have to give in, relive it.

"He took me to a shed in his backyard, I think. I could see the street from there."

"Okay," Joel said, as if to himself.

Tilly opened her eyes. "He lives in a neighborhood."

"Everybody lives in a neighborhood," Suzie said.

She saw Joel look at Suzie, give her three quick shakes of his head.

"When I said *neighborhood* I just meant that his place wasn't out in the country or something. He took me to his house. He didn't kill me in the woods like he did with you, Matthew." She offered him a small smile.

"Yeah, you said that already," Suzie said.

"Come *on*, Suzie!" Joel said.

Suzie flinched, then stepped back as she raised her chin.

"I'm sorry." He gave Suzie a small smile, leaned towards her. She looked off to the side of the room. He put his hand on her arm. When Suzie shrugged it off, Tilly wondered if Suzie felt the same electricity she did when Matthew touched her.

95

"If he took you to his house, maybe you could find it again. And somehow we could figure out how to call the police," Matthew said.

"Exactly. So, what we know is that he doesn't live in an apartment or some abandoned building. I wasn't brought to the woods, and his house looks like the kind of houses in my neighborhood—so he wouldn't live in one like I imagine Suzie lives in." Tilly felt the sting in her words, although she hadn't meant them to sound so critical.

"I caught the back of someone walking their dog just before they disappeared behind a hedge, so it must be a nice neighborhood, right?" Tilly added quickly, hoping no one had noticed.

"I was in a shed too," Joel said.

"The same one?" Tilly couldn't help herself.

"I don't know." Joel's lips compressed. "I don't remember a whole lot about it. I do remember staying after ball practice to work on my fastball. Jesse Pinski stayed behind with me as catcher. When we were done, he took off, and I went into the locker room to get my bag." Tilly watched Joel stiffen, the set of his jaw.

"He was in there. I didn't know he'd be the guy, of course; but he was there, fixing something." Joel fidgeted with the zipper on his jacket. "He had a uniform or coveralls on, something like that, and a hat. It was blue. Just like Tilly said."

Emotion played across Joel's face, then realization. "He mumbled something to me. I said, *What?* But he just mumbled again, so I went over." His voice dropped. "When I got close enough, he nailed me with a wrench or something. Then I woke up in the shed."

"Could you describe him?" Tilly asked.

"I didn't get to see his face; his hat was pulled down low."

"What did the shed look like?"

"It was dark. The windows were dirty." Joel closed his eyes while the others watched. He was shaking a bit. "I do remember a stack of boxes on the floor. And the floor was dirt like you said."

"Do you know what was in the boxes?" And she realized she'd interrupted again. "Sorry."

"No, that's good. You're helping me." Joel squeezed his eyes closed. "They were... they had wire in them. Yeah, I remember them now. There was cable wire sticking out of one." Joel moved his head around like he was looking around a room, his eyes still closed. "I can't see the name on the boxes." Joel opened his eyes and sighed. "I don't know—like I said, it was dark."

"Great job, Joel." Matthew gently slapped him on the back. "OK, Tilly. My turn, I guess." Matthew moved his hand to his mouth, his finger tapping his top lip. "I was killed in the woods just behind my house." He started to walk around the room, watching his feet.

"I was cutting through the woods, on my way to my buddy's," he went on. "We were going to binge-watch all the *Star Wars* movies. We planned to stay up all weekend. He had the old DVD movies, and I was bringing the snacks. I'd bought chocolate bars, chips and a giant package of sours. I had it all stuffed in my school bag with my toothbrush and a clean shirt, just in case I spilled something on this one." He took his finger and thumb and pinched his T-shirt, pulling away from his chest then letting it fall back. "Never did get a chance to spill anything, I guess."

"He came out of nowhere. He started asking a bunch of questions: *Do you have the time? Do you live around here? Where you off to?* His questions came so fast I couldn't answer any of them, and the whole time he walked towards me. Before I realized it, he grabbed me."

"Oh!"

Everyone looked at Kaylin. She covered her mouth. "Sorry," she mumbled from behind her hand.

"I'm the one who's sorry," Matthew said. "If I had stopped him, then you and Tilly would still be alive."

Tilly went to Matthew. It was her turn to comfort. She placed her hand firmly on his arm. "None of this is your fault." He shook his head. "It isn't." When he didn't stop or respond she found herself shaking him a little, wanting to shift his thoughts.

"Do you hear me? None of us are to blame, Matthew. None of us made this happen!"

"At least they know you were murdered." Suzie said. "They think mine was an accident. No one is even looking for my killer."

Tilly suddenly found herself feeling sorry for her. Even though the girl was rude and obnoxious, she was one of them and she was hurting. Suzie was probably just as scared and confused as she was. Like the rest of them she was probably missing her family.

"Suzie," Tilly shifted on the bed, inviting the girl to join her. "Tell us what happened to you."

Suzie shook her head slightly and seemed to be trying to get some of her brash confidence back. She had been all talk, but now that Tilly had given her the floor she retreated.

"Please," Tilly said and patted the bed beside her. Suzie gathered a breath and joined her.

"Well, as you know, I was the first to be killed. but I didn't go to a shed." She shifted and squared her shoulders a little, almost like an actor preparing to go on stage. "I was at my riding lesson. I have my own horse. My parents bought Fleet for me for my birthday. We made Grand Champion. He's a Hanoverian gelding, 16.6 hands."

"What happened at your riding lesson?" Tilly said, trying to get Suzie focused.

"I went to go get Fleet, but there was this guy in the alleyway of the barn. Each barn has only six or eight stalls: the owner likes small barns instead of one huge one. "Fleet, was the only horse in the barn because I had called ahead to say I'd be coming out to ride—that way they would leave him in his stall when they turned the others out."

Suzie rubbed her arm. "The guy was standing outside my stall, stroking Fleet's nose, talking to him. He must have heard me coming and turned around. He looked surprised, then went to a box of kittens that was outside the stall and picked one up. Now that I think about it, he was wearing a blue baseball hat."

"I went to go around him, when he spoke to me. He asked who owned the kittens and I told him they belonged to the owners and were barn cats." She opened her eyes. "They usually spay and neuter the cats, but this one had recently moved in and was already pregnant, probably just dumped off by her owner." She waved her hand, dismissing her digression. "I told him he could probably have one if he wanted, then I grabbed my kit from outside the stall and went to groom Fleet." She scanned the others. "My horse's name is Strawman War Fleet. But I just call him Fleet. They all have pedigree names and then their barn names."

"I was busy picking the dirt out of Fleet's hooves when I heard the guy speak again. I looked up, and he was at the stall door. A kitten in his hand. I was going to ignore him, but instead I asked him if that was the one he'd chosen. He told me he couldn't decide."

"I went to Fleet's other side and started to pick his front hoof, and that's when I heard the latch of the stall. I dropped Fleet's foot, turned around and found the guy inside the stall with me. Fleet started to snort a bit, and that was strange: he almost never does that."

"I told the man that he couldn't come in here, but he moved along the wall until he was on the same side as me. You know," Suzie returned her attention to the room again, "he wasn't very old. I'd say maybe twenty, twenty-two."

"Good information," Joel said.

"Did he kill you in the stall?" Tilly asked, aware she'd been blunt, but thankfully Suzie didn't notice.

"Fleet seemed to get more spooked the longer the guy was there. I tried to calm him while I asked the man to go, but he didn't go. I tried to shift Fleet so the guy would have nowhere to go but out. Fleet started to snort and toss his head. By now, I wasn't sure if the guy was going to hurt my horse, so I moved to the other side, to get to the door. Maybe if I left, he'd follow me. Fleet kept shifting."

"When I looked to see where the guy was, I froze. He had a knife in his hand."

Suzie seemed to shrink as she told her story. Tears slid down her cheeks, and Tilly wondered if this was the first time she'd thought of her death. Tilly shifted closer to her in an attempt to offer comfort.

"I wanted to scream, but I knew Fleet would get hurt—he's huge; he takes up most of his stall. I had to get him out of his stall since this guy wasn't going to go. I grabbed at his halter, but Fleet tossed his head and snorted. I was terrified he'd been stabbed so I grabbed at the halter again. Fleet tossed his head harder. The last thing I saw was his velvety muzzle coming towards my face. I heard my nose crunch, and then I woke up dead."

No one said anything. They let her cry.

There was a long pause before they went over what they knew: blue baseball hat, cable wires, a uniform. This gave them somewhere to start. They also knew that they were looking for a male, around twenty with long hair. But they still didn't know where he lived.

"Do we think he's a cable guy?" Joel said.

"He was a cable guy for me," Tilly reminded them. "He came in my front door—he was standing in my house!" What if Nathan had been home?

She suddenly remembered Nathan. She'd left him in his room when the conversation had turned to them discussing their deaths. "I need to talk to Nathan. I need to warn him!"

"But we don't know anything," Kaylin said as Tilly walked across the room.

"Keep talking, keep comparing. I'll be right back." She left the others and started down the hall towards his room. "Nathan," she called as she got closer to his door. He didn't reply. When she walked in, she found him sitting on his bed, reading.

Tilly smiled when she saw him.

"What have you decided?" Nathan asked without looking up.

"You have to be very careful, Nathan. Apparently, this guy wears a blue ball. Sometimes he wears coveralls or a uniform, like a plumber or a cable guy. I guess we don't really know, so if you see anybody like this, turn around and run home. You understand?"

"Yes, Tilly. You don't have to worry though; Dad won't let me go anywhere without him anymore. He even walks me to the front door at school now, and I have to wait in my classroom for him to pick me up now that the girl is missing." He dropped his head and corrected himself. "Now that Kaylin is dead, I mean."

Hearing Nathan talk about Kaylin being dead she started to realize how hard all of this must be on him. She had forgotten that he was just a little boy. Although at twelve he'd disagree about being little, but she couldn't help it. He was her little brother. She had to keep him safe. "Please listen to Dad."

As Tilly said that, she felt a weird sensation, felt her stomach clench, and had a sudden premonition of danger. She ran to her mother's room, Nathan behind her, the others arriving almost immediately from the other room apparently summoned by the same feeling. She was not surprised to see the gray haze. It was darker this time.

The haze was moving towards her mother's bed. Wispy tendrils sprouted from the front of it as it closed in. New ones appeared much like snakes' tongues tasting the air.

The haze moved above her mother. It pulsated, and changed in opaqueness as it did, the wall behind the bed disappearing behind the cloud as it thickened. Tilly felt a strong vibration, not sure if it was just her or if the room itself was vibrating.

"Do you feel that, Nathan?" She was hesitant to ask him.

"Yes," he said and side-stepped closer to Tilly.

Tilly's little group stood still, horrified, not knowing how to help or what to do.

Tendrils lowered themselves from the cloud and dangled toward Tilly's mother. The haze began to change to shades of green and grey.

Tilly's mother groaned, shifting in the bed.

"Tilly," Nathan pointed to threads of green beginning to lift from their mother.

The threads coming from their mother intensified in color. The haze seemed to hum now with vibrations that grew stronger, making Tilly dizzy. She felt as if she were being pulled from her body, or from her sense of being, whatever that was now.

The threads became streams of light. Her mother contorted, stomach lifting towards the haze.

She cried out. The haze rumbled. Tilly thought she saw her mother's skin sink within itself like sucking too hard on a juice box.

Tilly screamed. She ran to her mother, yelling for her to wake up. But, of course, her mother couldn't hear her.

"Make her wake up, Nathan!" She danced between her mother and her little brother trying to close the gap between them, drawing him closer to her.

Nathan started towards the bed.

"Hurry!" She reached out for him, desperate to push him towards their mother, but he jerked away from Tilly as he passed her.

"Mom, wake up!" Nathan called to her as he moved toward the bed.

In her haste to help her mum, she collided with Nathan. There was an explosion of light inside her head when they touched. She felt light but heavy, wanting to float away but was equally tethered. As she tried to clear her head, she realized specks of light were in front of her eyes as well and all around her. There was a rumble of sound, not like thunder but like waves on a beach, but so many waves that they all blended together.

And then pain, deep pain, of a kind that went beyond the physical. She couldn't breathe; and as the pain increased, the rumble increased. Specks of light blurred together now, making splotches of brightness and color.

She could hear a voice, but the rumbling blocked it out. She listened. It was familiar. She struggled to hear it.

"Get......" She strained harder to hear it. "... off, Tilly!" She remained as still as she could be, focused. "Get off me, Tilly!"

Nathan! She looked through the specks of light, trying to find him. He was so small, distant, pulsing.

"Get *off* me!"

But he was in front of her.

"I can't *move*, Tilly!"

She looked at herself. Her limbs were transparent, the room showing through her arms, the specks, and the splotches of light.

"Tilly!"

She took a breath and imagined herself stepping back.

As soon as she did, the lights faded. She became opaque again, her body again feeling like it had weight.

She looked for Nathan. He was half on her mother's bed, leaning on it, panting. Above them, the awful haze remained, but seemed to have retreated a little.

"Nathan!" She got as close as she could without touching him again. "Are you okay?"

He groaned.

"What did I do?"

"Just give me a minute."

Tilly was torn between Nathan and her mother. They didn't have a minute.

She glanced up at the haze, then looked around at the others. Everyone stared at her, having forgotten Tilly's mother for the moment. They just stood there, not knowing what to do.

"Matthew." She could feel tears on her face.

"I don't know, Tilly," he said.

"Talk to your mom," Joel said. "Keep talking until Nathan can help."

Finally able to take control of herself, Tilly turned back to her mother. "Mom," she cried, "please wake up." She looked to Nathan then back to her mother. "Please."

Kaylin and Suzie huddled near Nathan, trying to encourage him.

"Keep talking, Tilly," Joel said and moved to the other side of the bed followed by Matthew. Matthew tried to smile encouragement at Tilly, but Tilly saw that the smile didn't reach his eyes.

And above them all hung the haze as if the room had no ceiling. Threads of color still joined it to Tilly's mother, but at least it wasn't advancing anymore.

"Mom, please." Tilly crawled onto the bed beside, but not touching, her mother, the lesson about touching still vivid.

When Nathan groaned and pushed himself up beside the bed, she moved away, not wanting to repeat what had happened. He crawled up beside their mother. He took a quick breath and reached for her.

"Mom, wake up!" he tried to shout, his voice still weak from his collision with Tilly. He pushed at his mother, still trying to gather his strength.

Nothing happened.

He tried again, stronger this time.

Tilly's mother grumbled at Nathan.

Tilly let out a breath. Her mother was still alive.

"Wake her up, Nathan!"

"Mom, get up! Come on, Mom."

"What? What do you want, Nathan?" their mother mumbled, half asleep. "Go see your father."

"No, Mom. Get up!"

He pulled her into a sitting position. It seemed to be working. The threads stopped rising, and the haze was withdrawing.

"Mom." Nathan shook her and she flopped back and forth. "Please look at me!"

"What is it, Nathan? What do you want?" His mother still sounded groggy, but her eyes were open a little.

Tilly and her friends watched the haze shrink and then pass through the bedroom wall and out of the house. She patted the bed next to Nathan. "It's gone." Little vibrating waves slid up her fingers as she accidently brushed them against him, but they evaporated as they reached her hand.

"I'm going to follow the haze," Matthew announced, and disappeared.

"I'm coming too!" Joel said, and vanished.

Suzie and Kaylin stared at Tilly as if waiting for orders. Stunned by the sudden disappearance of the boys, and still horrified by what had happened to her mother, Tilly didn't know what to say to them.

"I don't want to go!" Kaylin said.

Who could blame her? Tilly still wasn't sure if Kaylin had any idea about what was going on.

"Suit yourself," Suzie said, not willing to be outdone by the boys, and then she disappeared as well.

Tilly looked to Kaylin who looked lost and confused.

"It's okay, Kaylin," Tilly said. "You don't have to do anything you don't want to. Why don't you just sit down for now?"

Kaylin moved to a chair and sat, while Tilly watched Nathan, who was still trying to get his mother out of bed.

"Mom, you gotta get up. Come on!" Nathan pulled the blankets back and twisted his mother, so her feet were hanging over the side of the bed. "Just for a minute, okay?" Grabbing both her hands, he pulled until she was sitting.

"Just leave me alone, Nathan, please. I'm so tired." Her body was limp, like all her bones had been removed.

Nathan looked at Tilly. She nodded. It was more than their mother had done in days, but at least the haze was gone. What else could they do for her?

Nathan let her lean back, settling her on the bed and covered her with the comforter.

"I love you, Nathan," she said, then closed her eyes. "You are such a good boy."

Nathan sat at the foot of the bed, watching his mother. Tilly sat on the other side of the bed. She watched her mom breathe, each movement like a small victory. But was it a victory? What had made the haze leave?

"Nathan, I have to find the others." She stood. "Kaylin, you can stay here with Nathan if you want." Tilly looked at Nathan to see him nodding in agreement.

"I do want to," Kaylin whispered.

Since the others seemed to be able to find Tilly no matter where she was, she hoped she could do the same with them. She had no idea how to start, so she closed her eyes and just concentrated on Matthew.

Matt, where are you? She wasn't sure if he'd be able to answer her. *Matt, I'm coming to you.*

A blast of light filled her head, like the millions of little stars, the points of light that exploded in front of her eyes when she had touched her brother. There was no sound. Then the little stars blinked rapidly and disappeared.

When Tilly opened her eyes, she was in a bedroom she had never seen before. A woman lying in a bed was arched painfully just like her mother had been. Above that woman was the haze, its tendrils drawing streams of green-yellow light. At the foot of the bed was Joel.

Suzie was shrieking, "Get away from her!" at the haze while Matthew tried to hold her back from physically attacking it. Tears streamed down Suzie's face as Joel tried to comfort her. Suzie was smacking Matthew's hands away.

For a moment Tilly was frozen. She had just watched the same thing happen in her own home only minutes ago. How could this be happening again?

"Get away from my mother!" Suzie broke away from Matthew and started towards the woman on the bed.

Tilly ran to Suzie and spoke urgently, "Talk to her!" She had no idea if it was going to help since it was Nathan who had woken up their mother. "Just tell her you love her."

"Leave my mother alone!" Suzie screamed at the haze.

"She's right," Matthew said. "She's right! Talk to her, Suzie. She needs to hear your voice."

"But I'm *dead*," she sobbed. "She *can't* hear me, I'm *dead*." She looked like she was going to collapse.

"She can." Tilly took Suzie's arm, holding her up. "She *can* hear you. She'll think it's a dream, but she can hear you." She gently guided Suzie closer to her mother's face. "Remember, I did it." Was it a lie?

When Suzie didn't move, Tilly shook her. "It has to be you," she whispered in the girl's ear. "Tell her you love her."

Tilly could see the haze darkening. She could see colors seep from Suzie's mother, like they had from her mom. Suzie stood frozen as her mother whimpered and contorted in the bed. Tilly felt her own heart pull back, trying to escape her chest.

More threads slowly extended from the haze, winding their way through the air to find, seek out the woman in the bed.

"DO IT!" Tilly yelled at the girl, shaking her. Hard. Then, softer, "Do it."

"Mommy," Suzie's voice shook, barely above a whisper. "Mommy, can you hear me?"

The new threads found their target.

"Sit down, but don't touch her." Tilly helped her, making sure there was space between the two. She focused on Suzie, not looking at Suzie's mother or the haze, forcing herself to stay calm. "Just talk to her. Tell her you love her."

"She knows that!" Tilly felt assaulted by Suzie's viciousness. For a split-second, she wanted to walk out of the room, but her own circumstances kept her from moving. She knew what Suzie was feeling.

"You need to stop acting like a child," she said carefully and clearly. "Just do what I told you."

"Listen to her," Joel said.

Suzie's closed her mouth, her eyes widening when she looked over at Tilly.

Tilly risked a look at the haze. It had darkened. It seemed larger.

"Tell your mother you love her," Tilly said firmly with encouragement and "tell her over and over—until the thing goes away."

At first, Suzie just stared at Tilly.

"Go ahead, do it." Tilly jerked her chin toward Suzie's mother.

Sitting next to her mother, Suzie said, "Mom, I miss you so much. I wish I could hug you." Suzie started to reach out but pulled back, plainly remembering what had happened to Tilly and Nathan.

"Suzie?" her mother said weakly.

"Mom."

Tilly could detect some excitement in Suzie's voice this time.

"Suzie. Where have you been?" Her voice sounded raspy, like it hadn't been used in a very long time. "I've been waiting for you."

The haze retracted some of its tendrils.

"Keep it up, Suzie," Tilly said, not wanting to intrude, but terrified that Suzie would stop.

"I love you, Mom."

"I love you, Suzie-Q."

By now the haze had pulled back from the bed and retreated to a corner of the room.

"Attagirl!" Joel said.

"You did it," Matthew said.

Tilly just smiled. She knew what Suzie was feeling.

"How did you know?" Joel asked Tilly.

"I didn't know," Tilly said. "It just felt right."

The three of them looked at the haze in the corner of the room. It hovered for a moment longer, then went through the wall.

Suddenly, Tilly surprised herself as much as the others when she jumped up and said, "I'm following it." She had no idea how she was going to do it, but that wasn't going to stop her, she had made it here, after all.

"Not without me!" Matthew said, right with her.

This time, Tilly found the jump much easier. When the sparkling of light retreated, she found herself in a room longer than it was wide, a giant picture window with a green couch running the length of it, a worn chair with an end table squeezed between it and a brick fireplace. A television on the opposite wall was paused on two guys sitting at a table, a snack in the hand of one of them, holding it over the other's arm.

"Do you feel that?" Matthew said.

"The static?" Joel asked.

"Yeah, like the electricity ball at the science center."

"Look!" Tilly shouted. They turned to look where she indicated. The haze hovered by the picture window. "Who lives here?" Tilly looked at the boys. "It's feeding off someone again." The gang shrugged. "We have to help them. Do you know who it is?" But again no one seemed to have an answer. "They must be upstairs." She started for the stairs then stopped as a man, carrying a can of beer and a plate with a sandwich, came into the room.

"Does anyone know him?" The man walked towards the chair. They watched the haze start to appear and move towards the chair.

"Someone needs to help him." She thought of Nathan pulling their mother up on the bed, and of Suzie needing to talk to hers.

"Wait!" Matthew said. "Something's different."

The man stopped behind the chair. The haze moved to hover above him, its tendrils dripping but not touching him. He stood for a minute, then looked towards the window.

They waited for him to cry out. Or fall. Something.

"Is he smiling?" They all moved towards the chair to watch.

The man set his plate on the table beside the chair but continued to stand for a moment longer. The haze continued to hover. He nodded then moved in front of the chair and sat down. "Perfect," he said and took a drink from the can of beer. "I don't mind waiting." There was no question about a smile this time. "I am ready any time. Just tell me when." He picked up the remote, pressed play and took a large bite out of the middle of his sandwich.

Matthew stepped up to the chair.

"Who's he talking to?" Tilly looked at the TV for a clue.

"I don't think he's in danger, Tilly."

"Matthew's right," Joel said and moved beside him.

They all watched as the haze moved back towards the window then slowly contracted and disappeared.

"Did it just evaporate?" Tilly said. "What the hell just happened?" She stood, not quite frozen, and looked from the man in the chair to the window. "Where did the haze go?" She had no sense of it now, and following it didn't seem to be an option.

"This is him," Joel said.

"Him?"

Joel pointed towards something on the coat rack by the front door. "It's the blue baseball-hat guy."

CHAPTER 20

Tilly felt her muscles stiffen and chill. She had been so desperate to save her mother from the haze, she had forgotten all about her killer. Now they'd found him.

Instinct told her to run from this place—except her body wouldn't move. Fight? Flight? Freeze? Her body chose to freeze. This was the guy from her doorway. This was the figure in the shed. She waited for him to see her and attack her again.

"He can't hurt us," Joel whispered. "He can't even see us."

Tilly wasn't as sure as Joel about that. She shook her head.

"I think Joel's right," Matthew said, he slowly moved to the window, looking up the street.

Tilly wanted to run as fast as she could, but she was stuck.

He reached for the remote and turned up the volume.

As repelled as Tilly was, she was also mesmerized by him for some reason. "Are you sure he can't see us?" Tilly asked, fighting panic.

"No, he can't." Joel walked in front of the television to prove this. Then he walked over to the man in the chair and waved a hand in front of the man who continued to shove the sandwich into his mouth.

How can this be happening? I'm standing in a killer's living room and he's watching game shows. Like a normal person. She stepped closer.

"I've seen him before, somewhere," Tilly said, more to herself.

"Oh, this is definitely the guy!" Matthew said.

"But I know him from somewhere else."

Joel circled the chair. "I think I know him, too."

"From the shed?"

"No. From before." Joel walked closer to him. "I can't remember. It's like I'm losing my memories or something."

"I know." Tilly was still scared, but tried to remember.

Joel turned away and walked around the room, plainly taking stock, then into the hall.

"Look." Joel said.

Tilly followed his voice. She found him pointing to a skateboard by the front door.

"I knew it!" He said. The skate park. He's been at the skate park." Then he disappeared through the front door.

"Joel?" she said.

"Are you all right, Tilly?" She felt sparks where Matthew touched her, and he immediately said, "Sorry."

She turned to look at him. She tried to answer him but couldn't get her mouth to work, so she just nodded instead. When Joel reappeared suddenly through the front door, Tilly almost dropped to the floor. "Whoa!" Matthew said.

"I checked his mailbox for an address or name. We got it," Joel said. "It's Phillip Coffey."

"Good. Can we go now?" Tilly felt her skin tightening as she looked back at the guy in the chair, feeling raw, like a bad sunburn.

Back in Tilly's room, they all huddled together while Joel filled Suzie in on what happened; but all Tilly could think of was how she wanted to shed her skin. After being near her killer, she wanted to shower, wrap up in a blanket, and crawl into bed. Would any of that help anymore?

Matthew said, "So now that we know his address—"

"All we have to do now is get it to the police!" Joel said.

"How are we going to do that?" Suzie asked.

"Tilly's brother," Joel said.

"What?" Tilly said.

"He's the only one who can hear us."

"No. No, not Nathan." Tilly shook her head. "No, not Nathan!"

"He has to," Matthew said.

Tilly kept shaking her head, refusing to risk her brother.

"They're right," Suzie said.

"He can't." Tilly looked at Matthew, furious.

"It has to be Nathan." Matthew knelt, to be eye-level with her.

"He can do it, Tilly," Joel said, softening his voice.

"No. He's too sensitive. He can't handle this."

"He's stronger than you give him credit for. Your brother is a special person, Tilly, and I've seen him at our practices and around the locker rooms. He's very smart and can take care of himself."

Whether Joel was right or not, Tilly was not going to put her brother in danger. "No! I'm done arguing. What if he was *your* little brother?"

"Are you guys talking about me?" Nathan asked from the doorway. Kaylin stood behind him.

"This isn't your business!" Tilly took a breath and slowed herself down. "I don't want you involved, Nathan. It's too dangerous. I can't let anything happen to you."

"This is my business too, Tilly. I can help." He looked around the room, looked at each one of them. "I can help all of you."

"He can, Tilly." Joel said.

"I'm going to tell Dad that I know." He started to turn in the doorway.

"Don't!" Tilly said.

"Dad!" Nathan yelled.

"Nathan." Tilly put her hands up, she couldn't let him say anything to their dad. He would worry even more about Nathan, and he already had enough on his plate. "You don't even know who this guy is." She added.

But it was too late. "Nathan?" Tilly heard her father call up the stairs. Nathan and Tilly stared at each other.

"See. I have to, now," Nathan said.

"Please, Nathan. Make something up. Tell him you need something."

"Like what?"

"I don't know."

"Nathan?" their father called up again. They could hear his footsteps coming through the dining room towards the stairs.

"Dad!" Nathan moved to the landing at the top of the stairs, his hands on the railing, he looked down. "I need to tell you something."

"Don't," Tilly whispered.

"I can help," he said over his shoulder to Tilly.

"It's not safe."

"Nathan!" their father called from the bottom of the stairs.

"I'll be okay, Tilly."

"Nathan? What are you doing?"

Kaylin stood next to Nathan at the railing and looked down at his father.

"He can't hear any of you," Nathan whispered. "But one of you has to give me *something*."

"Nathan. You can't. Please don't!"

"I have to," he said, heading for the stairs. "You heard Joel."

"Guys." Tilly looked at her friends for answers, but none of them spoke. Tilly wasn't sure if their silence was because they regretted what they had said about involving Nathan.

"I know who he is, Dad!" Tilly heard Nathan say as he reached the bottom of the stairs. She suddenly found herself next to him. "I know who the killer is!" He walked past his father and went into the kitchen.

"What? What are you talking about?" Their father followed him. "Sit down and tell me what you are talking about."

"Nathan," Tilly was waving her hands. "Don't!"

"I know who killed Tilly!"

Their father dropped into a chair next to him.

"Hold on a minute," he said, leaning forward, his hands braced on his thighs. "Okay, Nathan. Start at the beginning."

Nathan took a deep breath. "Tilly's *here*, Dad. She and the other kids that man killed. They know his name and address. They know who their murderer is. They can give me his name and his address. You can call the police and tell them to go there and arrest him.

"Slow down," He motioned Nathan to sit on one of the stools. "What are you talking about? What kids? Where?"

"Tilly's killer, Dad." He was vibrating in his seat. "They know who her killer is."

Their father dropped his head and it was obvious their father didn't believe him.

"You have to believe me, Dad!"

"Nathan, you can't have Tilly as an imaginary friend." He turned away, inhaling sharply. "And you certainly can't go around making stuff up like this." He turned back. "She's dead, Nathan, and you have to let her go. The police will figure it out." Tilly saw strain in her father's face; she wasn't sure if he was fighting back tears or fighting to stay calm.

"Nathan, please," Tilly begged him.

"I *know* she's dead! She's dead, but she's not gone. And I don't think that she *can* go until we find him, Dad."

His father ran his fingers through his hair.

"He's still killing, Dad. He killed Kaylin, and he's not going to stop."

His father rubbed his fingers back and forth across his forehead.

"Dad, I mean it. They know who he is. This isn't imaginary!" Nathan dropped his hands to his sides and then started to shake them as if shaking off water. "They know his name." He looked at Tilly. She *had* to tell him now!

Matthew and Joel joined Tilly in the kitchen, looking sorry for what they had let happen.

"Tilly." Hurt was plain on Nathan's face. "Tell me his name."

"Nathan." His father paused for a second.

Tilly watched, feeling helpless. Feeling responsible.

"It's Phillip Coffey." The shaking of Nathan's hands was getting stronger. "And we have his address."

"You can't just blame people without knowing for sure," their father said. Then he seemed to stop what he was going to say next, and then: "I am trying hard to be patient." He brought his hands up to his mouth.

"It's for real, Dad. I know the difference between imaginary and real, and this is *real*."

"OK," His father said, beaten. "All right. Let's say you know the difference—"

"I do!"

"How do *I* know that you know the difference? How do *I* know that if we call the police and I give them an address that they will find something there." He leaned in, closer to Nathan's face. "Calling the police is very serious—you know that. We could get in big trouble if this is not real."

"IT IS REAL!" Nathan's hands were inches from his chest, shuddering, shaking.

His father gently reached for Nathan's hands and loosely wrapped his around them, lightly, like you'd hold a frightened bird.

"You tell me what you know, and I will call the police. You do understand that we are calling the hotline that they've set up for tips about the murders, and I can't promise that they won't need to talk to you. Tips are supposed to be anonymous, but I can't promise that either."

"Yes, Dad." Nathan's shaking started to slow.

"You need to be as precise as you can, okay? You need to tell me everything. I need to know what we are getting into."

Nathan nodded.

CHAPTER 21

"You're lucky, Tilly," Suzie said, breaking the silence after they had been sitting on Phillip Coffey's doorstep, waiting for the police to arrive.

"Oh?" Tilly said.

"You get to talk to your family."

"Yeah, but,"

"No, I just watch mine cry and lie in bed all day, watching the energy-sucking hazy-vampire thing come to drain them."

"But . . ."

"My mother had an uncle that used to visit us when I was little. She hated him." Suzie was picking at the peeling paint. "She said that it didn't matter what the occasion was, but that every time he came to visit, the family would end up leaving, hating each other. It's like he sucked the life out of the room by digging up the past, calling out everyone's mistakes or faults, just killing everyone's 'buzz,' Mom called it. Everyone would wind up yelling or crying."

She started picking at her nail now. putting it up to her mouth to bite off the end she'd just torn on the step. "Her uncle's name was actually Chuck, but she liked to call him *Sorg Ata*, who she said was some soul-sucking demon in a book she'd read …or maybe it was a movie." She spit out the nail. "That haze is just like Sorg Ata. Ruining everything."

Suzie was right, Tilly thought. She missed her parents terribly, but at least she could talk to Nathan. He could see her and hear

116

her, and he could even pass on messages. She suddenly felt the need to apologize, and did so.

"If it wasn't for you and your brother, Tilly," Joel said, "we wouldn't have been able to let anyone know who our killer was."

"Or even that I *was* killed," Suzie said.

"What?" Joel said. Matthew turned away from the window.

"What do you mean?" Tilly said.

Before Suzie could answer, a car pulled up in front of Coffey's house. Two uniformed men stepped out and walked toward the front steps. Out of habit, Tilly and her friends stood up and moved out of the way.

Tilly turned and watched one of them ring the doorbell, while the other discreetly looked in the front window.

When the door opened, Tilly was taken aback.

"What the?" Joel said. The man who opened the door had short dark hair. He wasn't tall, probably as tall as Joel's mother who was five-foot-six, and he was probably as old.

"Who's he?" Suzie asked, looking around at the others.

"Evening," the man who had rung the doorbell said. "I'm Detective Anthony and this is Detective Coles. We'd like to speak with Mr. Phillip Coffey." The detective held up his badge.

"That would be me. Please come in, detectives," Phillip Coffey said, pulling the door open wider and shifting out of the way.

Both detectives stepped inside.

The four teenagers follow the detective into the house.

"Can I get you anything?" Phillip asked while nodding to the chairs in the living room.

"No, thank you," Anthony answered.

Phillip perched on the edge of the chair in front of the TV. A pile of magazines and newspapers were stacked beside the chair with a coffee cup sitting on top of it. There was no sign of the sandwich-eating young man that the group remembered had been sitting there earlier.

"So, what's all this about, Detectives?"

"We're canvassing several neighborhoods, asking if anyone has seen anything that may help in our investigation of the murdered children," Coles said.

"I didn't think any of those kids were from this neighborhood." Phillip slowly slid back in his chair.

"Any bit of information can help us." Detective Anthony said. "Sometimes people don't realize they've seen something that could help."

"Sure."

Tilly watched Joel disappear from her view, heading down the hall. She thought about joining him but stayed in the living room, wanting to hear what Phillip Coffey would say.

"What is it you do for a living, Mr. Coffey?" Detective Coles asked, glancing around the room.

"I'm a long-haul trucker for Larder Transport. I'm away from home a lot, sometimes weeks at a time."

"How long have you worked for Larder?" Detective Anthony asked.

"Only about a year. Before that I was maintenance supervisor at the sanitation plant." He leaned forward, elbows on his knees. "Then budget cuts came, and I got laid off. Politics if you ask me." He took a sip of his coffee. "It's always who you know, isn't it?" He put the cup down. "You sure I can't get you anything?"

"No, thank you," Detective Coles answered. "What did you do before that?"

"I did a little contract work with home heating. Boilers, that kind of stuff. I have my TSSA ticket. But then my knees started to go, so I had to give it up and took the job at the city."

"Do you live alone?" Detective Coles asked.

"No. My nephew lives with me."

"What's his name?" Coles continued.

"Benjamin."

"Coffey?"

"Yes, Coffey." Detective Coles scribbled in his notebook.

"That's gotta be him!" Suzie shouted.

"Ssh!" Tilly made a gesture to shush her.

"They can't hear me."

"But if you're interrupting, I can't hear them."

Suzie crossed her arms but stayed quiet.

"Maybe I will take you up on that offer, Mr. Coffey," Anthony said. "A glass of water would be nice."

"Of course. Let me get that for you." Phillip stood.

"You don't mind if Detective Coles has a look around while I join you in the kitchen, do you?" The detectives stood up, too.

Phillip stopped. "Wait a minute." His curious, friendly expression changed. "Are you telling me something might have happened to my nephew?"

"No sir. We are just here to check with you and your neighbors, gathering information."

"Good." Relief crossed Phillip's face, and he continued to the kitchen, Anthony behind him. "He's a good kid. Likes to keep to himself—but he's had a rough patch lately."

Phillip retrieved a glass from the cupboard, walked to the sink, and turned on the tap, letting water run. "His mother died about six months back. My sister. Has no idea who his father is." Glass full, he turned off the tap and handed the glass to the detective.

"Could we talk to your nephew? Is he home?"

"Naw. He works part-time at some funeral home. Not sure how a weird gig like that came along, but like I said, I'm gone for weeks at a time."

"That's where I saw him," Tilly shouted. "At the funeral home."

"What?" Matthew said.

"Shh," Joel said as he came into the living room. "Later."

Tilly had a hard time listening to the conversation. She wanted to tell them that she had seen Coffey's nephew at the funeral home. That her family had been in the same building as him. She needed to tell Nathan.

"I'm sorry, Detective Coles; did you want a glass too?" he shouted to the other room.

"No thanks," Coles' called back.

Detective Anthony lifted his glass to his lips and drank. As he lowered it, he looked out the back door window.

"I'm not sure I have anything that could help you," Phillip Coffey said.

"I'd like to take a quick look around your shed if you don't mind."

"Here we go," Joel said.

"My shed?"

"In case anything is out of the ordinary for you, we can't be too careful with things happening to our kids."

"Yeah, sure. I'll get my shoes."

Tilly watched Phillip retrieve his shoes and noticed Coles holding a skateboard.

"Hey, Coles," Anthony said to his partner, "I'm just going to check out the shed at the back."

"I'll come too," Coles said, putting the skateboard down.

Phillip slipped his feet into his shoes and walked back through to the kitchen. He reached for one key of several hanging on a row of hooks, then opened the door.

"After you, gentlemen," he said.

"I don't want to do this," Tilly said.

The detectives walked out, followed by Tilly, then Phillip, who closed the back door behind him. He followed the detectives down the steps and across the yard, unlocked the shed door, flicked on the lights then went inside with them.

Standing by the doorway, Tilly watched the officers as they looked around the shed.

Detective Anthony's phone went off, and he said, "One moment," as he took the call and left the shed.

Tilly tried to listen to Anthony's call, but could only hear his responses, which seemed limited to *uhum*, *yes*, and *all right*.

"Thank you, Mr. Coffey," Detective Anthony said, as he ended the call and stepped into the shed with Phillip and his partner. "We'd like to talk to your nephew as well." Anthony pulled out a card and handed it to Phillip. "He can come down to the station or if he'd prefer, we can speak to him here."

"I will let him know." Phillip slid the card into his back pocket.

"In the meantime, we know where to get in touch with you if we need to ask any further questions." Coles said.

"Sure, I'd be happy to help," Philip said, and watched the detectives as they left the property, then he turned and walked into his house, closing the door behind him.

"Tell me that didn't just happen," Matthew said, standing on Phillip's deck, a blank look on his face.

"Right house, wrong guy," Suzie said.

"You heard him; his nephew lives here," Joel said. "We saw the nephew, sitting here, drinking beer and watching TV like it was nothing. He's the killer and this guy is his uncle."

"I saw him at my funeral," Tilly said.

Everyone looked at her.

"What?" Matthew said.

"At the funeral home. I saw the nephew in the coffee room. And it was almost like he saw me—"

"Saw you?" Joel said.

"We need more evidence," Suzie said. "We need to make those detectives come back and see his nephew."

"More evidence!" Tilly said.

"Tilly," Matthew's said, clearly trying to calm things. "I want him caught as much as you do, but owning hats and using his uncle's shed isn't enough.

"Matthew's right," Joel said. "A skateboard isn't enough to prove that a killer lives here."

"We'll get him, Tilly!" Suzie said, giving her a quick nod. "Somehow!"

CHAPTER 22

Benjamin listened with increasing fear as his uncle, Phillip, told him about the police visit. He tried to pull up memories of the last few days. Then weeks.

"They left their card and they want to talk to you."

"Why me?" Benjamin Coffey asked his uncle.

"I don't know. To see if you've heard anything, I guess."

"What would I have heard?" Who had seen him? How had they found out where he lived? What had his uncle told the police? What had the police seen while they were here?

"Beats me. All I know is that they're going around asking people if they know anything." He handed his nephew their card. "I'd go with you but I'm heading back out tomorrow," his uncle said. "But I could hold off for a bit in the morning if you needed me to go with you."

"Naw, I'm good." Benjamin gave his uncle a cursory nod of acknowledgement and kept his attention on the TV while videos of his own rolled through his head.

He'd killed five kids. Although one was more of an accident, he'd set out to kill her and she died because of him. So, it counted. And the itch backed that up. The thought of what he had done energized him. They had all presented different challenges. Each one taught him something. But he'd been able to react quickly to events, and achieved his desire. The itch went away, but he also gained a sense of power. He was tired of being the only one suffering. It was like a voice was telling him that taking life would make his pain stop.

But his excitement turned to frustration. Now, someone was trying to stop him. Who had seen him? He needed to find out before whoever it was could give the police any more information. He had to stop them, or his pain would come back. And it wasn't just easing the intolerable itch anymore. He didn't want to admit it at first, but he enjoyed what he was doing-the excitement of watching his prey fight for freedom. He wasn't sure he could live without that. Or even if he wanted to.

He stood up from his chair and went to the front door, grabbed his blue cap, and said, "I'll be back later." He grabbed his skateboard and started down the street, heading for the skate park. He'd stay until dark, until his uncle went to bed.

Who had been sneaking around? Watching. Had it been that old woman down the street, with that annoying little dog? She always snooped around when Uncle Phil was gone. Maybe that bratty kid who delivered the newspaper. He's out while it's still dark and no one pays any attention to him. Ben was sure he'd kept an eye out for both of them. So, who could it be? Was it just dumb luck? Who did they think they were? Whoever it was, he was onto them now! "I can't let them take this away from me," he said aloud. He pushed harder. "You said I could have as many as I wanted!"

CHAPTER 23

"If the police are going to be able to nail this guy, we need to get more information for them," Joel said. They'd remained together at Tilly's house, in her room, after leaving Phillip Coffey's place.

"And how are we going to do that?" Suzie asked.

They stared at each. The silence spoke loudly.

"We have to do *something*," Tilly said, pacing, hands on her hips.

"We need to go back to his place," Joel said.

"There's nothing there: the police already checked." Suzie said.

"There has to be something there," Tilly said.

"How do you know that?" Suzie said.

Tilly fought down her frustration, but ended up saying: "Because I was there!" *I died there. There has to be* something *of me there*. She shivered and fought the fear creeping up her throat. "And Joel was too." She rounded on Suzie. "Why do you have to be so difficult all the time?" And saw hurt wash over Suzie's face. Suzie turned her back fingering the necklaces hanging from the mirror. "And don't touch my stuff!"

"That's a little rough, Tilly," Joel said.

Suzie dropped her hand, letting it land on the dresser.

"My watch."

"Sor-ree!" Suzie said, taking her hand off the dresser. She crossed her arms, protectively tucking her hands behind her elbows.

"No, Suzie." Tilly went to the dresser, stood next to her. "I mean I was wearing my watch the day I died. I haven't seen it since."

"Okay—" Joel said.

"It's got to be at his house."

"But the police didn't find anything, remember?" Suzie said.

"To be honest, it sounds like they didn't really look. Maybe young Coffey hid it," Kaylin said, uncrossing her legs and sliding to the edge of the bed.

"If we don't know where he hid it, then what good will it do?" Matthew asked. "Don't get mad, Tilly. I'm just saying."

But Tilly felt the sting of his statement. She knew he was right. She was scared and taking it out on her friends. Even though she was dead, she still feared Benjamin Coffey. In her head she knew he couldn't hurt her; but in her body, she could feel her muscles constantly in a state of flight. It was when her brain tried to remind her she didn't have a body anymore that she seemed to shift to fight mode.

"We need to go back to the house. Look around for ourselves," Joel said. "We weren't looking for stuff before, just his name and address. This time we could look around his house. Maybe even the shed."

"I'm coming too."

Tilly jumped at the sound of Nathan's voice. He'd been standing in the doorway.

"You can't come, Nathan, it's too dangerous," Tilly told him. "We can be there in a blink, and no one sees us."

"And you can't follow them," Kaylin reminded Nathan. "You're not a ghost." But her words trailed off as she spoke.

"We can be across the city in a thought," Tilly told him. "And gone just as fast if we need to."

"But what if you need someone real?" Nathan looked at Kaylin, turning her argument to his favor.

"To do what?" Tilly looked straight at him. "And that's my point. You *are* real."

"I was the one who gave the information to the police, remember?"

"Exactly. And you are our only contact with the real world. You can get hurt." She wouldn't say the other possibility. "And it might sound selfish, but if you do get hurt, we lose that contact. No. We're going, but you are staying here."

"I'll stay with you," Kaylin offered.

Nathan smiled at Kaylin, but Tilly saw the disappointment he was trying to hide.

CHAPTER 24

Benjamin Coffey walked over to the brick fireplace. When he had first moved in as a kid with his mother, he had wanted to roast marshmallows, but his uncle said he hadn't used the fireplace in years, that the flue had been blocked to keep the draft out.

He moved the ornamental iron screen to the side and knelt at the edge of the hearth. He picked a newspaper out of the kindling bucket on the side, now used as a recycling bin, and spread the paper out in front of him. Then he lifted a log out of the fireplace and placed it on the laid-out sheet.

He moved three more logs, then shifted in closer and used a worn table-knife to shift the bricks along the back interior wall. With his fingernail, he tugged at the corner of a brick until it slid enough for him to put his fingers on the top and bottom and slide it out. The hole it made left a space for him to be able to remove the brick that had been beside it and two others just below.

The opened cavity exposed a wooden box, which he lifted out, brushed off, and cradled in his lap. He ran his fingers along the embossed Wright Brothers' Model A Flyer on the lid.

He had won the box at a carnival when he was a kid. He'd been so happy that day. He'd never won anything before; but that day he managed to get all three rings on the red bottle. The carny wanted to give him a giant stuffed tiger, but he spotted the box and asked if he could have it instead.

"Are you sure?" the carny had asked. "It's just a box."

"Yeah, I want to see the box."

"Look kid, the red bottles get you more than that. You can pick anything. How about a different animal, or this?" The young carny held up a square mirror with a picture of a plant on it.

"Just the box, please."

Shrugging his shoulders, the carny handed the box to him. Once in Benjamin's hands, he turned it over and over, running his fingers along the top, feeling the outline of the airplane embossed there. He looked at the carny. "Thanks." And walked away.

The carny called after him: "You're crazy, man. You could've had *three* prizes. The box is just junk. I don't even know where it came from."

Ben didn't care: he was pleased with his find. It wasn't all that big, only about six inches deep, and he guessed wide and long enough to hold something a little bigger than a full sheet of paper. Maybe to store his cash or hide things from his mom. Not that she spent much time with him lately.

That had been a dozen years ago and although he could still feel the outline of the plane, all the color of it was gone, worn down to silver metal by years of his hands grabbing and pulling, opening and hiding.

Comics had filled the box, which became magazines about skateboards and motorcycles. Eventually, some of these magazines were tossed aside and replaced with porn.

But now, the box had gained a new purpose.

There were photos and small items. Some of the photos he'd taken himself, others he'd printed from the internet. It was easy to find an image of almost anyone these days. Everyone seemed more than happy to share their lives with strangers. He looked at the face in one of the photos, remembering the day he'd stumbled across a boy in the woods. He hadn't been looking, but as soon as he had spotted the boy, the itch was there, pushing him. He had to come up with a plan, quickly. The itch seemed to tingle, no stings or bites, rather little feet scampering across his skin.

He remembered the boy getting closer. Not knowing what to do, he spoke. He wasn't even sure what he'd said.

The boy didn't react, so he tried again.

"Nice day." He instantly chastised himself for that but kept talking. "Hey, don't I know you? You live around here, right? I've seen you at the skate park." He scrambled for what to say next as he walked closer to the boy, and then: "You seen my skateboard anywhere?"

"What?"

"I think someone stole my board, have you seen anyone around?" He walked closer as he spoke.

"No. I haven't seen anyone," the boy answered and kept walking.

"Wait!" What if he lost this chance? "Is that it there?" He pointed just off to the kid's left, and when the kid looked, his heart jumped. and the tingling ran up his spine. "There, in the bushes."

The kid stepped to the edge of the path and looked toward the bushes. "I don't see—"

Now. He sprang.

He blinked, memory evaporating to the past, and snapped his attention back to his living room. He dropped the photo back into the box, shifted some folded newspaper clippings, and lifted out a gold necklace, sliding it across his fingers, letting the pendant dangle from his hand. He watched it swing, then rolled the pendant into his other hand.

> Happy Birthday, Kay
> Love M & D

CHAPTER 25

Tilly's little group found Benjamin Coffey standing in his uncle's living room in front of the fireplace, wiping his hands on his pants.

Coffey turned and walked across the room to the front door, put on his coat, grabbed his skateboard, and a set of keys hanging on the rack. He left, locking the deadbolt behind him, and Tilly followed, the group with her.

He walked half a dozen blocks to a small skate park. There were a few other skaters who acknowledged him but kept to themselves. Coffey dropped his board, took off his coat and tossed it into the grass.

Joel looked at the group. "Let's go, people."

"Should someone stay here?" Suzie asked.

'You're right,' Tilly said.

"You got this, Suzie?" Joel asked. He turned to Matthew and Tilly. "Let's go check out the house."

Upon their return to the house, Matthew commented, "Everything looks pretty normal." There was a 1950s-era table and chairs in the kitchen. The counters were clean, a jar of jellybeans tucked in the corner beside a coffee maker. A dish towel with green frogs on it hung over the handle of the oven, and there were separate garbage bins for compost and waste.

"I just thought of something," Joel said to no one in particular. He looked to Tilly and Matthew. "Does it really matter if Coffey comes home while we are here?"

"What?' Tilly said.

"I mean, he can't see us, right?"

Tilly chuckled. "I guess we are still learning how to be ghosts."

A knock on the door made them all jump. Tilly almost screamed.

"Let me in, guys," they heard through the door.

"Nathan?" Tilly was sure her ears were playing tricks on her.

"Come on. Hurry up!"

What was he doing? Why was he here? She could tell by his voice that Nathan was bouncing on the balls of his feet. The thought of him standing on Coffey's front step made Tilly's muscles liquefy. He was supposed to stay away. "Go home, Nathan!" Tilly found herself frozen as if any movement would draw attention to him. "You can't *be* here!"

"Well, I am. So, let me in."

"Go home. I mean it, Nathan. Go home!"

"I'm not leaving, Tilly. Do you want to keep arguing about it?... With me out here on the step for the neighborhood to hear?"

Instantly, she was beside him, outside on the step.

"Let him in," she yelled to the others, trying to block the view of Nathan from the street, forgetting that she could not be seen.

"I'm trying, Tilly, but I can't unlock the door." Joel's voice vibrated.

"Joel!" Her vision started to blur; she fought to not lose herself. "Nathan, you need to hide."

"Something's wrong, Tilly. I can't unlock it." Joel's voice rose in pitch.

Tilly looked from the door to her brother, then back.

"We move things all the time. We open doors all the time." Tilly thought of her eraser, of picking up the phone. "Peek-a-boo!"

"What?" Nathan looked at her like she was losing it.

"Matthew, remember the lady at the park, you moved her hair. Think about how you did that."

She saw the doorknob turn. "Nathan, hurry." She motioned for him to get in front of the door, but the door stayed closed.

She grabbed at the knob. It turned left then right but the door didn't budge.

"C'mon! Open the goddam door!" she yelled.

"It won't open." Matthew shouted back from the other side of the door.

"It's a deadbolt," Joel told her. "We need the key, even on the inside."

"Find the key!" she shouted. *Why do I need a key? I'm dead, why can't I just open it with my mind? She concentrated.* "Nathan is standing on our killer's front step!"

"And if Coffey comes," Joel said, "Nathan can run home."

"How will we know if Coffey's coming?"

"Suzie is still at the park. She'll let us know." Joel said.

Leaving her brother on the front step, inside the house she tried the doorknob again. The door still didn't move.

"We can't leave Nathan out on the step," she said as she worked the doorknob again.

"Here." Matthew appeared with three keys, each hanging on a separate tag.

Tilly grabbed them from him and jammed one into the slot. Her wrist twisted but the key stayed straight.

"We've got this, Tilly. We'll get Nathan in." Matthew said.

"Let me try, Tilly." Matthew reached out to take the keys.

Tilly looked at her hand and watched as the key fell to the floor. She looked at Matthew.

"I'll do it," he told her. She watched him reach for the key. His hand swiped over it.

"What?"

"Maybe we've been dead too long," Joel said. His voice was unusually quiet.

"What?" Tilly could feel herself start to crumble. "What the hell are you talking about?"

"No," Matthew said. "He may be on to something." He reached for the key, this time making contact with it, picking it up. "Maybe the rules are changing." He tried the doorknob. It turned slightly both ways, just like before. He put the key in the slot and tried to turn the key. Nothing happened. "Maybe we are not moving things. Maybe we just think we are. Or maybe our signal gets weaker the longer we are dead."

"How are we going to get him in?" Tilly said. "He needs to go home. Nathan, you need to go home. Please." She could feel tears sliding down her cheeks.

"Just slide it under the door," Nathan said, so matter of fact.

"Nathan, someone will hear you," Tilly yelled, fighting the panic building in her, losing to it.

"Guys!"

"I can't." Matthew ran his fingers along the bottom of the door. "There's no space under the door."

Wait. Tilly took the key from Matthew and put it into her pocket.

"What are you doing?"

I'll just take the keys to him. She took a breath. "Nathan."

Suddenly standing beside Nathan, she heard a clink. The two of them looked down. Tears of relief streamed down Tilly's face as she watched Nathan pick up the key and slide it into the lock.

"Forget this, Nathan, just go home. Please."

Finally, the door swung open, and Tilly almost pushed Nathan into the house.

"Took you all long enough," Nathan said, closing the door behind him.

Tilly fought the urge to hug him. With Nathan safely off the step, she started to get her senses back, and realized the irony of the situation. How could he be *safe* inside a killer's house? Inside, he'd be trapped, but if he was outside, he could run. Nathan knew this too, but he had made it clear he wasn't going to leave the front step, and the thought of Coffey spotting her brother out there terrified her even more.

"How did you know he wasn't here?" Tilly asked.

"Well, to be honest, I didn't. I was just trying to follow all of you."

Tilly wiped the tears off her cheeks, waiting to be made fun of. No one did.

They had to find what they needed, fast.

"He's still at the park," Suzie said as she appeared in the room, She looked at the others as they all stared at her. "What?"

"We had a bit of a situation," Joel told her. "It's under control now."

"What kind of situation?"

"Shouldn't you still be watching him?" Tilly said, and she could feel her anxiety coming, back thinking that Coffey could just walk in.

"He's good for a bit. He and some other skaters just started a little jump competition." She shifted her gaze from Tilly to the boys. "What was the problem?"

"It took us a while to get the door open for Nathan," Joel said.

"Oh, hey, Nathan." Suzie seemed only now to notice him. "Why are you here? Shouldn't you be at home?"

Nathan could see the *see-I-told-you* look on Tilly's face.

"I guess I'll ask it again. What was the problem?"

"We couldn't get the key to fit," Tilly said.

"And then we couldn't even *pick up* the key," Matthew said.

"Why?" Suzie asked, plainly puzzled.

"Something has changed," Joel said.

"But you must have figured out something."

"Yeah," Nathan said. "Tilly brought the key out to me."

"He's right," Joel said. "She did."

"What changed?" Nathan said.

"I couldn't pick the key up! My fingers went right through it." She looked at Nathan. "Am I disappearing?" She looked at the others. "Do we just disappear when we are dead?"

"No." Matthew took her hands.

She felt the nips of electricity. She welcomed them.

"We can see you." He looked at the others, wanting them to reassure her. "And you did pick up the key, so whatever it was is gone."

"What if it comes back?"

"Maybe she's right," Nathan said.

"I don't want to just... disappear," Suzie said, and she sounded so young, almost like Kaylin.

"I mean, you guys could be changing," Nathan said "You've been dead for a while now. All of you." Nathan looked at Tilly in particular. "You are also beginning to accept that you're dead." He tucked the key in his pocket as he spoke. "Maybe that changes how you interact with the world."

"How can that change anything?" Tilly asked.

"Your energy is becoming more..." Nathan searched for the word. "You aren't so *humanish* anymore."

"Humanish?" Joel asked.

"Yeah. I don't know the word, but now, to me, you feel bigger, more spread out." He thought for a minute. No one interrupted him. "Before, your energy was concentrated on you, it was tight around you. Now it seems less focused on you, less about your body." Nathan's struggle for the words showed on his face.

"No, I get it, Nathan," Suzie said. "We keep thinking we are still alive. We keep acting like we are still alive. We aren't."

"So...?" Joel's invitation for her to continue.

"We need to start acting like the ghosts we are."

"But why can we pick up the key or turn doorknobs but then not do either?" Tilly asked, genuinely confused.

"I don't know the answer, I just know that the old rules don't apply anymore. I have no idea what the new rules are though, having never been dead before."

Tilly's first reaction to Suzie's comment was anger, but she stopped herself and thought about what Suzie had actually said. *New rules. Rules about being dead.* "You're right, Suzie."

Suzie smiled. Her shoulders shifted back; she stood a little straighter.

"Hate to break up the love-fest," Matthew said, "but we'd better get moving. Who knows how long Coffey will be gone!"

As Tilly turned to Matthew, seeing Nathan beside him, she slammed back to reality. Nathan was still standing in her killer's living room.

"How did you find us? How did you get here? You need to go home, now, Nathan. Where's Dad?"

"You told me his address, remember?"

"Where does Dad think you are? How did you get out without him seeing you? How did you know how to get here?"

"Google."

"Not funny," she said.

"I thought it kinda was," Joel whispered to Nathan.

"I went to my room for my afternoon meditation. It's the only time Dad lets me out of his sight." Nathan seemed pleased with himself.

"You meditate" Suzie seemed surprised and interested at the same time.

"My baseball coach is on us about mindfulness and stuff like that," Joel said, seeing her interest.

"That," Nathan added, "and my afterschool program does focused meditation, and we also do kundalini yoga and—"

"Nathan, this is so dangerous. How did you get here?" Tilly brought them all back to the topic, not willing to be distracted.

"He's okay, Tilly," Matthew said, trying to calm her.

"I rode my bike here."

Tilly went to the window.

"Don't worry, I left it behind the bushes at the park a block up," he told her. "And I knew you were still here because, in case you forgot, I can *hear* you. In fact, I can hear you a mile away."

"That's not the point." Tilly didn't know what else to say.

"So, what did you guys find out?" He looked to the others, ignoring his sister.

"Not much," Joel said. "I think we need to go out to the shed."

Tilly immediately looked at Nathan.

"Nathan, please just go home."

"I'll go check on Coffey," Suzie offered, "and see where he is. Make sure he's not on his way home."

"Thanks," Tilly smiled at her. She felt herself ease a little.

"As soon as Suzie tells you the coast is clear, you have to go home, Nathan. Understand?"

She walked around the kitchen, not sure what she was looking for but keeping an eye on Nathan as she did. Each time she passed the window and the door to the backyard, she felt herself drawn to the shed. She knew she needed to refocus her attention and look at all the same things again.

"Tilly."

She looked at her brother.

"Why don't you go to the shed? You know you want to. You are wasting time. Suzie will let me know when the coast is clear."

She didn't know if she could trust Suzie with her little brother. She didn't know if she wanted to. She thought of getting Nathan to come with her to the shed; but the thought of him anywhere near it made her skin crawl.

"I can't go with you, you know that."

Had he just heard her thoughts? Read her mind?

"No, I can read your face." Nathan looked out at the shed. He watched as Joel walked around the back of it.

"Suzie will be right back. Matthew can stay with me."

"Did I hear my name?" Matthew asked as he walked into the kitchen.

Nathan turned the upper part of his body leaving his feet planted. "Will you stay with me while Tilly checks out the shed with Joel? Until Suzie gives me the all-clear to go home?"

"Sure." Matthew looked at Tilly and seeing the look on Tilly's face, replied more seriously, "I mean, yes, of course."

Tilly hesitated, torn between the two choices: Stay with Nathan; go to the shed.

"Go, before he comes home," Nathan said.

"Go," said Matthew, backing him up.

The feeling of pain in the shed was so thick Tilly could barely move. She struggled to keep her thoughts wracked as she was with the remnants of her own fear. She saw Joel's face and realized he was probably feeling the same thing, given he'd spent time here before he died. And suddenly it was too much for her to bear: Joel's pain, her own, the flood of memories. She fled outside, bent over her knees.

Suzie appeared, almost knocking her over.

"He's coming! He's coming! I lost track of him for a minute. He's just up the street! I'm sorry, I lost track of him for a minute."

Alarmed, Tilly ran for the house, Suzie in tow, who kept yelling the news that Coffey was nearly here.

"Nathan," Tilly yelled "He's here!" She rushed through the kitchen to the living room and froze, horrified. "Nathan!"

But Nathan didn't move. He didn't make a sound. He just stood, staring at the fireplace.

"What are you doing? What are you waiting for?" She could barely push the words out. Nathan still didn't answer. She moved to face him and called his name again. He just stared ahead, still not acknowledging her. "He's coming! Run!" She was about to grab him when he finally turned his face towards her. "Run!" Now his face registered her what she was saying. He turned and sprinted through the living room, away from the front door.

As Nathan scrambled to the kitchen, Tilly heard the click of a key in the front door. Nathan turned the knob of the back door, but the door didn't move. Another deadbolt. He looked around and spotted the key rack, and careful not to make a sound, he lifted the key tagged *Back Door* and unlocked the door, slipping out.

Tilly motioned the others to follow, and together they hugged the side of the house, listening for any movement in the house.

"Where is he?" Nathan hissed.

Tilly stood. She was just able to peek in the window.

"He's in the kitchen. You need to run, quickly." She glanced at Nathan, to be sure he had heard her, then turned back to watch what Coffey was up to.

Nathan, stayed low, keeping below the windows, heading towards the front yard.

"Hurry!" Tilly was terrified to take her gaze off Coffee, but she had to make sure Nathan got away. She moved towards the front of the house as she saw her brother run for the sidewalk. She saw the huge hedge to the right and knew once he passed that, he'd be out of sight, and safe. She watched as he ran for the hedge; but just before he made it, an older lady in a green velour tracksuit walking her dog emerged from behind the hedge. Her little white dog started barking.

Tilly watched Nathan stop to avoid running into her. The woman looked at Nathan as if he was some street punk.

"You need to watch where you're going!" She shouted at him.

Nathan apologized and tried to get around her. As her yapping dog bounced around, it made it impossible to avoid getting tangled in its leash.

Tilly took a moment to look towards the front window of the house. She could see Coffey heading towards the commotion to investigate. "Run, Nathan, just run!" She yelled.

Joel appeared in front of Nathan.

"HEY!" The sound of Joel's voice was like thunder, it stopped Nathan instantly. The dog stopped too. "Go, go, go!" Joel made a pushing motion towards Nathan. "Get out of here."

Nathan looked down at the dog. It was focused on Joel.

"NOW!" Joel yelled.

Then the dog shifted his attention as Matthew appeared, too.

"You kids have no respect," the woman said coldly, reeling in the leash.

With the dog motionless, Nathan untangled the web around his legs and jumped over the animal. "Sorry," he shouted without looking back.

Tilly watched as Coffey stepped out onto the front porch.

CHAPTER 26

When he got home from the park, Ben Coffey placed his key in the lock and found the door unlocked, and wondered if he'd forgotten to lock up before he left.

He stepped inside, removed his hat and coat, and hung his keys on the hook by the door. But as he walked across the living room, he felt something odd, something different. At a quick glance he couldn't see anything missing or out of place. For one horrifying moment, he wondered if the cops had come back. Searched the place. Wouldn't they need a search warrant. Had his uncle given them permission? He looked at the fireplace. Had they found it? *Easy*, he thought. *Take it easy. Take a deep breath.* He paused every few steps to look around and *feel* the room. He did the same at the doorway to the kitchen. Stopped. *Felt.* Still nothing.

He turned and went to the kitchen counter, filled the kettle, and let it come to the boil. A cup of tea would calm his nerves, especially with a little shot of something in it. He knew where his uncle hid his booze. He reached across the counter and grabbed a handful of jellybeans from the jar on the counter, leaving the red ones behind—he hated red ones. As he popped a couple into his mouth, he heard a commotion out on the street.

Coffey looked out the kitchen window and could just see two people at the end of his driveway. At a closer glance he could see it was a boy, a woman, and a small dog, and the boy was tangled in the leash. He felt for the kid. While the dog ran around yapping, the woman shook her finger in the boy's face.

With his mouth still full of jellybeans, he left the kitchen and walked across the living room. He stopped to watch the little drama from the front window.

He laughed as the boy became completely entangled in the leash. He popped another jellybean in his mouth, but he stopped chewing when he noticed that the boy kept looking towards the house. The kid looked familiar.

Coffey almost choked on a jellybean when he heard the woman threaten to call the police. He couldn't let that happen.

He hurried to the front door, not knowing what he was going to do; but as he stepped out onto the porch the boy jumped over the dog and ran off down the street.

It was later that night when it came to him. *Her brother!* What was that dead girl's little brother doing outside his house?

CHAPTER 27

They all gathered in Nathan's bedroom to debrief. Tilly kept saying, "Oh my God," over and over.

"I'm fine, Tilly," Nathan said, dismissing her.

"Man, Nathan, that was insane," Matthew said, still roused from watching the event transpire.

"I would have shit myself," Joel added. Suzie giggled.

"He saw you, Nathan." Tilly looked at the others. "Coffey saw Nathan!"

"It'll be okay, Tilly," Nathan said.

"No, it won't." She wanted to shake him, but instead, she balled her hands, her fingernails digging into her palms. "You are not to do anything like that again. From now on you can't be involved in any of this."

"You can't stop me. In case you forgot, you're dead."

"That's the problem, Nathan, I'm dead. He's the one who killed me. And now he *saw* you."

"So what? I was just some kid outside his house. Big deal. He doesn't know who I am."

"He! Saw! You! It doesn't *matter* if he knows you." She ran the palm of her hand back and forth across the back of her neck. What had gotten into her little brother? "He can easily figure out who you are—or that might not even matter because he could just decide you're next."

Matthew came to her side. "Sit down, Tilly." He gestured towards Nathan's bed.

Despite her frustration she looked at Nathan. When he nodded in approval, she sat down.

"Well, we can't do anything about what happened now," Matthew said. He looked at Tilly. He smiled, his eyebrows pulling closer together.

"We'll just have to keep him close," Suzie said, looking at Nathan.

You didn't do such a great job when you were supposed to be watching Coffey, Tilly thought, biting her tongue. *But neither did I.* "Thanks," she said instead.

Tilly saw Nathan smile at Suzie, and a quiver ran through her as she watched Suzie smile back at him.

"I just said that Nathan mustn't follow us anymore," Tilly growled. She didn't want to recognize the emotion coloring her mood.

"Then I'll just have to stay with him." Suzie told him, "I've got your back."

"Sorg came back," Kaylin was standing in the doorway.

"What?" Matthew turned to her.

"Who?" Joel asked.

"Sorg," she said, sounding afraid to repeat it. "Isn't that what you called it? Remember? When you told us about your uncle?"

"Sorg?" Matthew asked.

"The haze." Suzie straightened and looked at Kaylin. "She's talking about the haze. It's a good name for it."

"You saw it?" Tilly asked. "Where?"

"After you guys left, I was lonely. So, I went home." Looking as if she had done wrong. "I couldn't help it. I miss my dad."

"That's fine, Kaylin." Tilly walked over to her and put her arm around her. Little vibrations ran through her arms. "What happened?"

"I went home to see my dad," she said. "I found him in the living room. He was staring at the TV. Just staring at it."

"Was the TV on?" Suzie asked.

"It was, but you could tell he wasn't watching it. He was just sitting there like he was sleeping with his eyes open."

Nathan slid along his bed, closer to the headboard. Kaylin sat in the opening he created.

"I called to him. I thought maybe he could hear me like Nathan does; but he couldn't. Then Sorg showed up. It was the same as when it was at Tilly's, but it seemed bigger. Maybe." She went quiet for a moment. "It was bigger, and greenish-black." She nodded her head. "It made this humming sound. It kept getting louder and louder. It hurt my ears." She covered her ears as she spoke. "I yelled at it to go. I started screaming at it. Then my dad seemed to snap out of it." Kaylin dropped her hands. "My dad sat up straight," she imitated her father, "and called my name.

"I told him I was right here, but he couldn't hear me." Her eyes filled with tears, her nose reddening. "I grabbed his hand."

Tilly covered her mouth with her hand.

"And when I did, he started shaking and then threw up." The tears had started to stream down Kaylin's cheeks. "My grandma came in then. She scolded my dad for just sitting in front of the TV all day, but then she hugged him and told him she'd make him something to eat." Kaylin wiped at her tears with the tips of her fingers. "I don't really like Grandma. She always gets mad if I get dirty or she complains how I'm sitting. I feel like I can never do anything right when she's around." She ran her palms across her cheeks. "She was like that when she came to stay with us after my mom died four years ago. I know my dad feels the same way. He and my grandma would argue all the time and he eventually asked her to leave. He doesn't know I know all that." She wrapped her arms around herself. "And now he's stuck with her, because of me."

"It's not your fault," Tilly said, trying hard not to burst into tears herself. She moved closer to her and opened her arms. Kaylin leaned in, rested her head on Tilly's chest and started to cry. Tilly cried with her, ignoring the fizz of electricity between the two of them.

"That's it. We have to stop this thing, this Sorg thing." Joel said. "We can't let it keep hurting our families."

CHAPTER 28

Tilly missed having Sunday breakfast, and she especially missed movie night with her family. They would take turns picking what to watch; Nathan always wanted a superhero movie of some sort. How many comic book movies could a person possibly watch? She missed popcorn stuck between her teeth and listening to her mother sing as she made supper.

This was not how she thought being dead would be. She was the dead one, yet she was the one missing everyone.

She watched her father trying to keep things as normal as possible for Nathan. They still watched superhero movies and he still made bacon and eggs on Sundays. Both were done in an awkward silence and without Tilly's mum, who hadn't left her bed since the funeral.

Tilly saw the same thing happening to Suzie and Kaylin, how their parents refused to get out of bed, and just lay there as if something had sucked all life out of them. But she didn't seem to have the energy to spare to worry about them with her own mother to worry about.

Tilly sat on the edge of her bed, looking out the window, watching birds flit through the trees.

"Are you okay, Tilly?" Nathan asked from the doorway.

"Yeah."

He came over and gently sat beside her, sharing silence for a while.

"I miss you, Tilly," Nathan said, barely above a whisper, not looking at her.

Tilly's laughter took her by surprise, just on the edge of hysteria, and threatening either a full-blown nervous breakdown or a fist smashed into something. And she laughed because Nathan had said exactly what she wanted to hear. Here he was, sitting next to her, yet they both missed each other so much. She missed fighting with him, babysitting him, taking him to school. She missed being a family.

"Are you all right?" he said again, watching her wipe her eyes with the sleeve of her shirt.

"Yeah."

They sat, watching the birds, and then she said: "Nathan?"

"Yeah?"

"Where are your imaginary friends?"

"You know they aren't imaginary, right?"

She nodded. "Am I a ghost to you?"

Nathan waited, and Tilly realized he was giving her time sort this out.

"Why can't I see your imaginary friends?" she finally asked. "I mean, I can see Matthew and Joel and Suzie and Kaylin, but what about others."

He waited again.

"Do you still have imaginary friends?" She finally looked at him.

"I do." He smiled at her. "But I haven't seen them for a while."

"Why?"

It was Nathan's turn to pause.

"What's wrong?" Tilly shifted, facing him, and realized she'd caused him upset. "I'm sorry."

"No, it's not you." He rubbed his hands up and down his thighs. "Shortly before you died, I started having trouble connecting with them…. I have things I can do when I want to block them."

"What do you mean? Block them from what?"

"It's hard to explain, Tilly." He started rubbing his hands together. "I block *me* from *them*." He watched her to see if she looked like she was believing him. "I've always been able to see, well, ghosts, if you want to call them that; but there are times they get in the way like when I'm busy at school or playing ball or at night when I'm going to sleep."

"Your lamp?"

"Exactly. But now it seems that even when I want to talk to them, I can't find them."

"Where did they go?"

"That's it. I don't think they went anywhere. I think it's me."

"What do you mean?"

"You guys are the only ones I can see. And I couldn't see the people you're with until after you... died." Nathan's forehead crinkled.

"Why not?"

"I don't know."

They sat in silence for quite a while, processing. Tilly tried to imagine what it was like for Nathan. How his imaginary friends could bother him at school or when he was trying to sleep. How he had to block himself from these imaginary friends that apparently were actual ghosts. Real ghosts. And now she was one.

"Do you want to watch a movie with me?" Nathan broke the quiet. "I'll let you pick. You haven't picked in a while." He smiled.

His offer was comforting, and also stung.

"I'd really like that, Nathan," She desperately wanted to hug him, something she couldn't do in either world.

"Great! You go pick one out and I'll start the popcorn." He dashed out of the room.

She gave him a minute then joined him in the kitchen. She found him at the microwave pulling out a bag bloated with popped corn. "Did you decide?"

"Surprise me."

She watched him dump the contents of the bag into a big red plastic bowl and followed him into the living room. "Close your eyes," he said as he put the bowl on the coffee table.

She settled herself on the couch and did as she was told, listening to the faint click of keys as he punched them on the remote. "Should we call for Dad?"

"Naw." Nathan paused as he scrolled through the screen's movie selections. "It's easier without him. Just leave him upstairs with Mom."

He was right. And that made Tilly's heart dip a little.

"Ok," he said, "got it." The opening credits revealed he'd picked one of Tilly's favorites. She wanted to cry but stopped herself. She'd been crying a lot, lately.

"Thanks, Nathan," she said, curling up in the corner of the couch. He nestled himself into the other corner, smiled at her, then turned his attention to the TV. Tilly's chest filled with love for him.

She watched as he pushed popcorn into his mouth, one piece at a time. He hadn't offered her any, she realized. Maybe he knew more about being a ghost than she did.

"You're doing it again," he said, bringing another piece up to his mouth.

"Doing what?"

"Staring at me."

She couldn't help it. She looked at the boy who always sat at the other end of the couch during movies, but she saw a different boy this time, one who was no longer her baby brother. "Sorry." She forced herself to look away and watch the movie.

Later, Tilly watched Nathan take his popcorn bowl to the kitchen, dump the unpopped kernels in the compost bin and put his bowl in the dishwasher. Their father came into the kitchen.

"Hey champ," he said to Nathan as he slid in beside him to put his dishes in the washer.

"I'm going to bed, Dad," Nathan said. "Good night." And he left the kitchen and headed for the stairs. She followed him up. While he went off to his room to change for bed, Tilly stopped to check in on her mother before she went to her room.

It was the same scene. Her mother lay in bed, shades drawn, a glass of water on the nightstand, a bottle of pills next to it. Tilly's mother took them at night to sleep; but now, sleeping didn't seem to be a problem—waking up was the issue. No one could wake her up for more than five minutes at a time; and even then, she wasn't really there—she'd mumble something, then go back to sleep. Tilly felt her mother was slowly disappearing.

She climbed up on her mother's bed and lay next to her, cuddling in close to her, but carefully not touching her. She lay quietly, focusing on her mother.

Tilly tried to slow her thoughts. She tried to forget everything that had happened in the last few days and just be present. As she lay there, she could feel the warmth radiating from her mother's body. She could see her mother's chest expand slightly with each breath.

As Tilly lay listening to her mother's heartbeat, she tried to count the beats. She wasn't sure what the proper number of beats was.

"I miss you, Mom," she whispered. "Nathan misses you too, and so does Dad. Come back," she told her, fighting tears. "Don't let *it* take you, too."

Benjamin Coffey had killed Tilly, and now, he was taking even more from her family. He would end up killing her mother too, indirectly, but she would be just as dead. What would that do to Nathan and her father?

Listening to her mother breathing, Tilly started getting sleepy. She realized that she rarely felt sleepy. In, out. In, out. With eyes closed, she gave in and let her mind drift, picturing herself in her pajamas, her mother in hers. She imagined morning sun shining in on them, a moment of safety and warmth.

In that wish, she could hear her father puttering in the kitchen, making breakfast, Nathan helping. Tilly and her mother would pretend to be sleeping so her father and Nathan could surprise them with breakfast in bed. Her mom would giggle. Tilly would hush her. Nathan and Dad would be coming down the hall.

"We have a plan."

Tilly opened her eyes and sat up. Nathan was standing by the bed. Matthew and Joel were behind him.

"We're going back to Coffey's," Joel said.

CHAPTER 29

"We need more information," Matthew said as the group settled in Tilly's bedroom.

"You're right," Suzie said. "Because even though we know it's the old man's nephew, there still isn't enough evidence to prove him guilty."

"And then what?" Tilly asked.

"Well," Joel said, "we know the police looked at the house but didn't find enough to even take the uncle in for questioning, so it's not like giving them another name will make it any different. That's why we have to go back."

"We have to watch him," Matthew said.

"What's the plan?" Suzie asked.

"We are going to hang out at Coffey's," Joel said, "and see if we can spot anything that we can tell the police about. Tilly, you said you thought he had your watch. Well, maybe we can find it. Maybe he has it hidden, and he'll take us to it."

"He has to do *something* that will give him away," Matthew added.

"And then what?" Tilly asked, knowing what they were going to say next.

"Then we give Nathan the information and he gets it to the police," Joel said.

"What if Coffey grabs another person while we are watching him?"

"Then we tell Nathan, and he *calls* the police," Matthew said when nobody spoke up.

"I don't know if Dad will do it again," Tilly said.

"You have a cell phone, right?" Matthew asked Nathan, who nodded.

"You know I don't want Nathan involved in this."

"He already is," Suzie said. "And before you get mad at me again, I said I would watch out for him."

"How, Suzie?" She forced herself to keep from snapping at the girl. "How do you plan to do that?"

Tilly saw her barb strike, watched Suzie recover and look straight at her. "I don't know, Tilly, but I'll do whatever it takes."

"I'm not sure that's good enough."

CHAPTER 30

How had the kid figured him out? How had he discovered where he lived? It couldn't be a coincidence that the brother of the dead girl was outside his house. He recognized him from the funeral home. But what did the boy know exactly? Had he been in his house? Coffey was sure he had been. He couldn't find anything out of place, but the house felt different in a way he couldn't explain. But that wasn't true, was it? The front door had been unlocked when he came home from lunch; he was sure of it. He went to the key rack. The second set of keys was missing, and his uncle was away, so he couldn't have taken them.

He needed to study this boy. Ben sat in the worn-out chair, staring at the fireplace. *I am going to enjoy this one.*

CHAPTER 31

When Tilly arrived inside Coffey's house, the boys were already there, sitting on the landing that split the stairs going to the second floor.

"What took you so long?" Joel asked, his elbows on his knees, chin resting in the cup of his hand. "Not like you to miss out on the action." Tilly kind of knew he meant it was unlike her to not want to be in control. The truth of that was a surprise to her.

"Dad was taking Nathan out to feed the ducks at the park. I just needed to go with them for a bit. Then I left them there to lie with my mom for a bit more and I seemed to fall asleep. After watching the movie with Nathan last night, I just wanted to spend more time with him and Dad. And my mother." Tilly wasn't sure if staying with her family was to ignore the fact she was dead, or because of what had happened at Coffey's house, but now she was also afraid she was going to disappear before everything had been resolved.

"Do you guys—I mean do *we*—sleep?" Tilly wasn't sure if this was something she hadn't noticed before or if it was a part of their changing.

"Sometimes I lose little pockets of time. I'm not sure if it's sleeping though," Matthew said. "I just figured it's a glitch when my two timelines meet. It messes with my energy and it's like I'm not here and not there. Kind of like a temporal displacement."

"What does that mean?" She wasn't sure she wanted to hear his answer.

"Ignore him," Joel said. "He's just being a show-off."

"Have fun?" Matthew said.

"What?"

"The ducks. Did you have fun feeding the ducks?"

"Oh. Yes. I did." She found herself smiling.

"Did Kaylin find you?" Matthew asked.

"Kaylin? No. Was she here?"

"She was, a little while ago. Maybe ten or fifteen minutes ago. She was looking for you. Guess she's not as good at teleporting as we are."

"Teleporting? You a closet sci-fi nut?" Matthew said. "Seems you've kept that one hidden."

"You're not the only nerd."

Weird, Tilly thought, *Why was Kaylin looking for her?* "Anything happening?"

"No," Matthew said. "Coffey is in his chair in front of the TV and just sits there eating and watching stupid shows. He talks to himself a lot."

"What does he say?"

"Mostly mumbles stuff about promises and family and itches. It doesn't make any sense."

"He must be getting ready to do something though," Joel said. "He muttered, *the next one* a couple of times."

"The next kid?"

"But he doesn't *do* anything. He just sits there, so I don't know if that's what it means Worst stake-out ever. Certainly not like in the movies." When Matthew and Tilly looked at him, he sat up. "What?"

His comment seemed out of place, but yet it was true.

"Did you know that he has garden gnomes? How weird is that?" someone behind them said.

Tilly spun around to see Suzie walking through the living room.

"Hey, Tilly," Suzie said when she spotted her, "is Nathan here too?"

"No." Tilly shook her head. "What's going on?"

"Kaylin was here. She said you were with Nathan." Suzie came closer. "So, I figured he was okay with you."

"Kaylin left," Joel said.

"Then she's with Nathan?"

"I guess so."

Tilly knew she had to let it go. If it took all of them to keep Nathan safe, then that's what it took. This was bigger than she could handle by herself. She also knew Kaylin needed someone right now, and she was glad her brother could be with her. The girl seemed calmer when Nathan was around.

"So, what do we do now?" Suzie asked as she sat beside the boys.

"Has anyone looked upstairs yet?" Tilly asked.

Nobody replied as she watched their attention shift to the living room. Her muscles tensed as she pictured Coffey sneaking up behind her. She turned to see what had caught their attention.

An empty plate in his hand, Coffey stood, looking out the living room window.

"Hmmm," Coffey said. "What are you up to now?"

Tilly, with the others in tow, went to the window, instinctively giving Coffey a wide berth.

"Nathan," Tilly shouted. A thump made them jump, and Suzie let out a little squawk.

"It was just Coffey's skateboard falling over," Joel said. No one acknowledged him. The only thing Tilly cared about right now was Nathan.

Coffey just stood at the window, watching Nathan slowly ride his bike up the street towards the house. She watched her brother drop something and then get off his bike to pick it up.

"Good one," Coffey mumbled.

"No!" Tilly was out of the house and next to Nathan in a blink. "What the hell are you doing?" she yelled at Nathan. "He can *see* you.

"Good, that's what I want," Nathan said through closed lips.

"That's what you *want*? Are you kidding me?" She moved around the bike as he got back on it and started to pedal slowly. "I told you to stay home."

"What are you doing?" It was Suzie this time.

"You said you'd watch him," Tilly spat at her.

"He wasn't supposed to be here. He was home with Kaylin, and your dad is there, too."

"It's not her fault, Tilly."

Tilly gave Nathan a look. "Go home Nathan. Please!"

Tilly saw the guilt on Kaylin's face as she and Nathan settled on his bed. She hadn't said a word to either of them as she followed them home; now they were settled in Nathan's room, with the door closed.

"So, you were a part of this?" Tilly tried to say calmly, not achieving it.

Suzie appeared in Nathan's room.

Dropping her gaze, Kaylin nodded.

Tilly walked to the window then back to the bed. She looked at the two sitting on the bed. Walked to the window and back. She looked at Suzie. She walked halfway to the window then turned to face them. "This can *not* happen again!" She was sure her face was getting red. "What were you two thinking?"

"I'm helping." He looked at Kaylin. "We want to help."

"Not by putting yourself out there, Nathan," Tilly's hands were in the air. "How do you think putting yourself in front of a killer is helping?"

"Tilly," Suzie said.

"What!" she shouted. Tilly chewed on her cheek, took a deep breath and slowly let it out. "What?"

Suzie didn't need to say anything. Tilly knew the girl was right. Yelling at them wasn't going to help: they all needed to fix this. She just needed to figure out how to keep Nathan safe while they did that.

"It's done," she said, not willing to apologize to her brother, making her feel small, but not caring about that right now—she needed to be right. She started to pace again, then realized what she was doing and stopped herself. "What are we going to do now?" she asked, more to herself than to those in the room.

"He saw you, Nathan," Joel said as he arrived in Nathan's room.

"And he knows *exactly* who you are," Matthew added, regretting saying it as soon as the words came out. He knew he should have waited to tell Tilly when they were alone.

CHAPTER 32

"What do we do now?" Tilly was pacing again, almost frantic. "How are we going to deal with this?"

"We'll figure something out," Joel said, sounding like he was trying to convince himself.

"Coffey's going to be following Nathan." Tilly fought panic crawling up her throat.

"But now we have the upper hand," Nathan said.

"Upper hand? How's that?" Tilly tried to control her voice.

"What do you mean?" Suzie asked.

"Now he will follow me, and we can keep an eye on him this way."

"There are four of us who always could keep an eye on him, Nathan. And none of us can be hurt by him!" Tilly ignored the irony in her words.

"But he could hurt someone else while we wait and watch," Nathan said.

"Nathan," Joel interrupted, "I get what you're saying." He smiled at the boy. "You do realize what you just did, right?"

Nathan nodded.

"Do you really?" Tilly asked him.

"Yes, Tilly, I do."

"And what is it?" she asked, not believing him.

"I don't want this to be someone else's problem. It's ours." He looked at each one of them. "I don't want another family to have to go through this." He now traced the pattern on his comforter with his finger. "We can do this. We can stop him— but sitting around and waiting for him to help us to stop him isn't going to work."

"I'm not sure I agree with what you did, Nathan," Joel said. "But here we are, and now we have to do something about it."

"Joel's right," Matthew said. "So, what *are* we going to do about it?"

Kaylin, who had characteristically been quiet until now, said, "Coffey's going to follow Nathan to some place where we can catch him. When we get him where we want him, Nathan can call the police on his cellphone, and they will have to investigate and hopefully arrest him."

"That's the plan you two hatched up?" Tilly struggled to reel back her growing anger. "All that sneaking around earlier! Letting Suzie think you were with Dad. Letting *me* think you were with Dad!" Tilly was surprised no one was trying to stop her. "You were a part of this?" she asked Kaylin. "Checking to see where I was, for Nathan?"

Kaylin sat quietly. For a moment she looked like she was going to shrivel up and disappear.

"That's what you two were up to?" Suzie looked from Nathan to Kaylin and back again. "Was it?" she asked, when neither of them responded, and finally they both nodded. "How am I supposed to keep my promise if you sneak around like this?" Suzie stared at Nathan this time. "I told your sister I'd watch out for you." She crossed her arms but this time her shoulders slumped as she did.

"All right," Joel said, "let's take a minute here." He went over to Nathan's bed to sit beside them.

"Watch out!"

Joel froze, looking around.

"Don't step on the mat!" said Nathan, pointing.

"What's going on?" From Joel's posture it was plain he was afraid to move.

"Just don't step on the mat," Nathan said, looking a little embarrassed.

"I don't get it." Joel said.

"Nathan doesn't like anyone stepping on the mat beside his bed," Tilly said.

Joel backed away from the bed.

"He just likes it that way," Tilly answered. "It's where Arthur sleeps." She looked at Nathan, giving him an apologetic look. Although she was angry at him for putting himself in this situation, she realized that she was the one who had done that. And Nathan's little idiosyncrasies just proved how much she needed to keep him out of it.

"Arthur?" Kaylin asked.

"Our cat," Tilly answered. "He died a few years ago." As soon as she heard her own words it snapped like a lightbulb. "You can see King Arthur?"

Nathan nodded.

"Your dead cat?" Suzie asked. She looked around the room. "Where is he?"

"Can you see him now?" Tilly leaned in while she asked him, her voice gentle.

He shook his head. "No. He's blocked too."

"Who's blocked?" Joel asked.

Tilly let out a sigh. She took in a deep breath and slowly told the others. "As you know, Nathan can see us." She paused for a moment, looking at him. He gave her a small nod. "He used to see other ghosts or…" The words caught in her throat for a minute. She hated saying it. "Dead people. But then something happened, and now he can't see the others. Not since we died."

"Maybe it's the same reason we can't see other dead people," Kaylin added.

Tilly was surprised by Kaylin's comment.

"So, all this time King Arthur has been sleeping on your mat?" Tilly asked her little brother.

"Sometimes he comes up on my bed; but when he gets too close, we end up giving each other a shock, so he usually just stays on the mat."

Tilly made a *humph* sound.

"Maybe we should get back to making a plan," Matthew said.

CHAPTER 33

"Nathan," Tilly called out from the bottom of the stairs, "ready to watch a movie?" When she didn't get an answer, out of habit she climbed the stairs to see what he was up to, wanting to not only be alone with him, but give him a break from all the drama. For that reason, she'd suggested everyone take some time to visit their own families, get some space from each other, and then regroup to come up with a solid plan. Although she realized that her idea was maybe more selfish than helpful, she also needed a break.

But when she entered Nathan's room, he wasn't there.

"Nathan?"

She checked his closet, knowing never to make assumptions about him, but also starting to worry there might be a problem. She checked the floor of the closet. No sign of him. Nothing. "Nathan," she said. Nothing.

That brought her to a search of the house: She found her mother asleep as usual, and her father in the living room watching a documentary about whales and dolphins.

She checked the backyard. Still no sign of him.

"Nathan!"

She stopped; fought her rising anxiety. She closed her eyes instead. Pictured him. And *moved*.

She was stunned to find Nathan in Coffey's kitchen. Kaylin next to him.

"Oh my god!" she said, rushing towards him. "What are you… why are… how did you get *in* here?"

He turned, startled. "Tilly!"

"How did you get in here?"

"I have the key." He tapped his front pocket. "Remember?"

"What are you doing? Why are you here? You need to come home. Where is Coffey? He could come back."

"He's at work. Kaylin checked."

"I don't want you here! I want you home, safe with Dad."

"We have to stop him, Tilly."

Tilly turned to Kaylin, hoping to enlist her help. Kaylin stared towards the living room.

"Kaylin, you know this is insane, right?"

Kaylin still didn't respond.

"How did you get away from Dad?" she asked her brother, gesturing him toward the door.

"He thinks I'm—"

And then suddenly Joel was there, alarm ringing off him like bells. "What are you guys doing here?"

"We were just leaving," Tilly said.

"You've got to go now!"

"What's wrong?"

"He's coming home!"

Tilly wished she could wrap her arms around Nathan and make him invisible. She wished she could grab him, take him with her, back to the house, drop him inside his room.

Nathan started across the room, headed for the front door.

Matthew appeared in front of the door. "What the hell are you guys doing here? I just went to your house." He gestured wildly at the door "He's right *outside*."

Nathan froze.

"He's coming up the walkway."

"Back door!" Joel shouted. "Back door! Fast!"

Nathan spun and ran for the back door, Tilly right behind him. She could hear the key in the lock of the front door. The bolt giving way. Nathan ran through the living room and into the kitchen. She heard the click of the door as it closed behind Coffey.

"Go!" she yelled. "Faster!"

Nathan reached the back door, turned the knob, and pulled. It didn't move.

"The key," Tilly shouted. "You have a key for this door too, right?"

Nathan looked at the door. His face went white. "That's not the problem." Just above the deadbolt was a padlock.

"It's new," came a voice from the living room.

Tilly's body went cold.

"Special gift for you."

She listened to heavy footsteps coming through the living room.

"I was told you were here."

Joel appeared to their left, in the dining room.

"Nathan," he shouted, "there is a door here that takes you through to the hall." He kept pointing to the door. "He's in the living room. Go to the door and when he comes into the kitchen, you run down the hall and get to the front door. Hurry! Before he sees you."

Tilly turned to see Coffey standing in the archway between the kitchen and living room. She grabbed at her chest, feeling like she was having a heart attack. Her mind took her to the first time she had seen him. She remembered him once again standing at the bottom of her stairs.

"Aren't you going to say anything?" Coffey asked Nathan, stepping into the kitchen, searching for him.

She fought to make her muscles move. She forgot about Nathan. Forgot she was in Coffey's kitchen, not in her own house. She screamed. A crash from near the counter brought her back. She watched jellybeans spin across the tile, shards of glass sparkling in the fall.

She remembered finding him standing in her doorway. How he had closed the front door, trapping her. Now she felt trapped again. She remembered throwing her bag at him before she ran as hard as she could for her back door.

"What the...?" Coffey looked at the counter and the glass and the jellybeans. Then looked back to the door.

She had no bag to throw at him this time. She watched as Coffey came further into the room, then glanced in Joel's direction.

"Oh, but what if I've locked the *front* door too?" Coffey said, seeming to know where Nathan was going.

Tilly watched as Nathan quietly slipped through the hall door. She watched Coffey follow Nathan's path. She moved from the kitchen into the living room in time to see Nathan reach the door. She watched him turn the doorknob, but the door didn't move. Nathan felt for the key.

"There's no time, Nathan! Up here!"

Tilly looked toward the staircase and saw Kaylin waving Nathan toward the stairs. Nathan pulled out his phone as he started up.

Coffey reached through the spindles and grabbed Nathan's leg. He tripped, dropping his phone and saw it bounce down the stairs.

"Where are you going?" Coffey laughed. "Nothing up there.

Nathan knew he had cornered himself.

Tilly saw Coffey grab Nathan. She watched him fall.

"Run!"

And with that shouted word, a sudden sound of breaking glass filled her ears. Pieces of the front window flew across the living room and hall. She watched Coffey duck, dropping to the floor, releasing Nathan's leg. Nathan was up again, taking the stairs two at a time.

As Coffey got up, Tilly tried to grab him. She threw herself on him and felt a blast of cold run through her. She lost her breath then crashed to the floor. Her limbs were lead, her heart a stone. Her head screamed in agony with pain that was dull, dark and dead.

Coffey stopped for a moment and seemed to look her in the eye. Was he smiling, or was he confused—or angry?

He just shook himself and started towards the stairs.

Tilly prayed she had given Nathan enough time to hide or get out of the house.

Tilly was gaining control of herself again. Joel was beside her now. "If he can't get out, then we need to find somewhere for him to hide."

Coffey followed her brother up the stairs.

"Hide! Find somewhere to hide! Call 911!" she called out to Nathan. "We need to find him a place to hide," she told Joel.

Nathan didn't answer her.

She appeared next to Nathan as he entered a bedroom.

"Hide!"

"Where?"

She looked around for a spot.

"Where's your phone?"

"I dropped it when he grabbed me!"

Tilly looked around frantically. *Under the bed? Too obvious. Closet? Trapped even more.* "Back door. Balcony," she told him. "Joel, look for a door."

Joel left in search for a way out.

Nathan ran into another bedroom. Seeing a door in its corner. he bolted to it— a bathroom.

Trapped.

Tilly watched as Nathan got into the tub, pulled the shower curtain halfway closed and ducked behind it. Pulling it all the way was too obvious.

"He'll find you here." Kaylin waved her arm, motioning for him to follow her, but he curled in the corner of the tub, trying not to create a shadow. Kaylin settled in beside him.

Tilly didn't know what else to do. She left and looked for some kind of exit.

"He's looking under the beds," Joel called out.

"Can I get by him?" Nathan asked.

"No.

She thought about grabbing Coffey again, but her first effort hadn't done much.

"He's coming this way!" Joel said.

She watched as Joel almost ran into Matthew as he appeared in the bedroom. "There is a makeshift fire escape. One of those emergency chain ladders by the bed in the back bedroom." Matthew told them.

"We need a door!"

"The ladder means there isn't a door, Tilly! Its for an emergency exit, like a fire."

She shook her head in frustration.

"You need to get to the bedroom in the back," Matthew told Nathan. "Past the stairs. It will be hard for you to not want to go down the stairs, but you need to go to the ladder."

They heard Coffey in the bedroom now, just outside the bathroom.

"Where are you, little boy?" he called. "You know I'll find you."

Kaylin looked around the bathtub. She looked at the shower curtain. She pointed through the opening of the curtain. "He's here," she whispered.

Tilly watched Coffey walk into the room, looking at the shower curtain. He walked to the opening without moving the curtain, then bent to look inside, as if teasing the boy behind it. Nathan jumped up, grabbed at the wall and cannonballed himself over the edge of the tub. He slipped, coming down hard on the edge and felt a bone snap in his right arm.

As he howled in pain. Coffey just stood laughing at him.

Nathan slowly got up, cradling his arm as Tilly ran towards Coffey—and this time Joel joined in. Their combined force knocked him off balance, slowed him down enough for Nathan to dash by him out of the bathroom, through the bedroom, and down the hall.

Tilly watched as Coffey stood still, staring. He seemed stunned for a moment. He shook himself. Leaving the bathroom, he looked around the bedroom, then hurried down the hall just in time to see Nathan disappear into a back bedroom. As Coffey reached it, Tilly saw that Nathan had opened the window and was about to throw the ladder out of it.

Coffey hurled himself across the room and tackled Nathan, knocking him to the floor. Nathan screamed out in pain from his broken arm.

Coffey climbed on top and straddled him.

Tilly screamed again and the bedroom windows shattered. Coffey tried to cover his face from the flying glass as Nathan managed to squirm out from under him. He tried to climb out the window, cradling his arm.

Coffey pulled Nathan's leg out from under him. Suddenly, light bulbs exploded, sparks flew from them and landed on the curtains. Nathan went down hard, knocking himself out.

"Get up!" Tilly yelled. "Get up fast!" But Nathan just lay there.

Coffey stepped back, tried to get his breath, to make sense of everything that was happening.

"We have to get a door open!" Tilly yelled at the others. "Nathan can't climb out the window with that hurt arm!" She knelt next to him. "We have to wake him up."

Coffey grabbed Nathan's collar and dragged him away from the window. He straddled Nathan again, this time wrapping his hands around Nathan's throat. "I wasn't expecting it to go like this, but you sure made it fun." He slapped Nathan. "And you aren't getting off that easy!" He slapped him again. "I want you *awake* for this."

Images flashed in Tilly's mind and the first was of her lying on her kitchen floor, Coffey on top of her, choking her. Then she remembered waking in the shed.

But then she also remembered the day she ran into Nathan in their mother's room. How they had somehow stuck together and how Nathan was unable to move until she was able to pull herself off him. And how it had happened again, downstairs, briefly, when she had tried to grab Coffey.

Tilly ran for Coffey. She slammed into him. This time wrapping her arms around him. He wobbled but managed to straighten up again still pinning Nathan to the floor.

Then, for Tilly, it went dark. She couldn't see. She felt like her head was in a vise, getting tighter and tighter. White spots blurred in front of her. She felt knives stabbing all over her body, burning her. She could feel Coffey struggling to get back up. But she could feel something else. She could hear someone else. They were screaming. They were in pain. She felt rage. There was laughter too.

Tilly could feel herself slipping, getting weaker. It wasn't supposed to be like this. *He* was the one who shouldn't be able to move. She'd lost all sense of time, and she didn't know if she could hold Coffey for much longer. She knew she wouldn't let go, though. She would do whatever she had to, to keep Nathan safe.

She heard her name and tried to find where the voice came from. It called to her again. She twisted her neck enough to see Joel. He was blurry and seemed to blink on and off. She tried to call out to him, reach out for him but she couldn't lift her arms. She watched Joel rush towards her, saw him clearly for a split second, felt him touch her—but then her vision went black, and the sound of crashing waves became deafening. She felt as if she had been ripped from her skin, if she even had skin. Then the sound stopped. Her head was free from the vise—and she opened her eyes.

She was lying on the floor a few feet from Coffey. He twisted and turned, but it all seemed to be in slow motion. He was solid, then blurred. The sounds he made were like growls and groans, like he was trying to yell or scream. Tilly realized he was blurred because it was Coffey and Joel blending together. Was that what had happened to her? She pulled herself up to step towards Coffey. "Joel?" She yelled at the blur. "Joel?"

She stepped closer. She started to reach out, wanting to pull Joel free, like he must have done for her.

"Don't!" She heard. "Don't touch us, Tilly." Joel's voice was muffled, blended with the bodies mashed into the blurry form in front of her.

"Joel!" Tilly screamed.

"Get Nathan out!"

Tilly heard banging. She didn't know where it was coming from. She didn't care. She went to her brother. "Wake up, Nathan!" she begged him. "Wake up!"

More banging.

The curtains had caught fire and Tilly remembered the exploding lightbulbs.

"Nathan!" Tilly took a chance. She grabbed him and shook him, quickly letting go, afraid she would blend with him like she had with Coffey. She didn't feel the vice or the stabbing pain, so she grabbed him again. Shook him again. "Nathan! The house is on fire. Wake up!"

Someone was calling her name, but she stayed focused on Nathan. When she grabbed him again, she realized there was no pain at all. She felt heavy and slow but felt no pain.

"The police," Matthew yelled at her as he stood over her.

"He lost his phone." She answered without looking at him.

"No, the police are here, fire trucks too," Matthew said.

"Someone must have called 911," Kaylin said.

"They must have seen the fire."

"Or heard the breaking glass."

Tilly was afraid to believe them. The room was on fire and Coffey was still here, so Nathan still wasn't safe.

"They're banging on the front door," Matthew said.

"Nathan!" Tilly said.

Coffey continued to twist. He was moving slower though. He seemed unaware of that there were firefighters in his house or even of the flames spreading across the room from the curtains.

"You ruined *everything!*" he yelled.

Tilly screamed again. More sparks came from the overhead light fixture and landed on the bed. The bedspread started to smolder.

Finally, Nathan's eyes opened. He lay motionless for a moment. Then he started to scramble to get up, using his broken arm, but he collapsed in pain.

The bedding was now on fire, but Coffey didn't seem to care.

"Tilly!" Nathan moaned. He was trying to get up again.

"We need to get out!" She felt so weak, just like her voice.

"Hurry!" Kaylin called from the door.

"The police are here," Matthew repeated.

Nathan stood. He watched Coffey shake and try to get up.

"Run, Nathan!" Matthew yelled.

"I can't," he said. "The doors are locked." He stepped back from Coffey.

"There is help downstairs!" Matthew told him.

Nathan took another step back. He slipped when his heel caught the curtain rod. He landed on the floor and Coffey reached out and was able to grab his foot, pulling him closer.

Nathan reached behind him, trying to pull himself away, but his broken arm gave out. His fingertips touched the metal rod. He picked it up and swung it, hitting Coffey squarely on his forehead. Coffey fell to the side and rubbed at his head.

"LEAVE HIM ALONE!" Tilly screamed.

There were more sparks, and Coffee fell back as if hit.

Nathan swung again.

And this time Coffey went limp.

The fire fighters burst into the room.

One of them helped Coffey to his feet and took him out of the room while another knelt beside Nathan and started to lift him as the fire spread around them. Nathan waved him away and sat up.

Kaylin rushed to him. "Are you okay, Nathan?"

Tilly did the same and gave him a quick hug before he could protest and before their bodies could register touch.

"I'm sorry," he whispered.

"I'm sorry, too," she answered.

"It's going to be all right now," the firefighter said to Nathan. "Can you get up? We've got to get you out of here."

"Yes. I'm fine." He hugged his arm to his side.

"I'm so sorry," Kaylin said, her face inches from Nathan's as they left the burning room.

Tilly saw him mouthed the word *okay*. She turned to thank her friends. She found Matthew standing at the window, ignoring the flames around him and watching the police cars, fire trucks and an ambulance on the front lawn. She could hear more sirens. The blunt wail of a firetruck horn.

She left him and went downstairs and out to the lawn to catch up with Nathan and the firefighter as they were met by the paramedics. She climbed into the ambulance as he was getting settled on the stretcher. She didn't speak to him; the space was tight for any kind of conversation. She watched as the medic placed the oxygen mask over his mouth and nose.

"I'm going to have to move your arm," The medic said. "I need to stabilize it until we get you to the hospital."

Tilly watched Nathan nod.

As the medic moved his arm as gently as she could, Tilly saw Nathan wince.

"They will get you fixed up, Nathan."

"I'm good," he mumbled behind the mask.

"Your father is on his way. He should be here any minute."

Nathan leaned back on the stretcher and closed his eyes.

Matthew and Kaylin gathered outside the ambulance. All Tilly could muster was a small smile when she saw them. "I think he's going to be okay."

"Nathan!" Tilly recognized her father's voice.

"NATHAN!"

She watched her father dodge past the firefighter and head towards her.

"Are you okay? Are you hurt?" He turned to the paramedic. "Is he hurt."

Tilly had never seen her father like this before. He was shaking and breathing heavy. He was frantic.

"He may have breathed in some smoke. It looks like he has broken his arm, we have set it for now but once they go over him, they will cast it."

"Are you comfortable?" She asked Nathan as she strapped him in the stretcher.

Nathan nodded.

"You can ride with us," the medic said as she slid further in to give their father room.

"I will see you at the hospital, okay?" Tilly said. She saw his quick nod of acknowledgement then climbed out of the ambulance.

"That was so scary," Kaylin said. She looked like she was trembling.

"I can't believe that just happened." Matthew said as he looked back at the house.

"Where's Joel?" Tilly asked.

"He's gone." Matthew said. She heard sadness in his voice.

"What? Gone where? With Nathan?" She turned towards the ambulance, watching as it drove down the street.

"No, Tilly," he said. "He's gone."

CHAPTER 34

The hospital room was dark except for the soft glow of the headboard's light. Tilly and the others stood close by Nathan's bed, but no one spoke. She watched as her brother woke up. He turned his head towards his father sleeping on a cot next to him. She felt her shoulders lower a little.

"We almost got him killed," Tilly whispered to the huddled group.

"He's going to be all right, Tilly." Matthew rubbed her shoulder, and she could feel the electricity from his hand heating her skin.

"He'll be traumatized for life!" She watched Nathan turn onto his other side and close his eyes again. "Coffey had him pinned." She pointed to her brother. "He hates even being touched. Coffey was choking him." And at that she could no longer hold back her tears. "He was almost killed, and it's all my fault."

"Tilly, you didn't mean for this to happen," Matthew said. "You—"

"He saved people, Tilly," Suzie said. "Coffey is going to go to prison because of Nathan."

"We don't know for sure about him going to prison," Matthew rubbed the back of his neck. "They still haven't found anything to connect him to *our* deaths yet."

"But when Nathan tells them—" Suzie stopped when she saw Matthew shaking his head. "What?"

"Nathan was in Coffey's house." He now had both hands clasped around the back of his neck. "Coffey may say Nathan broke in. He could say Nathan started the fire. Who knows what he'll say? He's going to panic."

"Matthew, please!" Tilly wanted him to stop talking.

"I'm just saying. We can't know for sure."

"Would you guys please stop, you're making my head hurt," Nathan said, without raising his head from the pillow. "I've had enough of you guys going on and on."

Tilly sniffed, wiping tears off her cheeks. The others smiled.

"Nathan…." Tilly started towards his bed.

"Yes, it *was* horrible," He whispered. He pulled himself up to a sitting position. "Yes, I was scared, terrified actually, but I'd do it all over again."

Their father shifted on the cot next to Nathan's bed, exhausted and deeply asleep.

"How did the police know to come?" Kaylin asked Nathan. "How did they know you were in trouble?"

"They didn't," he answered. He lowered his voice. "A neighbor called the police when they heard windows being smashed.

"Windows?" Matthew said.

"I guess the front windows smashed and then later there were other windows," Nathan said.

"I remember that," Tilly said, her and Coffey in the living room, ducking from the glass.

"I lied," Nathan's voice dropped even lower.

"You lied?" Tilly asked. "About the windows?"

"No. I said I was riding my bike when the chain came off." He looked down at his arm wrapped in plaster. "I told them that when I was fixing it, Coffey—but I didn't call him by name—came out to help me and the next thing I knew I was in his house and couldn't get out."

"Oh." It was so unlike Nathan to lie; but even as a lie, it reminded her of how Nathan had been trapped in the house.

"I feel horrible," he let out a big breath. "It's a lie, but I couldn't think of anything else to say."

"Where's your bike?" Suzie asked. Tilly could hear her trying to stay calm, the softness of her voice. "Is the chain fixed? What if they don't believe you?"

"I didn't know what else to do." He looked so small in the bed. "If they don't believe me, then he'll get away with it. I know I lied, and I'll get in trouble; but it's you I'm worried about." Nathan seemed to shrink the more he spoke. "What if my lie messed it all up?" Nathan seemed to be second-guessing himself. Tilly's heart hurt watching him.

"It's okay, Nathan." She ran her fingers over her mouth. "You did it for the right reason and no, he won't." Tilly corrected him. "He won't get away with it. He'll be caught."

"We'll figure something out," Matthew said. "You did great, Nathan."

He gave them a small smile. His face scrunched up as he shifted again. "I don't mean to be rude, but can you guys leave now?" He lowered himself back onto the bed. "I want to go back to sleep." He lifted his arm, heavy with a cast, and rolled onto his side, trying not to aggravate his bruised elbow or ribs. "I'm too tired to think about this anymore, and I'm too tired to block you. And I don't need Dad all over me again," he added, glancing at their sleeping father.

Block us? Tilly asked herself, remembering Nathan had told her he couldn't see anyone other than them, like something was blocking the other...ghosts. *Was Joel being blocked? If so, by what?*

"Sleep well," Suzie whispered.

"I'm going to Coffey's," Matthew said. "The police are searching the place. Coming?"

"Yes," said Kaylin. Everyone looked at her. "Is it okay?"

"Are you sure?" Tilly frowned, surprised. "You don't have to go. We can't know what we'll see." Up until yesterday, she wouldn't have worried about the girl—they were already dead. What could happen? But, she reminded herself, Joel was still missing.

Kaylin nodded. "I got Nathan into this too, Tilly."

They looked at Nathan. Tilly listened to her brother's soft breathing. She looked at her exhausted father. He seemed so much older. He had been through so much lately. She had forgotten how hard all this must be on him.

Her father had almost become hysterical when he arrived in the chaos at Coffey's house—fire trucks, police cars, lights flashing, Nathan sitting in the back of an ambulance, arm in a sling, wrapped in a blanket, shivering. She had watched her father collapse around Nathan and cry, Nathan letting him.

"I love you, Dad," Tilly whispered. "I won't be long," And left, Kaylin beside her.

CHAPTER 35

When they first arrived at Coffey', Tilly watched Suzie immediately go upstairs, hoping to find Joel there.

"He's *gone*, Suzie," Matthew said, entering the bedroom where they had last seen him.

"We are already dead, so how can he be dead again—if that's what you're trying to say." She walked around the room. "How could he just disappear?"

Tilly didn't know what to say. She stayed silent.

It was plain Matthew had no more answers, so he just stood next to her in an obvious attempt to offer support.

"How could he just disappear? Isn't that what you meant by *gone*?"

"Maybe Joel will show up," Matthew said, although there didn't seem to be much conviction in his tone.

Tilly turned at the sound of a glass breaking. She was a picture on the floor.

"Joel?" Suzie called out. She looked towards the ceiling, running the perimeter of the room. "Joel?"

They heard footstep on the stairs but quickly realized it was the fire inspector. They watched him as he walked the room, performing his inspecting of the house.

They could hear traffic come and go outside. Police officers were walking the grounds, a small fire crew remained in case something sparked up. Behind the caution tape, reporters were already on the story and neighbors came to look.

Tilly's attention returned to the marshal, but they all knew what they were waiting for. Waiting for Joel to come back. For him to give them a sign.

"I am having trouble finding any point of origin," the marshal dictated to his hand recorder. "Light bulbs are broken. I suspected sparks from the bulbs might have started it; but there are no scorch marks around the fixtures, no faults in the wiring or the breaker panel."

The marshal continued his inspection, but Tilly stopped listening. She became lost in her thoughts. She wondered why she had been able to separate herself from Nathan when they collided in their mother's room and was also able to pull herself away from Coffey when she shoved him yesterday in the living room but, where was Joel? The last time she saw him, he was entangled with Coffey. She heard Nathan's words again, ". . . block you." What did that mean?

"I'm going downstairs," Matthew said.

Tilly didn't know how long they had been sitting there, lost in their thoughts.

"I'm staying here," Suzie said.

Tilly couldn't blame her. She wanted to be here at the house when they found the evidence they needed to arrest Coffey. She wanted to stay and wait for Joel. She wanted to be at the hospital with her brother. She wanted to be with her mother.

"I'm going with Matthew, if you're okay on your own," Tilly said.

"I'll be fine," Suzie said. Her tone sounded anything but fine.

When Matthew, Kaylin and Tilly came into the living room, they found a corner to tuck themselves in, out of the way, an old habit of being alive.

The marshal must have given the *all clear* for downstairs because now they watched as people in white suits and booties photographed, moved, dusted, and bagged just about everything in the house. This time, the crime-scene officers bagged up Coffey's ball cap. They took photos of the key rack and bagged the keys, and they bagged Coffey's boots as well. They took swabs from furniture, railings and doorknobs, and looked behind photos hanging on the walls.

"Is this so they will keep him in jail?" Kaylin asked.

"He won't be getting out of jail," Matthew stated.

"No, Matthew's right," Tilly told the girl. "He'll be in jail for a long time, because of what Nathan did." Tilly paused. "They're bound to have their own information about Coffey, and I'm betting that this is an opportunity for them to see if they can link him to any of our deaths. They need to know if he's attacked other kids."

Tilly knew not all of this was true, but she didn't have the heart to tell Kaylin what had happened. Nathan told the police that Coffey had locked him in the house, and that was enough to get Coffey taken away for now, but they still had to prove that he had abducted Nathan—and that he was a murderer.

"You're pretty lucky to have a brother like Nathan," Matthew said. Tilly smiled at him. He was right.

One of the men in white carried a spray bottle and spritzed it on the fireplace mantel. Then he ran a purple light over the places he'd sprayed. They watched as he removed iron tools from a rack beside the fireplace. He sprayed each piece, moved the light over them, then set the tools beside their hanger. The man bent to spray the screen in front of the fireplace. He repeated the spraying, the light, and then moved the screen to the side. He leaned in closer to the fireplace opening.

"Dave," he called to a photographer in a matching suit. The man came over, looked at what the forensics officer indicated., "The fire was contained to the upstairs, right?"

"Yeah, the bedroom. What do you have?"

Tilly and her friends moved closer.

"Dunno, yet. Something though," and pulled out what looked like a pen, but as he pulled the end, it extended into a pointer of some kind. He pushed at a small pile of ashes and mortar that lay in front of the logs. Dave took several pictures of the pile and the inside of the fireplace.

When the photographer finished taking pictures, the forensics officer ran the pointer along the firebricks lining the firebox. He bent lower, leaning in further as he ran his pointer along the bricks on the back wall. Putting the pointer back into his pocket he took a bag from a kit and spread it on the floor.

"Got something?" the photographer asked.

He didn't answer, and instead removed the stack of firewood from the fireplace, one log at a time, Dave's camera clicking with each piece of wood.

"Not sure," he said, pointing to another small pile of mortar behind the metal grate. "Can you bag some of this up?"

"Doesn't look like ashes," the photographer said, bagging it.

"No." His voice had a far-off sound, like answering from reflex when you are deep in thought. He ran his pointer along the mortar between the bricks on the side of the firebox. Tilly could hear a dry, scraping sound. He then tapped the pointer on the floor of the fireplace making the little bit of dust it had collected fall off. He then ran it a second time along the mortar on the back wall of the enclosure. There was no dryness to the scraping this time. The pointer seemed to sink into the mortar rather than ride on top of it.

"Hand me a plastic bag," he said. "I don't think this is mortar."

Dave did and watched as he slid the end of the pointer into the bag and then tapped it on the ground, letting the collected bits fall into the bag. He handed the evidence bag over then leaned back into the fireplace, and, putting more pressure on the pointer, he started to dig at the mortar where he'd taken his sample.

After a few passes, unlike the dry mortar in the rest of the brickwork, it started to gather, balling up like playdough and falling to the floor. The photographer gathered two samples of the material.

The man with the pointer kept scraping, digging around the edges of a brick. Then another brick. It only took a few minutes before he had enough of the putty-like mixture removed to allow him to slip his gloved fingers in between the bricks and pull one out. Then another. One by one, he slowly dismantled two layers of the brick in the back wall of the fireplace, revealing a small space. He reached inside.

Tilly heard herself gasp when he pulled out a box and set it down in front of the fireplace. The sound of the camera zinging images seemed ominous.

"And what do we have here?"

He pulled off his dirty gloves, reached into his kit and pulled out a fresh pair. Once he had them on, he lifted the lid, all the while the camera zinging away. He gently pushed the objects around inside the box.

"My watch!" Tilly shouted. She moved in closer. "That's my watch!"

CHAPTER 36

Benjamin Coffey sat on a bench in a jail cell: three walls of blank concrete, the fourth of metal bars. When he stood at the bars, he could hear parts of conversations a few feet away. As he moved further back, it was like moving into an underground cave: nothing but the echoes of his breath.

Upon arriving at the police station, they had taken his photo, his fingerprints and bandaged some of his minor burns and cuts. He was sure the EMS tech had pressed unnecessarily hard on the lump that was growing on his forehead.

For the first hour, he had paced the small space. "This wasn't supposed to happen," he said. "I was doing it for you." He knew this wasn't true. Yes. Maybe at one time, at the start, when the itch wouldn't go away. When he had followed a kid and done the only thing that would make it stop. But he had to. He had to do it to make the itch stop. He had to make the kid pay.

Pay for what?

For what they did to me.

But what had they done? He realized he didn't care anymore. He realized he didn't even do it to make the itch stop. He almost welcomed the itch. It was familiar. It took away the dullness he felt all the time. It made him feel like he mattered. Powerful. Part of something.

From his bench, he watched the cops completed their investigation. They would be questioning him shortly. They had told him he could call a lawyer, and they said he could make another phone call.

But who would he call? His mother was dead. They had already contacted his uncle about the fire. He'd likely be arriving soon and he'd have to explain to his uncle how his house burnt down. He had no idea what the cops would have told him.

He thought of his boss at the funeral home. He had seemed to appear out of nowhere the day after his mother had died. Wanting to be buddies, offering him a job. Always offering to "take him under his wing." He wasn't interested in becoming an undertaker's apprentice, but he wasn't about to turn up his nose at some free meals and a pocket full of cash. The guy told him how his mother had once worked for him and because of that she had a funeral package at the funeral home. Everything pre-paid. His uncle was glad to hear that since funerals were expensive. A *necessary luxury* he had called it. An oxymoron. You had to bury a person who died, but not everyone could afford the cost of burying that person.

His fingernails scratched the meaty top of his arm, digging deeper each time, skin gathering beneath them.

"Where are you?" But there was no answer. He was utterly alone, jailed, likely in some very deep legal trouble. "I did this for you." He looked at the floor in front of his feet. "You *owe* me." And still there was no answer. He slowly looked around the room, checked the corners of the ceiling. He stood. "So that's it?" He turned a complete circle, searching for any sign of the entity that had consumed his life. "You need me."

CHAPTER 37

With Coffey arrested and in custody, and Nathan discharged from the hospital, Tilly went home to be near her family.

Matthew appeared as Tilly sat with her mother, waiting for her to get better, to get out of bed. "It's Suzie's mom," he said, the moment he arrived.

"What?" Tilly had been deep in thought. They had caught their killer, so she thought it was only a matter of time before she went to heaven. After all, that's what happened, wasn't it? People died and went to heaven, or that was what she had been told. She didn't know what to do next, so she waited.

"Suzie's mother is in the hospital." Matthew sat beside her. "The doctors don't think she is going to make it."

"But we caught Coffey!" She knew it sounded ridiculous. As thoughts, these ideas had made sense, or she could force them to make sense; but out in the open, the words made it all fall apart.

"We need to be with Suzie," he said and stood up, waiting for her to follow. She looked around, not wanting to leave her mother. She stood, looked back at her mother one more time, then turned to Matthew.

CHAPTER 38

Tilly found herself in a hospital room that looked much like the one Nathan had been in. Her muscles tensed a little. She remembered how her brother had looked and what had put him there. Suzie's mother was in a hospital bed with the sides up, surrounded by machines and an IV drip.

Suzie was sitting in a chair in the corner, Kaylin on the windowsill next to her. Out of habit she looked for Joel, then felt a tightening in her chest. A nurse was looking from machine to machine taking notes, her face showing no hints as to whether the information was good or bad.

Suzie looked at them; she had been crying.

"I'm so sorry, Suzie," Tilly said, not knowing what else to say.

"While we were running around, she was getting worse." Her tears started again. "I wasn't with her. I could have stopped it."

"Stopped it?"

"Sorg." Suzie lifted her head and looked at Tilly. "That dark haze. I could have stopped it." Her sobs were coming faster. "I could have kept it away from her. But I was too busy trying to catch a killer. What was I doing? I'm already *dead*. I spent all this time—" The sobs consumed her.

Tilly knew there was nothing she could say. *We got our killer caught. We stopped him from killing other kids, but we didn't stop him from possibly, more than likely, killing Suzie's mother. But Coffey isn't killing her mother. The haze that Suzie calls Sorg was killing her mother. What does it have to do with Coffey?*

185

"Matthew," Tilly whispered. When he looked up, she said, "I have to go but I'll be back."

"Where are you going? We just got here."

"To my house." She looked back at Suzie. "I think I need to be with my mom."

"I'll come with you," Matthew said, sensing her concern. They looked at Suzie, then to Kaylin. She gave them a small nod.

CHAPTER 39

Tilly was surprised how relieved she felt to find her mother sleeping. The feeling dissolved quickly when she realized Suzie's mom had now succumbed to whatever that haze called Sorg was.

"Is that going to happen to my mother?" she asked Matthew, knowing he didn't have an answer, but needing to put her fear out there. "Can I keep that thing away from her forever?" She sank to the foot of her mother's bed. Matthew squeezing in behind her. Tilly was getting used to the little tingles of electricity when they touched, looking forward to them, but she shifted a little to give him a bit more space.

He didn't speak. They sat in silence for a while, Tilly listening to her mother's slow breathing. They weren't the calm, slow respirations of sleep; they were forced, as if she labored.

"What if she's dying?" Tilly looked down. A tear fell, landing on her jeans, making a small dark blue circle. "I really thought catching Coffey would help." She raised her head and looked at her mother. "I thought that once Mom heard, she would...." She wasn't sure what she had thought.

Tilly started to feel herself vibrating, just enough to register the feeling. She looked at Matthew. He was looking at her.

"Do you feel it?" She stayed still, waiting to see if it would go away or get stronger.

"I think the haze is back," Matthew said, looking around the room.

Tilly's mother groaned.

"There!" Matthew pointed to the corner of the room.

Tilly's heart dropped as she spotted a blur where Matthew was pointing. It shifted from translucence to a muddy green haze. "No!"

"Get to your mother," Matthew said, pointing. "Get up beside her."

"Then what?" Tilly moved up near her mother's shoulders and leaned over to shield her mother with her body, careful to avoid contact with her. "What do I do?"

They watched the haze move further into the room, tendrils flicking back and forth.

It came closer.

"Matthew?"

"I don't know what to do!" he answered. "I'm trying to think!"

As the deadly haze moved over Tilly's mother and hovered, its tendrils flickered as some reached to touch her, others pulsed and changed in color.

Tilly's mother moaned and shifted in the bed.

Green light lifted from her mother as the haze expanded and contracted.

"Stop it!" Tilly shouted as she tried to shield her mother. And then the tendrils touched her, too. She felt a sharp jab of pain, then a cold, freezing stab. She shifted, trying to avoid the tendrils while still covering her mother. "Stop!"

"Tilly!" Matthew shouted. "It's going right through you!"

"I can't stop it!

"Leave her alone!" She tried to make herself as big as she could, all the while enduring more sharp, freezing stabs. "You can't have her!" But she could feel the awful haze slowly stealing her mother's energy.

Her mother cried out once more. Tilly looked to see the green of the haze turning so dark it was almost black. Her mother curled and cried out again. Tilly was terrified that her mother was going to die, right now—and she couldn't stop it. She could feel herself tiring.

"Tilly! You're disappearing."

Tilly struggled to understand him. What did he mean? *You can't have her!* Tilly shifted, then straddled her mother. *You need to wake up!* She focused on her mother's face. *You need to wake up!* Willing her. *Get up, get up!* "Get up. GET UP!"

Her mother twisted, groaning, gagging.

"Leave her alone!" Tilly yelled at the haze. "LEAVE HER ALONE!"

She felt it shift. Her skin no longer burned.

Terrified she was losing, "STOP IT!" she yelled. "STOP IT! STOP IT! LEAVE HER *ALONE*! GET *OUT!*"

The sound of her name being repeated finally made Tilly stop screaming. She looked toward the voice.

"It's leaving!" Matthew's voice was full of excitement. "Tilly, it's leaving!"

Tilly fell to the bed beside her mother, exhausted.

"It's leaving," Matthew repeated. He sat beside her putting his arm around her. Tilly felt his electricity, tiny snaps. She absorbed them, letting them tingle throughout her body.

CHAPTER 40

Tilly lay with her mother until her father came to bed that night, afraid to leave her side. She hoped she would know what to do if the haze came back.

She got up to check on Nathan. From his doorway she could tell he was asleep. She watched the stars from his bedside lamp glide across the walls in his room, listened to the soothing sounds of waves that it made, and let it all wash over her. She looked at the mat beside his bed, she found herself looking for the cat. No sign of him. She wondered if King Arthur was wherever Joel had gone. Or were they both gone forever? She noticed that the drawing on the wall had changed—it looked like a superhero now. She felt a tiny twinge, thinking how Nathan had moved on, but she was glad to see that he *had* moved on.

CHAPTER 41

When she left her brother, she went to see Suzie. She found her curled up like a cat at the foot of her mother's hospital bed. Tilly wasn't going to say anything, but then Suzie looked up.

Tilly attempted a smile, trying to ask how it was going without actually having to speak.

Suzie sat up, glanced at her mother. "They say she's in a coma." Suzie looked tired, her eyes dull.

Tilly moved to the side of the bed. "Can I?" she asked, putting her hand on the bed.

Suzie nodded as Tilly sat.

"I'm really sorry, Suzie." It sounded like such a hollow platitude.

"It's always been just the three of us," Suzie said. She started to pick at her cuticles. "We've traveled a lot because of Dad." She put her finger to her lips and chewed at the skin around her nail. Tilly stayed quiet.

"My dad's an astronaut, you know."

"I didn't know."

"So, we moved a lot when I was a kid, because first he was a fighter pilot in the military." She dropped her hand to her legs and started picking again. "Then when he became an astronaut, everyone wanted to meet him. People paid him all kinds of money to come and speak at their events." Suzie let out a little chuckle. "All kinds of money to listen to him talk. Weird."

"But he's an astronaut! That's a big deal, Suzie."

191

"Yeah it is, I guess." Suzie slid her hands under her thighs. "But see, to me, he's just my dad." She rocked back and forth, slightly. "I forget he's special to others. I forget he's a hero to some people. To me, he'd tell stories, the ones he'd tell me when putting me to bed. I'd kind of forget that the stories were real. While Dad was gone on these trips, it was just me and Mom. The more we moved, the harder it was for me to make friends. People already had friends and didn't seem to want to make more. I tried hard to get to know them, but after a while, I gave up. Mom and I did everything together. I think she had the same problem."

Tilly remembered when she first met Suzie. She wondered what it would have been like if she didn't have her friends or had to give them up. She wondered if that's why Suzie came off so cold and distant at first. Was she always protecting herself from getting hurt again?

"Mom and I were best friends. Then Dad retired and we stopped moving, and he only did speaking engagements. That's when I started riding."

Tilly leaned a little and let her shoulder touch Suzie's. Suzie let it stay. Little sparks shifted between them, but nothing like when Matthew touched her. Was Suzie okay?

"I'm going to lay down again, Tilly," she said as she shifted herself up the side of the bed, hovering close to the edge, carefully not touching her mother.

"I'll come back again later, Suzie." Tilly smiled at her, but Suzie had her eyes closed by then.

CHAPTER 42

Tilly found Matthew watching a movie with his little brother. She smiled at him; he smiled back. His brother looked about seven or eight. He didn't have red hair like Matthew: he was blonde but had the same green eyes. She settled herself into the loveseat across from them realizing that this was the first time she had gone looking for him: he had always found her. She was also starting to realize how selfish she had been. She had never asked anyone about their families. Until today. She had even forgotten Matthew had a little brother.

Matthew's brother laughed at something in the movie. Tilly looked at him.

"How's he doing?" She asked.

"He has good days and bad; mostly good." Matthew watched his brother try to stuff a fistful of popcorn into his mouth, most of it landing in his lap. "He doesn't understand what's wrong with our dad, why he works all the time now, why he doesn't tuck him in at night. He misses him. Mom does her best at keeping him busy though."

"Is she going to be okay, do you think?" Tilly asked him.

"Well, she cries a lot." Matthew smiled as he watched his brother pick popcorn bits off his shirt then tuck them in his mouth. "She worries about Dad. He isn't dealing with all this." He looked at Tilly. "I think he goes to work every day to pretend none of it is happening."

"Everyone's family is being torn apart."

Kaylin appeared, almost as if Tilly's words had called her.

"Oh. Hi, Tilly." She seemed surprised to see Tilly. "Can I stay here for a while?" she asked Matthew as she moved towards them.

"Of course," Matthew answered. "You are always welcome, you know that."

"I wasn't sure if you needed to talk to Tilly alone."

Tilly saw the girl's eyes shift, like she was afraid she'd said something wrong.

"Kaylin likes to join us sometimes," he told Tilly. "Is anything wrong?" His attention turned back to Kaylin.

"No," Kaylin said. She slipped in beside Tilly. "Everyone is sleeping." Her voice reminded Tilly of how young Kaylin was when her life ended.

Kaylin's words about how late it was struck Tilly. "Why is your brother up so late?"

"He's been sneaking out here to watch TV after Dad finally gets home." Matthew's hand hovered over his brother's head. Tilly was sure he was about to ruffle his hair. "He isn't sleeping well, so when Dad comes home, he wakes up."

Tilly sighed a little.

"He falls asleep on the couch but always seems to wake up before my parents get up. I think the sun wakes him."

Matthew settled himself back into the couch and turned to the television.

They watched the movie on TV for a bit, until Tilly spoke.

"How is your dad, Kaylin?" Tilly asked her.

"Pretty much the same as your mom." She shrugged, not taking her eyes off the TV screen. "Gram stays with him and my sister most of the time, but she's getting worn out."

Tilly didn't know what to say. There wasn't anything to say. She knew exactly how the girl felt. Both of them, and Suzie too, were all watching a parent slowly fade away.

Tilly looked at Matthew. He was spending his evenings watching TV with his little brother while his father lost himself in work. His little brother was slowly getting lost. So many people were hurting. And now Joel was gone, too.

Tilly kept all of this to herself. Instead, she rubbed Kaylin's knee, hoping to give her a little bit of quiet comfort. She realized she had started to need the tingle of electricity between her and her friends. It made her feel like she actually existed in whatever this new reality was.

She curled up in the corner and watched TV with the others.

CHAPTER 43

"Do you believe there might not be anything after death?" Tilly spoke so quietly she wasn't sure if either of them heard her, and she found herself hoping no one had. She had started to wonder if Joel again.

"You don't believe in heaven anymore?" asked Matthew.

"That day we were in my bedroom, when I remembered being in the shed." Tilly didn't know what she believed in anymore. Life had seemed so simple not that long ago. Now nothing was what she thought it was. "I said I thought you were…." She could feel her cheeks getting red.

"You thought I was…?"

"You were…"

"I'm just messing with you. Of course I remember." Tilly saw his playful smile she remembered from when they were kids. "You thought I was an angel."

She knew her cheeks were red now; she could feel the heat radiating from them.

"I guess," Matthew said. "I never gave it much thought, but there must be someplace we go after we die."

"I do believe in that," Kaylin said, her knees pulled up to her chest.

Tilly paused, wondering if she wanted to say the rest, and then plunged on. "I was always told that when you died you went to Heaven." She knew she had said this before, at least she thought she had. "I thought you were an angel sent to take me there." She looked at Matthew, found herself staring at his freckles, his kind eyes, his smile that made you feel like the center of the universe. He would make a perfect angel.

"Me an angel!" And he huffed a laugh. "Not likely."

"When I first saw the mist, Sorg," Kaylin said, "I thought *it* was the afterlife.... I mean...I mean I don't know if it's the same place as your heaven but I thought it was the door to my afterlife, you know?" She stopped, glanced at each of them. "You know how the air gets all fuzzy. I thought I was supposed to go to it." She wrapped her arms around her ankles and pulled her legs closer.

"Did you?" Matthew asked.

"Yes. I went up to it, but it started to make me feel sick. I felt dizzy, and like I was going to throw up."

"So, you stopped?" Matthew asked.

"No." She squeezed her legs. "I didn't know if that was normal, and I wondered if I'd be able to see my mother again, so I kept walking. But then I felt my skin getting hot, felt like I was on fire. It felt red. But then it felt black." She stopped, plainly searching for a way to explain.

"Red? What do you mean?" Tilly said. "You *felt* red? Or you *saw* red and black?"

"I don't know how to explain it. I *was* red. Like, angrier than I can imagine. Like I was going to explode. Then black... like outer space... not with the stars but like a black hole swallowing you up... no love anymore. Empty." Kaylin rested her chin on her knees, looking lost.

Tilly didn't push her this time. She hoped Matthew wouldn't either. She watched as Kaylin dropped her head so that her forehead was resting on her knees.

"There's something else." Kaylin said. "I think I saw Sorg at Coffey's house. I'm sorry I didn't tell you." She looked at Tilly.

"You saw Sorg?"

"I could sorta see it, but I could mostly feel it. I could *feel* the same red and black." She slid her forehead back to her knees. "It made *him* red."

"What?" The word was out before Tilly realized it. "Sorry, Kaylin. Let's back up. It made who red?"

"Coffey."

"Sorg made Coffey red?" Matthew asked. Tilly could tell he was trying to sort out this new information.

Kaylin nodded, her head still on her knees.

She watched as Kaylin rubbed her head back and forth across her knees, then took a deep breath.

"I saw it when Nathan was trapped in the house. It was in the bathroom with him."

"With Nathan? Or with Coffey?" Tilly forced herself to speak slowly.

"It was when Nathan was in the bathtub, hiding. It followed Nathan, but it was *with* Coffey."

That brought them all to silence.

She said it followed Nathan, Tilly thought, *but that it was* with *Coffey. We followed it to Coffey's. Coffey is in jail. It feeds off my mom. And Suzie's mom. Kaylin's dad too.* This wasn't making sense. *Suzie's mother is in the hospital. But it doesn't feed off Coffey. It made him red. It made him black. Where is it now?*

"But Coffey is in jail," Tilly said. "So that changes everything, right?" She wanted them to agree.

"Tilly," Matthew said, frowning, "Coffey isn't what's making your mom sick. You know that, right?"

"I guess I just hoped if we found our killer, it would help my mother want to get out of bed." She knew now she'd been kidding herself. "I wanted to believe that when we found Coffey it would stop all this. I wanted to believe it was all connected."

"But they *are* connected!" Matthew said. He held up his finger, seemingly following a logical sequence of events. "They are connected."

"What do you mean? Who's connected? My mom and Coffey? You just said they weren't." Tilly stared at Matthew.

"The haze, I mean Sorg. We might as well give it the name." He looked at Kaylin. "Sorg took us to Coffey's house." He counted off the point by raising a finger.

Tilly nodded.

"Then we saw Sorg hover over him but not feed off him." He raised the second finger. "I know I'm assuming things here. Maybe we can all only see each other because we were all killed by Coffey. And Sorg feeds off our families." And there his logic stalled.

"You think it was feeding off Coffey?" Tilly asked. "Didn't you just say it wasn't?"

"No, it's not *feeding* off him." Matthew was no longer talking to Tilly, he was talking to himself, nodding slightly. "When Sorg feeds, everything feels heavy and depressing, like Kaylin said." He shifted on the couch, sat forward, and hooked his thumb under his chin. "But at Coffey's house, the room felt *charged*. Like before a thunderstorm. There was no resistance, like when you peddle your bike fast enough so that you can coast." He turned to Tilly. "I can't explain it. But it didn't feel like *it* was feeding, it felt like *he* was feeding."

"He?"

"Coffey." He paused for a second. "Okay, maybe feeding isn't the right word. But it felt like Coffey was feeding, or maybe the haze, Sorg, was feeding Coffey."

"Wait a minute." Tilly wasn't sure she could process what Matthew was saying; in fact, she wasn't sure she wanted to process any of it. "I don't get it. What's the difference?"

"I don't know; but remember when your brother said Sorg was like a parasite?"

Tilly nodded.

"He said how a parasite needs a host, but in the end, it kills its host and then needs a new one." His eyes widened with excitement. "Coffey *makes* the hosts."

"The hosts for what? Matt, you are talking like a madman. Stop. I need you to listen to yourself." She took his hands, ignoring the tingles. "We aren't hosts, so how can Coffey make hosts."

"*We* aren't the hosts." He was looking past her again. "We aren't the hosts." And then his face lit with astonishment. "Our families are!" He pulled his hands out from under hers and grabbed her shoulders. "Coffey kills us, our families suffer, *it* feeds." He looked at her, vibrating with energy.

"They're working together?" Kaylin said.

"You're right. I remember him talking to himself." Tilly remembered moments in Coffey's living room. "So, does Coffey make hosts for it or does it *make* Coffey make hosts?" It still didn't make sense. The thoughts swirled in her head, making her dizzy, she felt like her body was spinning.

"I don't know." Matthew frowned. "I don't know if Coffey feeds it like a pet or if it has Coffey under some kind of spell and makes him do its dirty work."

Either way, we caught Coffey," Tilly said. "With Coffey in jail, he can't make more hosts." Tilly realized what she had just said. The words fell into place like pieces of a horrible puzzle. "But Sorg, the haze, can keep feeding on the old hosts."

"Until they die." Kaylin's said.

"Or, until we stop it." Matthew stood up.

"How are we going to do that?"

CHAPTER 44

"The thing draws on their energy," Matthew said. "We've seen it get stronger. It gets bigger and darker while its victims get weaker."

"But we know that part," Suzie said.

"Just because Coffey is in jail, it doesn't mean it will stop feeding. In fact, I think it will be the opposite." Matthew looked at them. "It won't have any new hosts, so it will need to feed off its old ones even more."

"Or maybe switch to other family members," Kaylin said, "like my grandma." Tilly saw the girl's eyes get shiny with tears. She wondered about her father. He was looking so tired. Would he be next?

"Some of our parents are getting sick while others aren't," Matthew said. "My dad spends all day at work, pretending nothing is wrong. Tilly's dad takes care of Nathan."

Are you saying it only hurts our mothers?" Suzie asked.

"No... no, I'm not," Matthew said. "And don't forget it's Kaylin's dad too."

"Then what are you saying?"

Matthew didn't reply and no one else spoke.

It was Tilly who finally broke the silence. "I think Matthew is right."

"He is?" Suzie asked.

"About what, exactly?" Matthew said.

"From the minute I went home and saw my mom, she's been in bed. I don't know about the days between the day I died and the day I came home, but since I've been home, she hasn't left her room other than to go to my funeral."

"Okay...." Suzie said.

"My dad has been doing everything," Tilly said. "Yours too, right?" She looked at Suzie.

Suzie nodded. "But not Joel's dad. His dad died when he was a kid."

"So his mother is—"

"His mother isn't in bed."

"How do you know that?"

"Joel told me. He said his mother had been going to church every day. And volunteering at the soup kitchen. He sometimes went with her."

"We need to block it," Matthew said. "We need to take away what it feeds on. If it feeds off our families' sadness and grief, which in turn makes them weaker, then we have to stop them from sinking further into depression. If we can somehow give them some joy, then maybe that thing can't hurt them." He looked at Kaylin. "Maybe it won't like the happy energy and our folks won't be useful to it anymore."

"How can we make them happy if they can't even get out of bed?" Tilly asked. She gave Suzie a quick glance.

"My grandma is getting sick; she's been sitting with my dad this whole time," Kaylin said.

"I'm willing to try anything," Tilly said. "Nathan told me that my dad is taking my mom to the hospital this afternoon—she's getting worse."

CHAPTER 45

Tilly and Nathan watched their father unpack their mother's things. She knew the hospital was the best place for her mother, but she couldn't help worrying that her mother would never go home. Nathan sat in the chair, swinging his legs, supervising his father's work.

"You should put her slippers by her bed, in case she wants to get up," he told his dad. Tilly smiled. It was nice to see some of the old Nathan. His innocence.

His father picked up the slippers that he had dropped on the bottom of the locker and placed them by the bed.

Nathan nodded. "Her housecoat needs to go on the end of her bed."

Their father flashed a small smile.

"What about her toothbrush? Is there a cup with a lid for her toothbrush?"

"Nathan, I've got this. Why don't you go across the hall? I can see a TV in there."

"By myself?" He hadn't been out of his father's sight since Coffey's arrest, and they both had been completely fine with that.

"Yes, by yourself. I'm pretty sure you'll be all right in the hospital by yourself." He turned to Nathan, looked him in the eye, then winked. "Just across the hall, though."

Nathan nodded. He stood, then went to his mother. He leaned in and whispered in her ear, then left the room.

Tilly followed him as he walked across the hall to the visitor's room, and once inside Nathan turned on the TV.

"You should probably shut the door," Tilly said.

Nathan turned, went back to the heavy door, and slowly closed it, picking up one of the pamphlets on a side table. Before he sat down, he gathered the cushions from the chairs in the room and piled them against the couch's wooden arm.

"You going to leave any for me?" Tilly asked.

He threw one across the room. It landed in the corner of a chair.

"Thanks."

Kaylin appeared by the closed door.

"Hi," she said to Nathan.

Nathan smiled and returned her greeting. He turned on the TV and started to surf the channels.

"C'mon, Nathan, talk to her," Tilly said. It had been a long time since she'd had to remind Nathan of his manners.

"That's OK, Tilly. I just want to be with you guys."

Nathan stopped on a documentary about sharks.

"I like sharks," Kaylin said. "Did you know that sharks have several rows of teeth and when a tooth falls out, another one moves forward to take its place? They can have three thousand teeth at one time."

"And they are picky eaters," Nathan added. "They like to taste their food. They take a bite and decide if they want to eat it. That's why swimmers can get bitten but not eaten. Although even a bite is usually bad enough for a person to bleed to death."

Tilly watched the two of them sitting on the couch. "I've seen this one," Kaylin said. Nathan, though, was captivated by the birthing habits of the Great White. While Nathan learned the dangers that young sharks faced, Kaylin picked up Nathan's pamphlet.

"My sister did this," she said, tapping the pamphlet.

"What's that?' Tilly asked. Nathan was still tuned into the show.

"Yeah, my sister, she had cancer." Kaylin opened the folder, scanned the inside and closed it.

Tilly moved to the couch and sat beside her.

"I didn't know you had a sister. What happened to her?"

"She's OK now. She's in remission. It was a couple of years ago." She handed the pamphlet to Tilly. "She got to have her wish through that program: Star Light Star Bright. We went to Fairy World. She got to dress up like a princess and have a tea party with all of the other princesses."

"How old was she when she got her wish?"

"Seven."

Kaylin took the pamphlet back and opened it, showing Tilly the photos of all the kids who had received their wishes. There were kids wearing tiaras, riding in race cars, meeting superheroes and athletes, and one even waved from a hot air balloon. There were captions like: *Dreams do come true!* and *I have the wish I wished last night.*

"Is there something you'd like to watch, Kaylin?" Nathan sat up to hand her the remote.

"This is fine." Kaylin set the pamphlet on the couch cushion and leaned back to give the shark show another try.

Tilly watched her for a minute then looked down at the pamphlet again. Under *STAR LIGHT, STAR BRIGHT*, she read, *Laughter is great medicine. Spread a smile.*

It hit her. "Grief!"

"Tilly?" Nathan said, looking at her as if she had two heads.

"Coffey killed us to create pain and suffering. Our deaths created *grief* for that Sorg thing!"

CHAPTER 46

"You read *what* in a pamphlet?" Suzie asked Tilly. "I don't understand what you're saying."

"Coffey killed us. Coffey is working with Sorg. Sorg feeds off our families." Tilly looked from one to the other of her friends. "Coffey made us—*this!*— and in the process, he made our families for Sorg. So Sorg can *feed*."

"But only my mom is sick," Suzie said. "Is my dad going to get sick, too?"

"We don't know for sure. We don't know if Sorg would switch to another person or not."

"People deal with death differently," Nathan said.

Everyone in the room looked at Nathan.

"What?" He looked from face to face.

"Nothing," Tilly said. She was reminded again of how she had seen him differently before all of this happened. "Go on."

"After a loved one dies, some people can't see a way out of their grief; it overwhelms them, there is nothing beyond it." He sat on his bed. He looked around to see if anyone wanted to object. "Your dad is dealing with this the only way he knows how, just as mine is." He looked at Suzie. "So far, he has managed to keep it together, trying to take care of your mother." He paused. "I don't know if he'll get too worn out if she doesn't get better, or if he'll just give in."

"Wow, Nathan," Mathew said. "That's pretty deep. I've never thought much about death before now."

"I wish I could say the same." He gave the others a half smile. Tilly could see past it. She thought, once again, of his imaginary friends. She could also see something else. She could see him curling his finger in and out, a sure signal he was holding back.

"What else, Nathan?" she said.

"Sorg is getting stronger." He looked at Suzie. "Sorg feeds on grief, which makes it stronger... and them weaker." He looked at Tilly. "Mom won't get out of bed. She's heartbroken. Instead of being given time to mourn and heal, Sorg steals her energy. Grief builds on grief, making her sadder. Making her even weaker.

"She doesn't want to get out of bed anymore. And that *thing*, Sorg, uses that, making it so that she won't get out of bed." He glanced quickly around the room.

"Our other parents somehow cope with their grief. It doesn't mean they aren't heartbroken; maybe it just means they aren't as easy to feed from." Nathan looked like he had run out of theory.

No one spoke for a few minutes, and then Matthew said, "Maybe our other parent *will* crack. Maybe they *will* get tired of trying to hold it all together."

"Trying to be the strong one," Tilly said. "Pretend it'll all be okay." She glanced at her brother. "But who will help my dad keep it all together? And your dads, or mom, or grandmother."

"And if they can't keep it together...," Suzie said, "do they become hosts?"

"It's like the pamphlet said: *laughter is the best medicine*. If sadness and grief, is making them weak, and that's what feeds Sorg, then we need to try to help people to stop being so sad. It may be the only way to keep Sorg from getting stronger. And while I'm at it, let me say that we're not the only ones who may have had to deal with Sorg; we've all heard the expression *died of a broken heart*."

But instead of there being a chorus of agreement, there was silence, broken finally by Suzie: "And how are we supposed to keep that thing from getting stronger?"

"I don't know yet. I was hoping we could come up with some ideas together."

"A lot of people had to come together to make even one of those dreams come true," Matthew said as he scanned the pamphlet. "I don't mean to sound pessimistic, Tilly, but how can the six of us do something that big?" He looked around at the little group. "Uh... five," he corrected himself, thinking of their missing member. "And four of us are dead."

"What if we have a tea party?" Kaylin said.

Everyone's attention shifted to her.

"I mean, it worked for my sister."

"A *tea* party?" Suzie said, the incredulity plain in her tone.

"It was just a thought."

"No, no, Kaylin. You're might be on to something: a tea party! No, wait, maybe not a tea party, but more like a—"

"A barbeque!" Matthew said. "Everyone loves a barbeque, right?"

"It would have to be for the whole community, or even bigger," Tilly said. "The more people, the better. Because, as it says in the pamphlet, *Happiness raises the spirits.* Get it?" She chuckled at herself. "If we make people smile, they forget to be sad, even for just a little bit; and if they aren't sad, then Sorg can't feed off them."

"But how do we get everyone out for something like that? And how can we make them smile?" Suzie asked. "How do I get my mother out to a party if she's in hospital and can't even get out of bed? She doesn't want to go to a barbeque and eat hot dogs."

"What if it's a memorial?" Nathan suggested.

"For us?" Kaylin asked.

"But I thought we were supposed to make people happy? Doesn't a memorial make people sad?" Suzie said.

"People want to talk about their loved ones," Nathan said. "The hardest part of Tilly being gone is that no one ever wants to say her name to me. They think it will upset me, but what I feel instead is Tilly never existed. Like the earth opened up and swallowed her and her entire existence with it."

"He's right," Kaylin said. "When my sister was sick, no one would say certain things, or they'd whisper, as if that way it wouldn't be true or hurtful. People are also scared to talk to me about my mom. They think it will upset me. But I like talking about my mom."

"We just have to make it about life. A celebration of *life*, not about death," Nathan said.

"You think people will celebrate us?" Suzie asked, sounding confused.

"Yeah, I do," Matthew said. "But we could also make it about anyone else someone might want to remember."

"Maybe people can make posters of the people they want to celebrate," Kaylin added.

"And tell stories."

Tilly watched Nathan and Kaylin build on each other's ideas, getting each other more excited as they went.

"And have a balloon release," Suzie said. "I've seen that done before, and it looks so cool."

"Not balloons," Kaylin said. "They pollute and kill turtles."

"No, they have biodegradable balloons," Nathan said. "I saw a show on them."

"We will have people write down names or special notes on rice paper," Suzie added. "And put it in the balloon."

"What do you think?" Nathan turned to the group.

"I love it," Tilly said. "You guys are great." But she could see Matthew chewing on his lip. "What is it?"

"I love it too," he said. "I'm just not sure how we are going to get this going." A hint of concern crossed his face. "It's a big job for one boy," he said, looking straight at Nathan.

"He's right, Nathan. This is all on you."

"I can do it." Nathan stood, his shoulders straight. "I have to do it, for you, Tilly, and for Mom, and for Kaylin's dad, and Suzie's mom." He looked around at the group. "For all your families."

Tilly was so proud of her brother. In this moment she realized she had never seen him as anything other than her little brother. He had been the *boy* she needed to protect, the *little* boy with imaginary friends. She'd felt guilty at times because she wished he could be normal, hated him because he wasn't. But now he stood in front of her, no longer just a boy. After what he had done, he was her hero, and what he was willing to do for her now made her heart expand.

"You are amazing, Nathan!" she told him.

And one after another, the others agreed.

It was decided. They needed to get the whole community on board, to try to make everyone happy again. It seemed an impossible order to fill, to get an entire group of people together to celebrate instead of mourn. What no one would say was that they needed to stop Sorg before it found someone else like Coffey, someone to kill for it, to start this all over again.

CHAPTER 47

Tilly had been sitting at home, watching movies with Nathan and her dad when Matthew brought the news that Suzie's mom had died. Nurses had pushed everyone out of the room as they tried to save her. But Suzie had remained unseen, standing by her mother's bed, had watched the whole thing take place, and had eventually crawled into bed beside her mother. Matthew said Suzie had screamed at the nurses out of grief when they pronounced her mother dead and recorded the time on a tablet. He said she had said she didn't care anymore. And that she just wanted to be left alone. She dug herself in her bed and cried.

"Tilly, I told her it's more important now more than ever. To get the community together," Matthew said. "I know she's taken Joel's disappearance hard; and now with her mother's death, I wish I could be better at comforting her."

"Matthew, you are amazing at helping; you helped me so much." Tilly said. "Let's go get her."

Now, they were in Suzie's bedroom. Tilly was distracted by the size of it. Large enough for a four-poster double bed, dressers, a desk, and even a couch and two chairs. She assumed one of the two closed doors led to a walk-in closet while the other was likely to her own bathroom. Sunlight from large windows reflected off a wall of trophies and medals.

"It won't work if we're not all there," Matthew said.

"It's too late. Mom is dead! So, we *won't* all be there, because my mother is already dead."

Tilly couldn't imagine what Suzie was feeling, but she knew she had to get Suzie on board, fast. How could everyone have gotten death so wrong? Everyone always talked about a light, and Heaven, and love, and peace. Where was her peace? Where was Suzie's—or Suzie's mother's for that matter?

"Suzie, I have no idea how you feel right now, but more people may die if you don't come." Tilly shifted to face her. She swallowed. "My mother will die." She looked at the others. "So will Matthew's family and probably Kaylin's. I'm pretty sure knowing that doesn't help you." Her voice cracked. She looked at Suzie, letting tears slide down her face. Suzie's mother's death only reinforced to the others what was coming sooner rather than later. "What will happen to Nathan, or Kaylin and her sister without their dad?"

Suzie pulled a hand free and wiped her cheeks. New tears covered them as quickly as she wiped them.

"And what about your dad?" Matthew asked her.

"What?" The sound was muffled by her moving hand.

"Your dad. If your mom got sick because you died then what about your dad? What if he gets sick now because he's lost both you and your mom? Grief breeds grief remember. If your mom can't feed Sorg anymore then maybe your dad would have to take her place."

"You don't know that!"

"That's harsh, Matthew."

"I can't say it will happen. But I can't say it won't. Sorg needs it. I'm sorry we didn't figure all this out sooner, Suzie. I'm sorry we didn't save your mother."

Everyone stayed quiet, trying to give Suzie some space, some time to think. They all knew Matthew was right: if they didn't stop Sorg, the deaths would just continue. It would kill the rest of their families and they'd watch their families die one by one.

"It will keep taking from us," Tilly said quietly, not wanting to agitate Suzie. She wished Nathan could be here to talk to her since he and Suzie seemed to have developed some kind of connection. "It will keep taking from you."

Suzie remained silent. Suzie wiped her face with one arm. Suzie looked around at the group, eyes puffy, nose red. She wiggled to the edge of the bed and stood beside it.

"Let's do this." She no longer looked broken, now she looked angry, furious.

"That-a-girl." Matthew winked at her then gave her a tiny smile.

"But I don't understand," Kaylin said.

"What don't you understand?" Tilly asked.

"Where's Suzie's mom?"

That surprised Tilly. She stepped towards Kaylin, reaching to hug her. Kaylin didn't move into the gesture. "She died, sweetie. Don't you remember?"

"What I mean is where *is* she? We're all dead and *we're* all here. So, where is *she*?"

The group stood speechless. Suzie's expression changed. Tilly couldn't read it.

It was Matthew who broke the silence. "It took a while for you to find us, Kaylin. Maybe she's on her way."

Tilly wasn't sure if this answered Kaylin's question.

"She will find us," Suzie finally said. "If I know anything about my mother it's that if she's looking for me, she'll find me."

Tilly saw a flash of pride behind the deep pain in Suzie's eyes.

CHAPTER 48

Suzie, Matthew and Tilly waited as everyone gathered outside the church. Kaylin had stayed behind with Nathan.

At first, Suzie hung back with the others; but when the hearse arrived, she went to her father's side. They watched as the pallbearers lifted the coffin out of the back of the hearse and carried it up the stairs.

Matthew and Tilly waited outside the doors until the coffin had been moved inside, then entered the church and slowly started down the aisle.

Tilly felt a weight when she entered the church. It surprised her since she hadn't felt it at her own funeral. It was like trying to walk in water: it took twice the energy to get half as far. It made her head feel cloudy, as if it had been stuffed with cotton balls. She looked at Matthew. He nodded as if acknowledging her struggle.

She considered joining Suzie, but thought her friend might need space, simply to be a girl grieving for her mother, even if it was only for a couple of hours. She and Matthew found a place to sit on an empty pew at the back of the church and settled in.

Tilly's thoughts returned to her own funeral. She was surprised at how easy it had been, how she hadn't taken it seriously, how she had played with Nathan. She should never have done that. The pain in this room today was suffocating. Was this because of Sorg? Was it getting stronger? Were all these people under Sorg's spell?

Tilly felt weird. She felt short of breath, and that her head was still stuffed full of cotton. She looked around the room. There was no sign of Sorg. She tried to clear some of the cotton but couldn't. It seemed to be replaced as fast as she removed it. "Do you think Sorg—" She caught movement near the ceiling from the corner of her eye. She didn't need to turn to see what it was. Tendrils, like tentacles of an octopus began to reach out ahead of a growing haze, touching, seeking.

The church darkened, as if a cloud had passed in front of the sun. People shifted in their seats. Sorg's thickening, pulsating mass moved further into the room, stretching out unseen by the congregation, tendrils tasting the air. Sorg's deep hum began, unheard by those in the pews.

Thick threads of color began lifting from the unsuspecting mourners. Tilly thought it could have been beautiful, like Northern Lights, if she hadn't known the ugliness behind it. She turned to the sound of an infant crying. She saw a little girl looking directly at Sorg as its feeler touched her head and slowly slid down her face and shoulder in a disturbing caress. She screeched, face red, trying to push herself away from her mother who struggled to pull her in and comfort her.

"She sees it," Tilly said, pointing towards the child who was now hysterical.

The mother gathered up the child and left the church, which only muffled the little girl's howls. Sorg's tendrils finally pulled away from the child as the door closed behind her. It sought out a new soul.

Tilly and Matthew watched as some of the mourners seemed to shrink, much the same as her mother had, but others became increasingly restless. Sorg shifted over the mourners, reaching out to them as if trying to choose. The colors that lifted from them were also different. The more restless a person was, the darker the green, like seaweed. Quieter mourners provided pale, washed-out colors. Sorg's deep hum filled the church.

"Look at Suzie's family, compared to the others," Matthew said.

He was right. Thin, dull threads were coming from Suzie's family. She looked at Suzie's father. Threads from him seemed to pulsate. Was he fighting it?

"What do we do?" she asked Matthew.

Suzie turned towards them.

"I just don't know," Matthew answered.

Some of the women began to sob, and more children started to cry. The church grew darker, making the streams and threads almost spectacular.

Tilly saw Suzie stand and turn to face the back of the room.

"Get out! Get out!" Suzie's face now looked like the screaming infant's, red and swollen with fear. "Leave us alone! Why are you doing this?" She looked as if she was starting to collapse, but she dropped to her knees in front of her father.

"You need to go, Dad," she begged him, unheard. "Get out. You have to get *out* of here!"

Her father didn't move. His thread still spiraled pulsing color to the haze above.

Tilly and Matthew moved toward Suzie.

"Daddy, *pleeese!*"

And suddenly her father looked right at her.

"*Daddy?*"

He blinked then put his hand to his forehead and rubbed it, gently shaking his head.

"Daddy? Can you hear me?" She leaned closer to him. "Can you *see* me?"

Tilly looked at Sorg. It was thicker, opaque. Its vibration made a steady hum as its tendrils continued feeding. A new tendril appeared, expanded, hovered over more pews.

Some of the mourners stood. They excused themselves as they pushed past those seated beside them and started down the aisle towards the door.

"You have to go, Daddy!"

"Oh, Suzie," he muttered.

"Yes, Daddy, I'm right here." She stood up. "Come with me."

"I'm so glad you're not here."

Tilly saw Suzie's body sink. She looked heavy, leaden. Defeated.

The humming that had begun with Sorg's appearance now became so loud that Tilly instinctively put her hands over her ears. There seemed to be no way to dull it. The room grew darker, and she was no longer sure if the dimming was only something the dead could see. It didn't matter either way—everyone needed to get out before Sorg sucked them clean.

"Keep trying, Suzie!" Tilly didn't know what else to say. She was grasping and she knew it. How would they get everyone out?

"Daddy," Tilly heard Suzie say, but she didn't look over until she heard Suzie's father begin to choke and splutter.

"Suzie, don't," she yelled; but it was too late. Suzie's father had thrown up on the floor between his feet. Suzie was taking her arm from around her father and had a horrified look on her face.

"It's all right," Tilly told the girl. "He'll be OK—just don't touch him again."

"I didn't mean to...." Suzie looked at her father. "I'm so sorry, Daddy."

"Just don't touch...." And suddenly it became obvious to Tilly how to get the mourners out of danger. It was horrible to do, but it had to be done. "Wait a minute!" she said, "Touch *everyone!*"

"What?" Suzie asked.

"Touch as many people as you can," Matthew repeated. He seemed to know where this was heading. "It doesn't have to be everyone." He sprinted to the other side of the church and started touching every third person who immediately began to retch and bend to vomit.

When the minister saw what was happening, he started to speak a little faster. He continued speaking as most of the mourner hurried down the aisle and left the building.

Once outside, people seemed to get control of themselves again. Tilly's little group looked around, but there was no sign of Sorg.

"I'm so sorry we had to do that, Suzie," Tilly said. "I didn't know what else to do."

"It's all right, Tilly. It worked!" She sat on the edge of the step, her father at the bottom, white-faced and leaning against the railing.

The pallbearers slowly slid the coffin into the hearse and closed the door. The minister announced that in light of what had just happened, perhaps only immediate family should proceed to the cemetery. He looked ruefully back at his church that now would need a lot of cleaning.

"Should I go in the car with my dad?" Suzie asked the others.

"It's up to you," Matthew said. His statement reminded Tilly of the day she and Matthew had sat on the funeral home's steps. How he quietly encouraged her, not pushing her to do anything, but at the same time seeming to know it was exactly what she had to do. "Would it make you feel better?"

Tilly appreciated his tact.

Suzie was hugging herself. "I think I will....You guys will be there, right?"

"Of course," Matthew said.

Tilly nodded.

Suzie watched the sky as the young minister spoke. Tilly only half listened, focusing her attention on the crowd, and praying Sorg wouldn't reappear. An arrangement of red, pink, and white roses lay on Suzie's mother's casket. She watched Suzie stand next to her father, both lost in their own worlds, grieving in their own separate ways for the woman they had lost, but unable to comfort one another.

She watched as family members walked up to place a flower on the casket, touch Suzie's father's arm or shoulder, then retreat to their vehicles, until eventually it was just Suzie and her father left. Tilly waited, giving Suzie a moment with her father. When he stepped towards the casket, Tilly went to Suzie's side. They both turned away as he knelt in front of it.

"I wish I knew what to say to you," Tilly said.

Suzie's father stood up, wiped his eyes, and started towards his car.

"I have to go with him," Suzie said.

"Of course."

CHAPTER 49

At home again, Tilly watched her father make supper for himself and Nathan. Her brother watched silently from one of the bar stools while Tilly pretended to still be a physical part of the family. As her father stirred pasta, she and Nathan shot each other looks behind his back.

"It's almost ready. Got the table set, Buddy?" her father asked without turning from the stove.

"All set."

Her dad moved from the stove to the sink and drained the macaroni.

"You're pretty quiet tonight," he said as he dumped on powdered cheese and stirred it in.

"I guess."

She watched as her father scooped the orange pasta into two bowls and brought them to the island. He placed one in front of Nathan and the other in front of him as he slid into his chair.

"So, what's on your mind?"

"I want to hold a memorial," Nathan stated.

"That's a good idea, buddy. We could do it in the backyard—"

"No. I want it to be *big*. I want it to be for *all* the murdered kids, or even anyone else who's died."

"Oh?" Tilly's dad's hand stopped, and he put his arm on the counter, a few elbows of macaroni falling back into the bowl from his fork. Surprise was in his voice. "I have a feeling you aren't thinking of our backyard then."

"No. I want to have it at the park. We'll have a ceremony, but we could have face painting and a barbeque and maybe even a band."

"Whoa, whoa! That's pretty big. You sound like you're planning a fair, not a memorial for your sister."

"I told you, Dad, it's not just for Tilly."

"I don't know about all this, maybe you should scale it back a bit."

"NO!"

His father lowered his hand and let his fork drop into the bowl. He wiped his hands on his napkin then tossed it down onto the counter.

"I understand you've been through a lot." He set his elbows on the counter and wrapped his hands together. "I thank God that nothing happened to you when you sneaked off like you did." Tilly could see he was choosing his words carefully. "It was incredibly dangerous, and we've talked about that." And now he was fighting anger. "I am grateful for what you did, but you can't keep doing this. You can't keep trying to make it up to Tilly. You have nothing to make up *for*. You can't bring her back."

He paused for a second. "I think it's time you let this thing with your sister go. It will only keep upsetting you unless you deal with it by just letting go."

"I know you still don't believe me, but Tilly was *here!*" Nathan was fighting his own emotions. "And I can't let go, not yet, not until we do a memorial barbeque. And it's so *everyone* can let it go. I don't want people to think of *him* when they think of Tilly." He squirmed in his seat.

Tilly's dad was silent, looking down at his food.

Nathan continued. "It's not just about me. Or Tilly. People need to be remembered for how they lived, not how they died, and we should be able to talk about them without feeling like we have to be sad, or worried that we might upset someone by talking about them. I want to *talk* about Tilly. I don't want to have to act like saying her name is a bad thing."

His father leaned into his hands, slowly bumping them against his lips. He sighed and pushed his food away.

"I'm tired, Nathan. Maybe we should go to bed."

"But, Dad."

"No, you should go now." He stood up and removed Nathan's half-full bowl from the counter. "Go."

Nathan slid off his stool and went to his room.

"I don't think he's going to let me do this," he told Tilly when they reached his room.

We'll figure something out, Nathan. Maybe Dad is right. Maybe you should stop this. Leave it up to us." She felt her heart breaking for him. "At least sleep on it."

Nathan turned on his special lamp and lay on top of the covers.

Tilly watched Nathan's eyes follow the faint stars gliding across the walls. It would be a few more hours until dark, but she watched Nathan's lids slowly start to lower.

When she was sure he was asleep, she took the throw off the chair and placed it over him, then headed downstairs to find her father.

She found her dad sitting in the living room. He had one arm across his stomach, with the elbow of the other one resting on it, a finger rubbing his forehead. The TV was off, and there was an untouched cup of coffee beside him.

He exhaled a long, deep breath.

Tilly moved to the chair beside his. She nestled into the corner of it, pulling her legs up to her chest. She wished she could hug him.

"Oh, Tilly," he mumbled.

She dropped her feet to the floor, leaned forward.

"I don't know what to do." His hands were cupped in front of his mouth.

"Just let him do it, Dad," she answered him, knowing he couldn't hear her.

"He can't keep going on like this." He lowered his face into his hands. "I can't keep going on like this."

"Please. Dad. You have to let him do this." She begged her father. Wishing he could hear her.

"What is he thinking? A barbeque? For the whole community?"

"It's not just *a* barbeque, Dad! You gotta *hear* me."

"What if we do it and it fails? What if no one comes?" He lifted his face from his hands. "It will crush him." He ran his hands up his face and through his hair, leaving them on top of his head. "How can I let that happen?"

"People will come, Dad, I believe they will." She leaned closer to her father. "He can handle it, whatever happens, he can handle it. He's *tough*." Tilly finally knew Nathan would be fine. She saw that, and she needed her father to see that now. For Nathan. And for himself.

"I'll just have to tell him no." He slapped his hands on his legs. "He'll have to deal with it."

"Please, Dad, don't say no!" Tilly dropped to the floor in front of him. She knelt at his feet. "We have to do this. You have to let him."

Her father stood up. Tilly shifted to the side. He picked up his untouched coffee and walked to the dining room. He stood at the patio doors. He took a drink of the cold coffee as he looked out into the backyard.

"He says it's for you, Tilly, but he needs to stop obsessing." He shifted the mug to the other hand.

"No, Dad, please."

"I just wish I knew what to do. I wish someone would give me answers."

"You have to do it, Dad, you have to let him." Tilly could feel herself becoming desperate. She knew that if they didn't do this, then Sorg would win and more people would die. Her mother would die. "Please, Dad. You need to believe in him."

"He isn't the only one who misses you, Tilly. I miss you too!"

She saw her father's nose redden, just like hers did when she was starting to cry.

"I'm right here, Dad." She stepped closer to him. "I'm right here and I am trying to give you the answers." She stood beside him. She saw tears overflow and run down her dad's face. It ripped her heart out to see him cry. She couldn't watch any more. "DO IT!" she yelled. "PLEASE!"

Both Tilly and her father spun around at the sound of glass cracking.

"What the...?" her father said, setting his coffee cup on the desk. He bent down to pick up a picture frame lying on the floor.

Tilly watched as he turned it over. It was the picture of her, zip-lining on their last vacation.

He stood, smiled, then started to laugh. But the laughter quickly turned to sobs. He dropped to the floor, and with his back against the wall, he covered his mouth, trying to muffle his sobs. The frame was on his lap.

Tilly moved to his side. She sat as close as she possibly could without touching him.

"I'm so sorry, Daddy," she said through her sobs. "I've hurt everyone so much. I wish I could go back and change it all."

"Oh, Tilly!"

She wiped her tears. She leaned into his ear.

"I love you so much," she whispered.

Her father's sobs slowed.

"I miss you, and Mom, and Nathan."

His head lifted but he stared straight ahead, half tilted.

"Tilly?"

She gasped. Did he hear her?

"Dad?"

He turned his head further, his eyes towards the floor.

"Tilly."

"Yes." A gulp of air followed.

"What do I do? Tell me what I need to do."

"You need to let him do this," she whispered. She prayed for him to hear her. "You need to *help* him do this." Louder this time.

He sat without moving, Tilly couldn't tell how long.

She wanted to repeat it over and over, but stayed silent.

When he still wouldn't move, she reached out and put her hand over his, hovering. She could feel little tingles and wondered if he could as well. She was ready to pull back if he started to react. She could see his mouth moving but couldn't make out any sound. She stilled herself, remembering her funeral, the mourners, and how she could hear their thoughts. She strained to hear her father's.

You are right.

Tilly snapped back to her thoughts. She pulled her hand away.

Her father stood up slowly. He picked out the few shards of glass that were left in the frame and set them on the table. He placed the glassless photo back on the shelf.

You are right, Tilly. "He needs to do this."

CHAPTER 50

When Nathan came down for breakfast, his dad had a stack of pancakes ready for him.

"Hop up," his father said, patting the bar stool.

Nathan climbed up, ignoring the food and watched his dad return to the stove. Tilly came over, leaned on the counter and smiled at Nathan.

Still cooking at the stove, Nathan's dad said, "I made a few phone calls last night to see if we could book the park for your barbeque."

"You did?" Nathan's smile spread from ear to ear.

"I had no idea if you could even book a park, and it turns out you can't." He flipped the last of the pancakes then came to the counter. "Seems you have to get a *permit* to have an event." He poured orange juice into both their glasses. "I called your coach, and he gave me the number of the park administrator—and the park's yours! I'll have to go in to fill out some paperwork and he's going to make some calls tomorrow, but basically you just have to pick a date." He slid a sheet of paper with a barely legible list of dates next to Nathan's plate.

"Did you hear that Tilly? He said OK."

"Nathan," she scolded him.

"Tilly already knows." One by one, their father slid the spatula under the pancakes, stacked them on a plate and set it in front of the empty seat at the counter.

Nathan looked at his dad.

"We had a chat last night." He sat down and poured syrup over the stack.

"You *saw* her?" Nathan looked at Tilly.

She smiled again, not sure what to believe at this point.

"Let's just say she helped me change my mind, and leave it at that," He winked. "Now, eat." He set the syrup down then picked up his knife and fork.

Looking back and forth from Tilly to his father, trying to find some sort of confirmation of their conversation, Nathan scrunched up his nose, trying to ask her again, without repeating his question out loud.

Tilly just shrugged her shoulders playfully and winked.

Nathan couldn't get breakfast into him fast enough. With his last bite still in his mouth, he ran upstairs and started his laptop.

"We've got a lot to do, Tilly!"

He opened a design program and started creating a flyer.

The local print shop made copies of Nathan's flyer for free. Then he convinced his dad to drive him around the neighborhood and help to staple them to telephone poles and construction-site walls. They dropped them off at stores, tacked them to coffee shop bulletin boards, taped them up in apartment-building lobbies and any office building that'd let them in. His father called the newspaper, and they told him they would place an ad for the event free of charge. The local radio station offered the same.

They recruited the help of the Badgers ball team to spread the word. Nathan gave them a bundle of flyers to pass out.

Sunday, August 23
Winslow Park
2:00 P.M.
Bar-B-Q, Face Painting, Games & Balloon Release
Come to celebrate the lives of lost loved ones.
In memory of the lives of
Tilly, Matthew, Suzie, Joel & Kaylin
&
Loved ones you have lost.

Everyone was excited. Now they had something positive focus their energies on.

CHAPTER 51

Today was the day, ready or not. The Badgers, Joel, and Nathan were setting up picnic tables with bright, neon-colored tablecloths donated by a local fabric shop. Tilly watched as the ball players competed with each other, snapping each cloth out in front of them, then letting it float gently down onto the table, to see who could do it in one fluid movement. Then they placed a mason jar in the middle of the table with strips of paper and five colored markers.

Tilly's father, who had recruited some of his friends to help with the cooking, were setting up the barbeques while Nathan put up easels for posters. He had made a poster for Tilly with pictures from some of their vacations and her last school photo. There was also a picture of Tilly being wrapped in toilet paper from when he had wanted her to be a mummy to go with his vampire for Halloween. He had used five rolls to get her just right. Another photo showed Nathan holding a birthday cake and Tilly crouching down next to him, her smile the center of attention instead of his cake. It was his eighth birthday. It was his favorite photo.

She watched as he propped his poster on the easel and hoped that others would fill the other easels. she noticed that a bouncy castle was being inflated, and the face painting station was all set with several local artists who had volunteered within minutes of the radio announcement.

It was ten o'clock and everything was going as planned. The only thing left was for people to come. For Suzie and her dad to come. When Tilly and Matthew went to check on them at Suzie's, they found that not everything was going according to plan after all.

"He just sits there," Suzie said, staring at her father. "It was bad enough to watch him before, but now it's horrible." Suzie seemed so small curled up in a chair, feet tucked under her, arms wrapped around herself, her loud voice now barely the squeak of a mouse. "I don't know what I'm supposed to do!"

"He has to come to the barbeque." Matthew tried to keep his voice soft. Suzie seemed like a spooked animal since her mother had died. You didn't know how she was going to react.

"How am I supposed to do that?" she asked. "How am I supposed to tell him he needs to go to a celebration of life when we just buried Mom?" She looked from Matthew to Tilly. "Besides, I can tell him until I'm blue in the face, but he can't *hear* me." She looked back at her father. "He is a hero. He's flown to the moon but…"

She trembled, her pain obvious. Tilly moved to her side. She thought of her father and wondered how he must feel. Tilly placed her hands on Suzie's arms. Tilly felt a snap of an electric shock, stronger than usual, but resisted pulling her arm away. It turned to tingling.

Suzie's sobs slowed as she took deep breaths. "How can I help him?" Tilly could feel the tingling in her fingers lessen. Tilly could swear that she felt Suzie fade, just for a split second, like a radio station losing its signal. She wanted to ask her if she was all right, but she knew how ridiculous that would sound, and couldn't figure out how to word the question any differently. Tilly looked at Matthew and saw concern on his face, but she couldn't tell what he was thinking.

She felt it again. She was sure of it this time. Suzie had *dimmed*. Suzie was losing hope. What would happen to her? Could Sorg feed off her as well? Or would her energy just fade away with grief? Is that what would happen to all of them if they didn't move on from whatever grief they were feeling? Tilly needed to get help.

"Matthew." She nodded to the corner of the room and joined him there. She looked at him and then at Suzie, who never looked up. "I have to go."

When Tilly arrived at the park, she was surprised at how many people were there. The games had started, and kids were jumping in the bouncy castle and having their faces painted. Kaylin was watching a young man and woman do some magic tricks.

Someone had brought a sound system, and a blend of hip-hop and remixed eighties music filled the air, making the celebration feel even more festive. A group of local high school students were weaving patio lights through the fence and the branches of the surrounding maple trees.

Tilly found Nathan pouring soft drinks. So different from the quiet, withdrawn boy he used to be, today he was smiling and chatting to everyone. He seemed so grown up.

"This might work." Tilly forced a half smile, wanting to believe in Nathan's vision—but they needed Suzie and her father here, too.

"Positive thinking!" Nathan said, reading Tilly's face, and not caring who could hear him. He smiled at her.

More people were showing up. Even most local businesses had decided to close early. Crushed by the string of murders, the local community had caught the spirit of the moment.

"Suzie's with her dad, I don't know if they'll come," she told Nathan. "Matthew stayed with her."

"Did you see the posters?" Nathan was saying to a woman as he handed her a drink.

"What?" Tilly said.

He glanced at his sister and then smiled at the woman as she turned to walk away.

"Did you hear me?"

"Okay." Nathan stepped back from the table. "Vincent, can you take over? I'm going to go check on the posters." It was one thing to say a few seemingly random things into the air in front of someone, but to have a conversation with yourself was another. Vincent slid into the newly empty spot and grabbed another can from the cooler for the next person while Nathan wove his way to the easels, Tilly following.

There were at least a dozen posters propped up on the easels.

"There're so many!" Tilly was in awe, for a moment forgetting why she'd come back to Nathan.

"People made up posters for their loved ones just like we wanted them to. Isn't it great?" He was actually grinning.

"I love my poster, Nathan!" she said when they arrived at them. There were photos of things she had forgotten, like sitting on the couch when she was five years old with Zeus the Moose, her favorite stuffed animal—and another of her diving off the high platform at the pool.

"Dad and I made the poster, Tilly."

"It's amazing." She couldn't stop looking at it. She felt her heart swell.

"And Joel's is over here." Nathan pointed to the next easel. "And Matthew's is over there," continuing to point. He shuffled past her. "And this is Suzie's. I think she'll like it—it has her horse."

When Tilly saw Suzie's poster, she knew Nathan was right. Suzie would love it. Right in the middle of it was a picture of her holding up a trophy with a golden horse on top and a huge ribbon clipped to her horse's bridle. The other photos were of her winning a variety of events like swimming and dance, but seeing pictures with Suzie and her parents standing in front of the Eiffel Tower or the Statue of Liberty made Tilly's heart sink. Suzie had lost so much. Who could blame her for not wanting to come?

"Who made it?" Tilly asked him.

"I don't know. It was just here."

"And Kaylin's?" Tilly asked. She followed Nathan.

When she looked at Kaylin's, she was reminded of how young the girl was. Her hair was in pigtails in her school photo. And the rest were of her and her sister playing or making silly faces for the camera.

"One, two, three, testing, testing!" A voice boomed through the park.

They turned around.

"Testing, testing."

A man was standing on a small platform, a podium in front of him. Tilly realized it was Principal Mullen from her school.

"I'd like to thank everyone for coming out today."

People slowly stopped talking and gathered around him.

"It's a beautiful day and everyone has done a wonderful job organizing this event."

The crowd clapped.

"You all know what today is about. We have suffered some tragic losses over the last few months." He paused. "But today isn't about the loss of our loved ones, it's about what our loved ones *mean* to us. Each and every one of us was touched by at least one of these people and our lives were changed because of it."

Nathan and Tilly walked towards the podium.

Poor Mr. Williams, burying his wife yesterday." She heard a woman say. "And so soon after his daughter's death."

"His wife died of a broken heart they say," another answered.

"There is a rumor that the Coffey kid killed Suzie, too."

"No. Her death was an accident, with her horse."

"Was it?"

"You can't just make stuff up like that!"

"Whatever."

Tilly looked at Nathan. He didn't say anything.

"Anyway, I'm not up here to give any speeches—so, enough from me." But Principal Mullen continued at the microphone.

The crowd laughed at his small joke since he obviously wasn't finished.

"I just wanted to say that if anyone has any stories they'd like to share, feel free to come up and do it. I'm sure we'd all love to hear the stories. The mic is open."

No one moved.

"Also, the food is ready, and we will be letting the balloons go at exactly five PM; make sure you've picked yours up and be sure to fill out a wish." He opened his arms. "Enjoy!"

As he stepped down, the crowd around the podium slowly dispersed. No one was ready to be the first one up.

Tilly looked around. She watched the faces of the people around her. Listening to them. Feeling them.

"Did you hear what happened at the church?" It was a man Tilly didn't recognize.

"I know, it was awful," another added.

Tilly could feel the air getting heavier, the festival feel was slipping away. Just as at her funeral, Tilly began to hear random thoughts from those around her.

I'm not sure why I even came here today.

What was Mr. Anderson thinking letting his boy get involved with this, after everything he'd been through?

I wonder if there are more kids dead somewhere.

"Nathan, we need to get Suzie and her dad here or I don't think this is going to work."

Those poor kids, their families destroyed, and someone thinks a party will help?

Tilly felt her chest getting heavy, her fingers started to itch.

"Oh, man! I think it's coming," she said. "I can feel it."

The duo looked to the sky.

From a distance it looked like a rain cloud, but they knew better. It slowly moved closer to the field in the park, changing shape and color as it did. Tilly could feel the air change.

"Do you think the change in mood is attracting it or is Sorg changing everyone?" Tilly asked.

"Who?" Nathan asked.

"I can hear them, can't you?" Tilly looked at her brother.

"No. Hear who?" He looked confused.

"The people around us."

Nathan was quiet. He looked around the crowd. He looked at his sister.

"You can *hear* them?"

"Well, I can't *hear* them. I can *feel* them. I can get an idea of what they are thinking." She paused. "More like the feeling behind what they are thinking."

"So, what do you think it is? Are they attracting that thing or is it changing them?"

"Both." Tilly realized, answering her question.

"It's trying to crush the party," Nathan said.

Kaylin was suddenly beside them. "What's happening?" she asked. "I thought it was working."

"We think it's Suzie's dad," Nathan said. "I think everyone is concentrating on Suzie's mom's funeral and not the festival, in sympathy with her dad's grief."

"He needs to be here, then. They need to see him instead of talking about him; stop focusing on all the grief," Tilly said. "We need to get this back to being a celebration of life, not death."

"What if it's not enough?" Kaylin asked. Tilly realized the girl was right. How could one more person make a difference? How could Suzie's dad change *any* of this? Tilly was feeling defeated, and the party hadn't even started yet. How could a bunch of dead kids fix anything?

"Tilly!"

Nathan's voice snapped her out of her head and back into the park.

"You aren't helping!" He was inches from her face, overpowering her, making her step back.

"It's doing it to you now." He got back into her face. Making her step back again.

"What? What do you mean?"

"That thing. It's in your head and you are letting it steal your power."

"It can't—"

"Yes it can, and it is."

"But I'm dead—"

"That doesn't mean anything." He stepped back and gave Tilly some room. "*You* are energy. *I* am energy." He pointed to the crowd. "*They* are energy. And that's what *it* wants."

"You're saying it'll steal our energy too?" Kaylin asked.

"I don't know if it can steal it, but if your energy starts to weaken, either because of it or because of what you think or feel, then does it need to get stronger? It's already stronger than these people, but that's because *it* believes in *them*, in their power, their energy."

"You aren't making sense,"

"Yes, he is, Tilly." Kaylin spoke up with a wisdom Tilly wouldn't have believed she had. "It's all about energy, or… vibration. Sad, mad, jealous, shame, fear, pity, they are all *low* vibration and that is its food supply. When we doubt ourselves, that is low vibration." She looked at Nathan. He nodded. "How do bullies get their power? They don't have to be stronger than you, they just have to make you feel weaker than they are."

"But it is powerful," Tilly argued.

"Yes, it is, but it doesn't have to use all its energy to defeat us if we defeat ourselves for it. If we weaken ourselves, then it makes it easier for it to just step in and win."

"So, we raise the vibration?" Tilly finally asked.

"Yes, by being happy, grateful, calm, nonjudgmental, loving. That's what Nathan wanted from the start." She looked at Nathan again and he nodded.

"But that still doesn't fix the problem," Tilly said, looking towards the sky. "Sorg is coming, and people are still complaining. How is Suzie's dad going to change that by coming here?"

"I don't know if he can, but we need everyone we can get. We need to get people to forget for just a minute," Nathan said. "We need them to live in the moment, the right now, right here so that maybe we are stronger than it for just long enough to figure out how to defeat it."

"Plus, Suzie's dad is an astronaut," Kaylin added.

The others looked at her.

"I just mean that sometimes adults take other adults more seriously, especially a famous one like her dad. Maybe if he comes, then he can distract them better."

"I'd better go get them then," Tilly said.

CHAPTER 52

When Tilly arrived at Suzie's house, she found her watching her father as he poured himself a drink from a not-entirely-full bottle of bourbon.

"I don't know what to do," Suzie said. "I don't know how to help him." Matthew sat next to her, their shoulders almost touching.

Tilly sat on a chair across from them. This was going to be tougher than she thought. *How are we going to get him out of the house? How are we going to get him to want to come to the barbeque? He can't hear us. Can Suzie make him hear her somehow?*

There was a knock on the door.

Suzie's father ignored it.

"I've never seen him like this." Suzie swallowed. "Even at my funeral, he was so strong."

"Strong for your mom," Tilly said, picturing her own father making dinner for Nathan. Trying to keep it all together.

Another knock.

"Go away," Suzie's father yelled at the door.

"Mr. Williams, I'm Tilly's brother."

"Nathan?" Tilly asked.

"I'm busy. Go back to your party," Suzie's dad yelled, but some of the sharpness left his voice.

"I need to talk to you!"

Tilly watched as Suzie's father got up to walk to the door, turned the handle and let the door swing open behind him as he walked back to the couch. Sitting, he returned to his drink.

"How did you get here?" Tilly asked. "We're across town?" He continued to surprise her.

"One of the Badgers drove me," he mumbled.

"Mr. Williams, I know this is not a good time," Nathan said, sitting at the other end of the couch. "But we need you to come to the park with us."

Suzie's father looked around the room for the *we*.

"Mr. Williams, it's really important."

"Look kid," Williams said gently, "I just buried my wife, and my daughter not long before that. Forgive me if I don't feel like going to a party." He slumped further into the couch.

"But, it's a lot more than a barbeque."

"Yeah, I get it. It's a party to celebrate families. And life. If you haven't noticed, I no longer *have* a family." He waved his hand around the room, a hand still holding his drink. "Or a life."

"But that's the thing, Mr. Williams, that's where you're wrong."

"Wrong?" said Suzie's father.

Nathan had sounded confident when he said, "Listen, you just need to come."

"Please listen!" Suzie shouted at her father.

"I'd like you to leave now, please." Suzie's father stood, pointed to the door.

Nathan braced his feet.

"Suzie wants you there." He stood straight. "And I'm pretty sure your wife would want you there as well."

"Okay, I've had enough of this!" Suzie's father slammed his drink on the table, liquid sloshing.

"Mr. Williams," Nathan said, standing his ground. "You need to listen to me. You need to listen to Suzie."

"I beg your pardon?"

"Mr. Williams," he started again, slowly and softly. "I met your daughter." He stopped. Waited. He looked at Suzie, who looked scared, but smiled and nodded at Nathan.

"Suzie wants you to go. She says you need to go." He looked towards her again for confirmation.

"I don't *need* to go anywhere! And even if you were a friend of my daughter's, she's *dead*, so she can't tell you anything."

"Careful, Nathan," Tilly said, unsure if Mr. Williams was about to cry or to lash out.

"Tell him, Nathan," Suzie said. "He's listening. He's hurt." She looked at her dad. "He would never hurt anyone, and I know he wants to go but he's afraid."

"Afraid of what?" Matthew asked.

"He's scared he won't be able to hold himself together out there. He's afraid of letting me down."

"How do you know that?"

"I just do. I know him." Suzie walked over to her father and stood beside him. "And I can *feel* him."

"Suzie is right here," Nathan said, "and I can see her. And hear her."

"That's enough!" Tilly watched Mr. Williams's lips working, his eyes close, and then he let out one long, shuddering breath..."You need to go."

"You can *feel* him?" Matthew asked.

"Matthew," Tilly said, "Let Nathan talk."

"But—"

"No!" Suzie shouted. "Tell him if he doesn't go, he'll have to dry the dishes."

"What?" Nathan looked at Suzie.

"Just tell him." She pushed forward with her hands.

Nathan dropped his chin to his chest. He took a deep breath then looked straight at Mr. Williams. "If you don't come to the festival, Suzie says you'll have to dry the dishes."

Suzie's father looked as if he had just been slapped. A second later he was angry again. "Get out!" He pointed at the door.

Nathan looked at Suzie.

"Touch him," Matthew told her. He reached out as if to push her. "Just lightly."

"I can't."

"Tell him that our favorite thing to do is to go to the boardwalk by the river and eat ice cream."

Nathan repeated Suzie word for word.

Her father stared at Nathan.

"Tell him my favorite is Holy Cow."

"She says—"

"Tell him if he gives me one scoop of Holy Cow ice cream, then he can have Ba-moo-moo Nut."

"Touch him, Suzie," Matthew repeated.

"Tell him."

"If you can feel him then maybe he can feel you," Mathew blurted.

"But I don't want to make him sick."

"Just lightly. Just lightly touch him when Nathan tells him."

Suzie moved closer and slowly lifted her hand. Barley touching him, she ran her hand up his arm and paused at his shoulder for a moment then moved it towards his heart.

"Tell him."

"Okay. She said if you go to the festival, you can get Ba-moo-moo Nut ice cream." Nathan gave Suzie a sideways glance. "She'll have Holy Cow."

The man didn't move. He didn't speak.

"Daddy?" Suzie started to cry. "Can you hear me?"

"Keep talking, Suzie," Matthew said.

Nathan watched as Mr. Williams started towards him but then turned away with his back to him. Nathan let it sink in; hoping Suzie's words would mean something. Mean enough. When he turned back to Nathan, Mr. Williams was rubbing his right hand on his temple. He lifted his other hand and rubbed the other temple, too.

Nathan jumped when Suzie's father moved again, not sure if he should get out quickly, but Mr. Williams just walked towards the chair beside Nathan and sat on the edge, still rubbing his temples.

"Can she hear me?" He looked at Nathan, his eyes watery.

"Yes, Daddy, yes. I can hear you." Suzie crouched at his feet.

Nathan nodded. "Yes, she can."

"I swear I just felt her." His face was blank. His gaze moved around, as if trying to focus on a thought.

"You did." Nathan stayed still to let him process what he was thinking, what he'd just felt. "She touched you."

"Suzie?" Her father's words were a whisper.

"Yes, Daddy. I'm here." She moved her hand towards his chest again. He gasped and now tears that had welled up began to roll down his cheeks. His hands went to his chest.

"She's in front of you," Nathan pointed to the floor. "She's sitting on the floor."

"Suzie, I've missed you so much. I'm so sorry." He started to cry. "I should have watched out for you better. My job was to protect you. I'm so sorry." He cupped his face with his hands.

"Tell him to go to the barbeque," Suzie said.

"Mr. Williams. You need to come to the barbeque. I know you don't understand all this. I'll try to help you to understand, but Suzie is stuck here, just like Tilly and others. They can't go to wherever is next for them because of Sorg. It's a barrier and a danger that we've named Sorg."

Nathan shot Tilly a look of regret. Her expression matched his.

No one spoke while Mr. Williams wept into his hands. Tilly's thoughts kept returning to the park, afraid of what Sorg was doing, but they couldn't push too hard or they could lose Mr. Williams.

Although it felt like hours, it was only minutes before Suzie's father lifted his head, his eyes red.

"My wife? Mary. Is she here too?"

Nathan shook his head.

"Can Suzie talk to her?"

Nathan shook his head again.

"When you say, *whatever is next for them*, what do you mean?" He shifted in his seat. He appeared open to trying to process what Nathan had said.

"Gently," Tilly reminded him then reprimanded herself; of course Nathan would be gentle: that's who he was. She was the one who stomped around, not always considering what others wanted or needed.

"Suzie was killed by the same man as my sister." He waited to be sure Suzie's father was keeping up. "That man killed at least three others."

"Killed?" Mr. Williams rubbed his hands together. "You believe that?"

Tilly was afraid they had just lost him.

"We think," Nathan paused at his choice of words. "We think that this man was under … a kind of spell from this…some kind of entity that feeds off grief." He watched the man's face. "The more pain and suffering that man could cause, the stronger it made the entity." He waited for questions, or anger, any response.

When Suzie's father didn't speak, Nathan continued. "The entity fed off your wife's grief, and now that your wife has died, it wants *you* next to feed it."

"NATHAN!" Tilly said. He had gone too far.

Suzie's father slowly looked at Nathan. "This entity is now feeding off me?"

"Yes, and off everyone who is sad or grieving. We've called it Sorg Ata just to give it a name."

"Sorg Ata?" Mr. Williams shot to his feet. "Why would you say that?"

"Sir?" His change in mood surprised Nathan.

"Why would you name this," he paused, "this *thing* Sorg Ata?" They couldn't tell what he was thinking but they knew he was angry at them?

No one spoke.

Then he started to laugh. "Suzie. Did *you* name him? Is that where they got *Sorg Ata?*"

Everyone looked at each other.

"You named him after your Uncle Chuck?"

They now laughed with him.

"Let's go get him then." Mr. Williams dumped his drink in the sink and headed for the front door. "Come on, Nathan." He stretched out his arm and gestured the boy towards him. When

Nathan arrived by his side, he set his hand on Nathan's shoulder and guided him out the front door.

And Nathan let him.

CHAPTER 53

The first thing they noticed was how dark it had become. Sorg was no longer like a rain cloud off in the distance; it now hovered over the activities. People lingered in small groups, but some of the parents were beginning to remove their kids from the games.

"What if it's too late?" Kaylin asked the others on their return.

"It's not; people are still here," Nathan said. "We can change this."

Tilly was surprised by the confidence in his voice. She was proud of him. He had grown so much these last few weeks, or maybe it was just that now she was finally seeing who he really was, and that she was the one who had grown. She laughed at herself. *He's the only one who can see* me*, and I finally can see* him.

Nathan smiled at her when he caught her staring.

"Come on," he called to everyone around him. "Let's go." Nathan ran towards the podium.

"Hello," he said as he took the microphone, quietly at first.

No one looked.

"Hello everybody! Can I have your attention, please?"

When the microphone let out an ear-piercing squeal of feedback, people looked towards him.

"I know it's getting late and you're probably starting to wonder why you're here." He looked around the crowd and saw some nods.

"I'm telling you that if you stay, I know the day will get brighter."

No one seemed to agree with him.

"Okay, so how about you stay because a lot of people put a lot of work into this and besides, if you leave now, you'll miss the balloon release." Humor or guilt. Whatever worked.

Some people sat down again on the lawn. Some kids ran over for more free hot dogs.

"There's a storm coming," someone called from the crowd.

"What do we do?" Kaylin asked.

By now, Sorg had settled itself over the gathering, tentacles flicking, skimming people. The wind had picked up, flapping the edges of the bright tablecloths. Then Tilly watched as the obscene cloud started to feed off the people they had worked so hard to gather. Threads of color drifted up from some individuals like the steam off Nathan's mac 'n' cheese, drifting to the outstretched tentacles ready to snatch them. So many colors, all different shades, each person's essence intertwined with the next, creating a breathtaking composition.

A gust of wind knocked some of the easels over, sending their posters scattering. A couple of men ran to get them. A toddler started to cry as a poster blew by, missing him by inches.

Tilly could feel the electricity in the air. Her fingers prickled; her scalp itched.

"Looks like the clouds are going to open up on us," one of the men said. "Better get to cover."

"So, what if it rains?" Nathan spoke into the microphone. "We'll just get a little wet."

People started to gather their belongings. There was a rumble in the air.

"Listen!" His voice was sharp this time. "I need you to listen to me, please."

Some people stopped to listen, but most continued to pack up.

The sky darkened. The wind whipped up again, sending paper plates and empty soda cans bouncing along the ground. Tilly watched as a balloon elephant blew past her. She looked over to the balloon station and saw them packing up, no one in line for any more animals.

"So, what if it rains?" Nathan said, the mic sending more painful feedback.

A man stepped up on the platform and started to move Nathan aside.

"All right, kid, time to shut 'er down." He reached for the microphone. Nathan pushed his arm aside.

"No." He spoke clearly and confidently. "So, what if it rains? So, what if it blows?"

"You won't be saying that once the rain starts hitting this." The man reached for the cord. Once again Nathan blocked him.

"Maybe our sound man is right."

Tilly looked at Nathan.

"Sure, maybe rain isn't the best thing for this mic, but I'm not afraid of getting wet." He looked around as he spoke. "Like my mother always told me, I'm not made of sugar. I won't melt. And she's right. None of us will melt."

The crowd didn't seem to agree—or care.

"Remember when you were a kid? Remember how you felt like a rebel if you stayed out in the rain?"

Some of the people in the crowd stopped and looked at him.

"Remember how it felt, like you had just conquered the world."

"Yeah, man!"

Tilly looked for the voice and saw the pizza delivery guy pumping his fist in the air.

"See, *he* remembers!" Nathan smiled. "We can't let a little rain ruin this evening."

The colored threads feeding Sorg deepened in intensity. Sorg grew wider, thicker. Tilly heard a baby crying.

"We came to celebrate our loved ones." He shifted again as the sound man reached for the cord. "After everything they went through, are you going to let a little rain stop you?"

Tilly was surprised at how his words came out as a condemnation.

"Sure, I wish it was still sunny out, but it's easy to be *happy* when it's *sunny*." He paused. "Nothing about why we're here today is easy. Today isn't about *easy*. It's about life, and right now life sucks. Right now, *easy* is just going home and doing nothing." Another pause. "You can do *easy* tomorrow. Today is about *life!*"

The man trying to shut down the stage stepped back.

People stopped where they were and began to listen.

"My mom is lying in bed, probably dying of grief because of what happened to my sister, Tilly. Remember reading about her in the papers?" He looked over at Tilly. "Suzie's mom was buried yesterday. They say she died of a broken heart when Suzie died." He shifted on his feet. "We don't show someone how much we love them by how long we grieve for them. That's not what they would want. We don't keep memories of those we've loved alive by crying or by visiting gravesites; we keep them alive by talking about them, telling stories about them." He looked for Suzie. "If we don't celebrate them today, when that is what we all came here for, then when will it be? When *can* we celebrate them?"

Then Tilly saw Suzie's father walk out of the crowd to the front of the platform. He smiled up at Nathan.

"Because of a storm, we'll go back and hide in our houses and maybe hide our feelings as well by never saying their names so as to not upset anyone—but I want to say their names *now!*" He stopped.

"Joel," someone yelled from the thinning crowd.

Nathan smiled.

"Kaylin," a little blonde girl called out.

"Tilly," Tilly's father said, speaking only to Nathan.

"Matthew," Nathan said.

"Kaylin's mom," Tilly said. She knew only her friends could hear her, but it was for Kaylin.

And soon, other names were being called out from the remaining crowd of people. Many names. Names of friends and of family, gone, but remembered by those who cared.

"No matter what happens today, we need to remember these people, the people we lost before them—and the people we love who we will lose in the future." Nathan looked at his dad. "Because death does *not* have to kill the *living.*"

CHAPTER 54

Sorg Ata grew dense above the crowd as Nathan spoke and the crowd called out names. Sorg made the air thick. Though the crowd only saw a storm, Tilly and her friends saw more tendrils stretching out beyond Sorg's mass, searching out more energy. Tendrils stretched the length of the crowd, even finding targets on the outskirts.

Tilly's father jumped onto the platform and knelt in front of his son. He wrapped his hands around Nathan's upper arms.

"I am so proud of you!"

"But it's not working!" Nathan answered him quietly.

As the wind picked up and the sky got even darker, people were grabbing corners of the tablecloths and pulling them together, gathering everything that was on the tables. At the barbeques, others tossed food into containers and coolers, trying to save what they could.

Sorg's tentacles worked above the crowd, continually feeding, draining, forcing some of its latest victims to sit where they were as it stole from them even the energy to move.

The ballon station was getting packed into a truck. The tarp covering the pre-filled balloons flapped, threatening to release them prematurely. Someone collected the rest of the strewn posters.

Tilly could feel Nathan's energy ebbing. Her heart broke knowing after everything they had done, she hadn't been able to save his vision, his idea. She crouched down beside him and her father.

"I'm so sorry, Nathan," she told him.

"It's ok, Tilly, you tried. We all tried." He looked from her to his father, then back again.

"Suzie Williams," Suzie's father called out over the PA system. The three looked behind them.

"She is my daughter, and she means the world to me. I could be home and who would blame me—but I'm here. For Suzie. For young Nathan here. And for my wife, who I buried just yesterday."

Some people stopped to listen.

"Even when my wife was pregnant with Suzie, my Suzie was a little firecracker, always wanting things her way." He talked into the mic above the wind that whistled in the speakers. "We spoiled her rotten, but I wouldn't have had it any other way." He looked behind him, smiling at Tilly's family. "One year she decided that she was only going to answer to *Princess Suzanne*. Whenever she saw her name written on anything she'd take a pen and write Princess in front of it."

"Look!" Nathan pointed.

Some of the crowd had stopped and were listening.

But Mr. Williams put the mic into its stand and left the podium.

"Matthew, my son's name is Matthew," came a loud new voice without the mic. The man who had collected the posters stood in front of the platform holding up Matthew's poster as the wind threatened to rip the others from his grip. Suzie's father took them, and handed the mic down to him. "One day I went into the bathroom and there were lines drawn all over the mirror. I asked him why he did it." He climbed up on the platform and took the mic. "He told me he was connecting the dots. I didn't know what he meant until he leaned in closer to the mirror. *See*, he said. And then as his face matched up to the lines he had drawn, I could see the lines went from one freckle to the next."

As a woman joined him, he wiped his face with the back of his hand.

"I'm Matthew's neighbor," she stated. "I don't have any children. I live next door to Matthew, and when he was around four years old, every morning he'd come across the lawn to my house, bright and early, and have breakfast with me. This was shortly after I'd lost Ralph, my husband. I'd ask him if he was hungry, and he'd always answer yes." The woman exchanged smiles with his father. "Well, it seems that as soon as he had finished breakfast at home, he'd head over to my place for breakfast *again*. Apparently, his mother had found out and told him, from now on, to tell me he had already eaten. I let this go on for a few more weeks and when I asked him why he didn't do as his mother told him to do, he replied that he didn't think that I should have to eat breakfast alone since it was the most important meal of the day." Her voice cracked during the last few words.

Tilly, Nathan, and her father walked around to the front of the platform and listened to Matthew's neighbor tell her story. Tilly's unseen friends joined them, including Matthew.

"I didn't realize I was setting myself up when I agreed to this," Matthew said to the others. He pretended to be embarrassed, but the smile on his face gave him away.

There was a thump as one of the folding tables hit a garbage can, knocking it over. Those nearest tried to collect the blowing contents.

Then Principal Mullen got back onto the platform. Matthew's neighbor handed him the microphone. He looked around at the small crowd.

"We may have lost some numbers, but I say after all the hard work that was put into this day, we should start this party all over again. Besides, we have clouds and wind, but so far... no rain!" He raised his hands in the air. "Are you with me?"

"Let's *party*!" a young man answered.

"Let's *eat*," another said. And there was thin laughter from the small crowd.

Principal Mullen motioned to Nathan and returned the mic to him.

"I know this hasn't gone as planned," Nathan said into the mic, "but I promise you that if you stay, it has to get better. So, let's get this party restarted."

"Let's do it!" the pizza guy agreed.

"Why not?" Matthew's dad joined in.

Nathan said, "So, like Matthew's breakfasts, let's eat... again."

Some of the crowd laughed.

Tilly felt the mood shift a little, but they were a long way from safe. The sky was still darkening. A lot of people had retreated to the field house, others had left altogether. But what made her heart sing was that a line had begun to form at the microphone. She watched as the first person, a tall man with wide shoulders wearing a baseball jersey, took the mic and started to speak.

"Cathy was my daughter. You won't remember her. She died in a car accident when she was fifteen. We'd go fishing every weekend once the season started. But Cathy would never put a worm on the hook because she didn't want to hurt the worm." He brushed his grey hair back each time the wind whipped it in his face. "She wore pigtails for two years and wouldn't leave the house until they were perfect. They had to fall in *front* of her ears so that no one could see them—she thought her ears stuck out." He chuckled. "And every year she'd make a carrot cake for her rabbit's birthday."

Cathy's dad handed the mic to the next in line.

Tilly listened as people continued to speak and then followed her brother to the hot dogs.

A man with a slight German accent was speaking. "Every night before we went to bed, my wife and I would say what we were grateful for that day." He was as wide as he was tall with a curly beard that dusted his chest every time he opened his mouth. He owned the corner store where Tilly bought penny candy, the only store that still sold it. "I would always say that I was grateful for *her*. She'd get mad because I'd use the same line every night, and she said that was cheating." He paused. "She died two years ago. I still say this every night before bed."

"Your wife was always happy to see me when I came into your shop," a man shouted from the crowd. "She made me feel like more than just a customer."

"Thank you."

Nathan tried to spread mustard on a hotdog, but a gust of wind splashed it over his hand as soon as it left the bottle. He stuck the tip down inside the bun and dragged it between hot dog and bun getting mustard all over the cap.

But despite all the efforts, Sorg seemed to be growing again. The wind was still picking up. Tilly could see the threads of color slipping from some of the people in the crowd. She watched as an older woman lifted her foot towards the platform. A gust knocked her off balance. She started to fall backward but was caught by those behind her. They helped her up and stayed with her as she spoke.

"Jackson died three years ago. He was thirteen and used to come to my house for piano lessons. He'd always stay for milk and oatmeal raisin cookies afterward. He knew I loved the company more than he loved my cookies."

"Don't know why people put raisins in cookies," Tilly said to no one in particular.

"He didn't realize I knew he was spitting the raisins in his serviette."

Tilly laughed.

The sky drew darker.

"I don't think this is working!" The wind was gusting so strong that Matthew had to yell to be heard.

Tilly looked at the crowd. Their threads of color still streamed upwards. But the threads themselves seemed to be duller.

"Not many people know this," a new woman said. "But when I was young, my older sister died. I have missed her every day of my life, but I stopped crying long ago." She stood proud. Her tight curls pulled back onto a ponytail that bounced with each gust of wind. "I stopped crying because it bothered people. I stopped letting people see me cry because that's what I thought I was supposed to do. I didn't stop crying because I felt better or because I didn't miss her, instead, I cried alone in my room. I cried in the shower. I cried thinking of all the things we'd never get to do together and for the things she would miss out on. Eventually I stopped crying, not because it didn't hurt, but because I started thinking of the cool things she *did* do, the fun things we did together." She paused. Tilly wondered if she had meant to say all of this to a bunch of strangers. "I still cry sometimes, but now I like to imagine she is with me on all my adventures. Because she *is* with me, and I feel her with me. I'm sorry. I don't think I'm saying this very well." She paused again. Everyone seemed to wait for what she would say next.

"I just mean: I miss Cecelia but I am not going to pretend she never existed just to make others happy. I celebrate her every day, in my own way. In ways like this." And she gestured to include the park and the crowd below. She set the microphone down and turned to leave the stage.

Nathan ran to the platform; and without breaking stride, he jumped up and hugged the woman.

"She's right," he yelled. "We can keep them here, the ones we've lost, stuck on earth through the pain and hurt we feel, or we can set them free and share their love and their lives." Nathan looked at his father working his way back towards the platform. "I'm not saying we won't miss them or that it won't hurt like…." Nathan stopped. "There will always be a hole in my heart." He looked at the woman who had spoken and repeated her gesture. "You can't ignore that hole, but don't let it swallow you whole."

A deep rumble made everyone look up.

CHAPTER 55

Tilly and Nathan watched as people looked around after the loud rumble, undecided about what to do. For a few moments, everyone seemed to forget the storm around them. But now the reality of the darkness and wind... well... Tilly's heart sank, and she knew Nathan was feeling it too. Everyone had tried so hard. But Sorg was winning.

The wind whistled through the microphone. The sound covered his voice.

"He's trying to scare you."

Tilly saw her brother's usually stiff posture soften in defeat.

"We can't let him."

Even though no one was hearing his words she had to stop him. She had to stop him from embarrassing himself with stories of evil spirits that no one would believe; but mostly she had to stop him from beating himself up.

She went to her brother and placed her hand over the mic.

As she did, an ear-piercing screech ricocheted through the air making everyone cover their ears with their hands. The amplifiers kept screaming until Tilly realized she was the cause of it. She pulled her arm back and watched people slowly lower their hands as the feedback lessened and then ended.

"Sorry," she said to Nathan.

Nathan gave her a half-hearted smile, an attempt to make her feel better.

They watched as once again people resumed packing. The sky darkening more.

"It's over," said Nathan, his voice barely above a whisper.

"No, it's not! It can't be." Leaning forward, she accidentally set off another round of deafening feedback from the mic. She jumped back quicker this time.

Nathan stepped away from the mic and walked towards the edge of the platform.

"We may as well go too."

"WAIT!"

Tilly and Nathan looked up to see Matthew running towards them.

"Wait! You got it, Tilly."

"Got what?"

"Turn on the lights."

"What?"

"Remember, in Coffey's house?"

"What?"

"You made the windows explode. You made the lightbulbs explode."

"The light bulbs?"

"You were the one who set the house on fire. You made the light bulbs explode. In Coffey's house."

"No, I didn't."

"And now you just set off the microphone."

"Matthew, I have no idea what you want me to do. And I'm too tired to solve riddles."

"Come here." He beckoned to her as he moved toward the edge of the stage. "Come. Come."

Tilly followed. She didn't have the energy to fight him.

"I don't know how you do it. I don't know if it's because you get mad, or scared, but you need to make those lights come on." He pointed to the string of lights hanging from one of the trees.

"Why do you think I can do any of this?"

"I didn't understand it at first," he said. "When I saw it happen at Coffey's, I couldn't understand why the lights exploded. But when they did, it looked like there was a stream of

253

electricity between you and the lightbulbs. Like the zap of a shock when you walk on the carpet then touch something." He took a breath. "But I now realize, you are the big ball of electricity."

She stared at him, as the haze robbed more daylight around them. Tilly saw more people looking to the sky.

"The spark comes from you. You… your energy hit the light bulbs and made them explode. That's what caused the fire. C'mon, Tilly. Use your energy to make these lights come on, but don't bust them."

"What's the point, Matthew? And besides, Nathan can just plug them in."

"Just do it. But try not to bust them this time."

"I wasn't trying to break them *last* time. I was mad. I was scared. I didn't even know I was doing it. And I don't know if I can do it now."

"Just concentrate."

"I don't see any point to all this."

"Please, Tilly. What have you got to lose? Make them as bright as you can."

Tilly jumped off the stage and ran to the string of lights. She reached out to grab it but looked at Matthew and Nathan. When they nodded, she wrapped her hand around the cord and slowly closed her hand around it. And nothing happened.

"Concentrate!"

Tilly focused on her hand. She felt the smooth electrical cord beneath her curled fingers. She imagined herself as a battery and that she was pushing energy into the green plastic. She pictured it going through the plastic coating and sizzling into the wires.

A snap of energy shot through her hand. There was a little blue spark of light as she let go.

"Ow!" She rubbed her hand.

"Nathan," Matthew said, ignoring Tilly. "When I give you the signal, turn on the sound system." He turned to Tilly. "Do it again Tilly."

She continued to rub her hand.

"Don't be such a baby. You're already dead, for Pete's sake. Just *do* it."

Tilly laughed and reached for the cord. She didn't have to imagine anything this time. As soon as she touched it, the lights came on. Their pale light contrasted against the darkening sky. People looked at the lights for a moment but then continued to hurriedly pack their belongings.

"Make them brighter."

She squeezed tighter.

"Brighter."

She was afraid of breaking them.

Brighter, Tilly."

Instead of squeezing she focused on herself. She closed her eyes and imagined pushing an invisible wave out through her hand.

And the lights brightened.

"Great. Now see if you can make them flash."

Tilly wondered what he would ask for next. She tried to pull back the energy in a rhythm.

"More!"

She pulled back more.

"Perfect! Now keep doing that."

Tilly slowly opened her eyes and watched as she made the bulbs brighten and dim. Yellows, blues, greens and reds repeated themselves over and over not just in the single string of lights, but all around the park. Sorg had made the sky darken but that only made the lights seem to glow brighter, like lights on a Christmas tree.

She looked over to Matthew for his approval. He was looking at Nathan. He nodded to him. Nathan turned on the sound system.

"We weren't supposed to do this 'til later but there may not be a later." Matthew left her and Nathan.

The music was barely loud enough to be heard over the wind. She watched Nathan turn the speakers. She thought she heard the sound of a South Asian guitar. She pushed through her memory to find the name of the instrument but came up blank. Instead, a scene of her ninth-grade music classes played out for her. Each month her teacher had invited a band representing a different culture to join the class so the class could explore music beyond what they heard on the radio.

It frustrated Tilly that she was having trouble putting words to the scene. The cotton balls in her mind were returning. Sorg wasn't happy.

She saw Nathan smile and turned to see the cause. It was some of the Badgers, in their uniforms, heading towards them. She reminded herself of her lighting director job as the players spread out in front of the remaining crowd. Each stood with their left knee slightly bent, their hands tucked slightly behind their legs. Some of their toes tapped in time to a musical intro that now played loudly from the speakers.

As a singer began, the uniformed baseball players started to bounce. Each player ran his hand through his hair then snapped it towards the ground, pointing. Then a two-beat bounce, then a shift to the opposite foot, right hand through hair, but this time rolling hands in front of them like a group game of patti-cake.

Tilly smiled, almost forgetting the lights. She squeezed her hand and let go, impossible not to do it to the beat of the music.

Those who remained watched the players and couldn't keep from smiling any more than Tilly could.

The boys hopped a quarter turn to the right and repeated the moves. They did this until they had completed a circle. When the singer hit a high note, five more players joined the group, bouncing to the beat.

The sky darkened. A gust of wind blew dust, cans, and some more plastic cups through the crowd. It broke the spell made by the dancers until Nathan turned up the sound system even more, emphasizing a woman's voice that now joined the song. This seemed to cue more dancers: five girls in baseball uniforms.

Each girl positioned herself between two male players, sliding seamlessly into the choreography.

Tilly recognized the song from a movie she'd seen with Nathan. He studied anything and everything that had to do with baseball after Joel's team had let him join. This particular movie had sparked his interest in cricket too, not that there were many opportunities for cricket around here. She watched as the crowd became mesmerized by the fifteen dancers. Some in the crowd were unconsciously moving to the beat, others quite aware of themselves.

A gust made the string of lights bounce in the branches. Tilly worried the lights might shatter if they banged into each other or a branch, so she concentrated on them. They brightened, but now, somehow, seemed less vibrant. She looked at Nathan, who was looking up. She followed his gaze and saw that the park's overhead lights had come on.

"Tilly," There was concern in Nathan's voice. "Are you doing that?"

She looked at the lights then her hands. The cord for the patio lights was in her hands but the cord wasn't connected to the park's lights. She shook her head.

The sky darkened further as Sorg continued its work on the crowd. But now, the threads seemed to be thinner, less robust.

"Keep trying," she yelled towards Sorg. "The darker you get, the brighter these get." She looked at the lights. "You're making my job easier." The park's lights brightened.

As if in response, another gust shook the branches, making some of the patio lights clink. She instinctively held her breath.

Those dancing were joined by more dancers. While some paired off, others were hoisted up in the air, adding more moves to the routine. As each musical number finished, the next began seamlessly.

When did they plan this? This is so cool.

Tilly looked at the crowd. It seemed to have grown in size. Everyone was now clapping in time to the music. Little kids were mimicking the routine while toddlers just danced, uninhibited.

When the wind picked up again blowing garbage cans over, no one but Tilly noticed. Everyone was absorbed in the performance in front of them.

"No one cares, Sorg!" she yelled to the cloud above them.

And Sorg responded. This time the wind whipped hard at the lights in the trees, smashing some. Tilly concentrated, wrapped both hands around the wires and concentrated. She visualized energy leaving her hands and running along the wires entering each light bulb. She watched as each bulb glowed brighter—even those that had been destroyed.

"You are not going to win!" she shouted to the sky.

But it grew even darker. She saw the tendrils searching. Their once-thick mass that had snatched up energy, pulling up light that had seemed to vibrate as it left, had now become only wispy threads bobbing over the heads of the crowd, as if bouncing with the wind, unable to control their paths.

When the wind gust again Tilly held the wires tightly. Sorg seemed to be weakening, but something felt different. There was a sense of *fear* in the air, although it wasn't coming from the crowd. Tilly felt a sudden *suffering* that ripped through her so fast and fiercely that she almost dropped to the ground. *Fear, hurt, betrayal,* all swirled around her, burning. She saw faces flash, then quickly disappear in flames. She heard a scream so loud it made her tremble. Then fear turned to the rage of a cornered beast. Tilly felt it pulse through her. And she saw Sorg. Saw it for what it was. No, for what *she* was.

CHAPTER 56

A rumble now vibrated both the air and the ground. Tilly saw people look up, while others look at each other confused; most continued to clap to the beat of the music. She saw Nathan bend over the sound system, checking to see if any more volume was possible. Kaylin was beside him, bouncing with the music. Tilly watched people returning to the park, joining the crowd in the increasingly jubilant atmosphere.

Near the stage, the baseball dancers continued to glide, clap, spin and stomp to the beat. Some broke from the group to grab the hands of the nearest spectator, inviting them to join their performance. The newcomers mirrored the dancers as best they could; but when they couldn't keep up, they joined the laughter of those who watched them try and fail, and then created their own choreography.

Sorg continued to threaten the party, stripping away bright tablecloths. Papers blew everywhere and the canopy over the barbeque flapped wildly, where Tilly's father fought to try to disassemble it. More bulbs clinked and cracked. A baseball hat blew by.

Despite the growing darkness, Sorg's tentacles flipped around, trying to find a target. They stretched over the crowd, pulling bits of color from the group but were seemingly unable to tap into any one source.

"I think it's working!" Matthew yelled above the noise.

"She's female!"

"Who is? It's going great!"

Sorg was definitely weaker, but Tilly was afraid it wouldn't take much to turn the tables, especially after the rush of hate she had felt.

"Sorg's female." She felt trapped by the wires she was holding to control the lights. She wanted to do more. She wanted to *move*, to take Sorg on, face to face. "You need to tell everyone! She wants revenge."

Matthew looked towards the dark cloud over the group then back at Tilly.

"What does that mean?" He jogged toward her. "How does that change anything?" He looked up at the cloud. "We need to stop her or him or it, or *whatever* it is. Come on." He waved at her to follow as he started towards the others.

"I can't!"

"Yes, you can." He stopped and ran back to her. "You are powerful, Tilly. I know you can keep those lights on. You don't have to hold the wires to do it."

She looked at her hand and then the lights.

"Do it."

She closed her eyes and pictured it in her mind, her hands holding the wires, the electricity running through them and through the wires. She pictured slowly letting go, watching sparks jump from her hands to the green plastic.

"Open your eyes."

She wasn't ready. She had to make sure it would work.

"Tilly. Open your eyes!"

She squinted, slowly lifting her right eyelid a crack.

"For Pete's sake, open your stupid eyes!"

She opened them. And the lights still glowed. Brilliant yellows, blues, reds, and greens.

"It worked!" She threw her hands in the air. "It worked!"

"You're more powerful than you think." But, strangely, what she saw on his face was compassion.

"There's something about you, Tilly. It's different than Joel was, or Suzie, or me."

She stepped back. She looked at the lights then back to Matthew.

"What do you mean? We're all of us dead, aren't we?"

He nodded. "But you can *do* things. You did it at Coffey's house." He pointed to the lights. "And you're doing it here."

"But *you* can do things." Tilly remembered the little boy at the park, now a dimming memory.

"No, I mean you can DO things." He put his hands out, palms up and shook them slightly. "Any of us can make a person sick by touching them or by lifting their hair, but you can manipulate *electricity*."

A snap made them both look at the lights. There was no sign of any of them breaking. The second snap made them look towards the trees. She quickly realized some of the branches were cracking now under the pressure of the wind. She looked at Sorg. She saw *her* tendrils. They weren't hovering over their intended victims the way they used to, but now seemed to grab at people. She saw one attach itself to a middle-aged woman, like the suction of a leech. Colored threads pulsed from the woman, and Tilly could see the woman's expression change quickly, her posture starting to slump. Tilly couldn't just stand here and watch: if Matthew was right, she had to *do* something!

As she neared the woman, she could feel the victim's energy drain away toward Sorg. It was almost like watching the fuel gauge on one of Nathan's racecar video games. Not knowing what else to do, Tilly wrapped her arms around the woman, trying hard not to touch her. She imagined she was a blanket, a bulletproof vest being draped around the woman, protecting her.

Tilly felt a dozen needles pricking her back: Sorg's tendrils still sucking the woman's energy. Tilly dug in deeper and focused on being a shield, Matthew's words in her head: *You can control electricity*. Tilly felt Sorg's energy trying to get past hers. She felt a probe searching for a weak spot. She also felt a wave of grief that almost overwhelmed her. She fought it. She felt the blast of grief curl and twist into anger, then rage. Tilly felt sick to her stomach. Her thoughts dulled; she couldn't focus. A blast of *hate* blinded her. Tilly felt the woman she was shielding lurch forward, so she stepped back, afraid she had hurt her. She waited for the woman to be sick.

But she wasn't. Instead, the woman stood taller. And Tilly's eyes opened in surprise as she watched the woman head towards the crowd to join the fun again.

Tilly looked at her hands.

"See?" Matthew said, suddenly at her side.

"She's female!" Her excitement made her shout this in his face.

"What?" Matthew looked to the woman as she disappeared into the crowd. "Her?"

"NO, *Sorg!*" She could hardly form the words. "Sorg Ata is female."

"You told me that already, Tilly!"

Tilly withdrew to her thoughts, trying to put them into words as she went, walking as she did, leaving Matthew to try to keep up. "She is female. She's angry. She's hurt. Betrayed." Tilly turned back to Matthew. "She is very angry, like *revenge* angry."

Matthew listened, not knowing what to say.

"I don't know if she means to be killing. But it's just like you said before: a parasite needs a host to live, but often ends up killing its host." She trailed off. Matthew still stayed quiet. "She is hurt and needs to feed from the pain of others to survive, but she kills in the end."

"Don't we already know this?"

"Yes, but she does this driven by that pain inside her, not just to feed. She is trying to heal herself."

"From what?"

"I don't know." Tilly looked around the park. "When she touched me, I saw kids' faces, and a man… and fire. There were flames. She was burned. I felt the flames." But as she looked around now, she saw Sorg's tendrils still seeking out new energy, but now in a crowd feeling joy, not the pain of grief. Her gaze shifted to Matthew. "I blocked that woman!" Listening to herself say this made her feel excited and strange "I blocked her from Sorg—and it worked. Maybe you can too."

"I can't, Tilly. I'm not like you."

"How do you know? I didn't know I could. Come on. We have to try."

She followed one of Sorg's tentacles to an old man standing all by himself, apart from the crowd of dancers. He looked lonely.

"Do it, Matthew." She pointed to the man.

"*You* have to."

"No, I can't get everyone. Just try."

He stepped up to the man. He looked at Tilly and she gave him a nod. He slowly lifted his arms, careful not to touch the man.

"Imagine you are wrapping him in a blanket," she told him.

She watched him close his eyes as he mimed wrapping the man. She looked to the tentacle above him. It wasn't changing.

"I told you." He dropped his arms. "Nothing."

"Do it again." She thought of the patio lights. She stepped behind Matthew and jabbed at the meat of his upper arms when he didn't raise them. "Do it!"

"Fine."

She was sure he was rolling his eyes. She placed her hands on the back of his and slowly raised hers with him, careful not to put pressure on them to touch the man. She pictured her energy entering Matthew's skin and into his muscles. She focused on love, how much she loved her family, how much they loved her. She visualized her energy running through Matthew's arms and out his hands, sparks of electricity flickering from his fingertips.

"Wow!" His voice was full of amazement.

"Picture that energy wrapping around him," she whispered in his ear.

"This is so cool." She could feel his body trembling.

"Pay attention and be careful."

She carefully pulled her arms away from his, then dropped them to her side. She stepped back and watched.

Small sparks jumped from his fingertips to the man. She was surprised how much it reminded her of Sorg's tendrils, except Matthew's were so white they were blue at times. Matthew's face lit up like his sparks. He watched them jump the small space between him and the old man.

"Are you seeing this, Tilly?" He didn't take his eyes off the scene in front of him.

"Yes, Matt, I'm seeing it!" She was excited for him. She was excited about what this meant. Who knew they had it in them all along?

"We have to tell the others." He slowly dropped his hands and stepped away from the man. He watched the old man's posture improve and the deep lines on his face soften. Sorg's tentacle pulled away. It slowly retracted into the dark cloud. "You have to help the others to do this, too."

Matthew's words stung a little. They reminded her of Joel. She had gotten used to her small circle, used to them having each other's backs. She refused to think of what this would have been like without them. They had been there for Suzie, but Joel's absence was a huge hole. No one wanted to talk about it, but she knew they all felt it.

"Tilly?" Matthew's smile slowly faded as he watched her. "Tilly?" His eyebrows started to press together, creating small creases just above his nose. "What is it?"

"It's okay," she started to answer then realized if she didn't talk about Joel then he was truly gone. "It's Joel."

"What do you mean?"

"It's just that I know he would have loved to run around hugging everyone."

Matthew laughed. "You are so right. I can see it now. He'd run around acting like a superhero, and probably even give himself a silly name as he did."

Tilly smiled, then laughed.

"Come on then, let's do it," Matthew said, and trotted across the field, looking back to make sure Tilly followed before he went too far.

As Tilly and Matthew explained to the others what they had done, the wind, which had fallen off, picked up again. A gust made the lights jerk up and down, some banging against the tree, shattering. Tilly saw people look over at the broken lights. She stopped and stood still. With her eyes closed and her arms against her sides, she concentrated on the broken lights. She spread her fingers apart and started to hum. As her face slowly tilted towards the sky, the broken bulbs started to glow.

The sky tried to darken, so she focused on the park's lights, counterbalancing Sorg's darkness with her newly discovered light.

The crowd turned back to the dancers. And more joined them.

"Matthew, you show Suzie and Kaylin." When he looked at her with hesitation, she said, "You got this."

Mathew found Kaylin, and she watched him closely as he recreated what Tilly had shown him. Suzie saw what they were doing and came over to join them.

As they worked their way around the crowd, wrapping Sorg's victims in love, the wind seemed to die down a little. Tilly began to think that they were winning when she saw Sorg's dark mass compress itself and darken further. Now, green tendrils again stretched from her, down to the crowd itself. Once again, ominous tendrils wove through the crowd, looking for something—someone—to attach to. When a tendril found someone vulnerable, it pulsed as its victim bent over, clutching their stomach. Tilly ran to the closest thread and wrapped herself around Sorg's victim. The tendril retreated for a moment then went in pursuit of another victim.

"There're too many," Tilly shouted to the others.

As the lights started to dim again, Tilly stopped and stared at the crowd. There were so many people to cover. With only four of them, how could they keep up? Sorg had them outnumbered.

"We can do it." Tilly looked over to see Matthew staring at her from across the field. "We *can*." He smiled at her. She felt a sting behind her eyes. She could feel tears building. He had such faith in her. She wanted to make him happy, she wanted him to be right, but she didn't believe in herself as much as he seemed to.

She looked at Sorg's awful tendrils moving through the crowd, her friends hugging strangers.

When she felt cold taps all over her, she instinctively looked around. There was nothing there, but she saw dots on the ground. With a sinking heart, she realized that it was finally starting to rain. It couldn't be! They were losing. She watched as drops slowly started to change the color of everything around her, the wetness making it darker.

She looked at Nathan. He was still working the crowd. He was working so hard, and all she could think of was how she was going to let him down. He must have sensed her, because he turned around and looked back at her.

The wind picked up again, blowing debris across the grass. Papers caught in the lights and branches and blew against the legs of the still-dancing crowd. She saw the lights dim.

She looked at Nathan again, He was still watching her. He smiled and she realized how much she loved him. She loved him so much that she'd do anything to protect him; she knew that now more than ever. He waved. She could feel that love so strong it was as if he took it out of himself and placed it directly inside her. She could feel her face getting wet and knew it wasn't the rain.

She smiled back at Nathan. She was stunned to see a thread leave her and shoot towards him. It wasn't ugly like Sorg's threads: it was like a wisp of white she'd seen come from Matthew a few minutes before, like the flow of sparkles that follows a magic wand. The second before that thread hit Nathan, she was terrified by what she had done—but the moment it touched him, it burst like chrysanthemum fireworks, her favorite. The light went everywhere. Tilly watched as her light lit up the sky and slowly arched its way down over the crowd. She watched Nathan's face as his gaze followed it.

The crowd seemed unaware of the burst of light, but all of Tilly's little group saw it and stopped to watch. Tilly saw the breathtaking shimmering light fall around Sorg. Each time one of the trails of light touched one of Sorg's dark green tendrils, that tendril immediately withdrew and retreated into the haze. As the umbrella of light lowered, Sorg seemed to shrink to escape it.

"Look!" Tilly heard Matthew shout.

They were all watching it now. Sorg's dark green was becoming less opaque. Tilly was surprised to find herself moving to get closer to it. She walked through the crowd until she was directly under what remained of Sorg's darkness. She stood, like she had earlier, arms at her side and face to the sky. She hummed.

She could feel Sorg's sadness so much it was almost overwhelming; but she stayed with it. She felt loss and loneliness. She started to feel Sorg's inner rage, so she raised her arms towards the sky and shut the anger down. She tried to remember how it felt when she looked at Nathan earlier. She focused on her family and her new friends and sent all of that love toward the sky to replace the anger.

Tilly felt quick jabs in her ribs and stomach. Her head felt stuffed with cotton balls again. She shook her head but left her arms up, making herself as tall as she could.

The sky rumbled again.

"Tilly," Matthew called to her. "Are you okay?"

Tilly saw a man's face flash in her head, which brought more jabs. She could feel her body start to shake as it absorbed a flow of hate coming from Sorg. She took a deep breath—and slowly let it out. Her body stopped shaking. She took another breath and let it out, too. The jabs were weaker this time. She took a third breath and held it for the count of five, focusing on her body and the energy she felt when she thought of her family, her new friends—then slowly let her breath out, visualizing it spreading through the air as she did.

And then Tilly heard voices in her head, children's giggles. She kept her eyes closed and listened. The voices started singing a song that Tilly didn't recognize, but she knew it was an old nursery rhyme. She felt herself smile.

By this time, Tilly's little group—and Nathan—had gathered around her to watch the display of light that only they could see.

"What is she doing?" Suzie whispered to Matthew.

"Just leave her," Nathan replied.

Then Tilly heard other voices cut in, teasing, mocking voices, making fun of her. Tilly could feel the mockery, knowing it was Sorg they were making fun of. She was shocked when she realized she felt sympathy for Sorg. She had been a person. Others had made her suffer for their enjoyment. Tilly pushed her love towards Sorg again.

The voices changed back to those of children. Tilly could see them now. Their little faces looking at her, at Sorg. There was a name at the tip of her tongue, but she couldn't quite make it come forward. The children danced around her, then curled up on her lap when she sat down, some playing with her hair. "I love you," the smallest one said as she leaned over and kissed her on the cheek. Tilly's hand went to her cheek.

"Tilly?" Nathan said.

Tilly felt her body soften. It lightened. She felt a wave of love wash over her.

"They love you," she said out loud. "They want you to come and be with them again."

"Tilly," Nathan called again.

"Who is she talking to?" Tilly heard Kaylin asked the group, her voice sounding off in the distance. Tilly brought her attention back to the voices inside Sorg.

"They want you to be happy. You need to go to them," Tilly said to the nameless woman they'd been calling Sorg. She watched the children hold out their hands, waiting to touch her. Tilly reached out her hand, but not her hand, Sorg's hand, and saw one of the children take it, then others place their own hands on top. Tilly felt a surge shoot through her, up her arm into her chest and then out through her feet and the top of her head. She knew she was crying.

"Goodbye," she said then let herself fall to the ground.

"Tilly," Nathan dropped next to her but didn't touch her. "Are you all right?"

After a long silence, Tilly nodded, slowly opening her eyes. She looked up to the sky. It was clear and blue. She looked at the others who huddled around her, concern on all their faces. She smiled to try to let them know she was fine. She looked at Nathan again. He reached out and put his hands on hers without any of the electric shocks that she had come to expect. A wave of exhaustion washed over her, but so did a sense of peace.

"Is Sorg gone?" Kaylin asked.

"I think so." Tilly's voice was barely above a whisper. She felt energy surging through her, but she had to focus to speak. She felt that if she didn't concentrate, she would dissolve into the air around her.

"She's gone for now, at least." Kaylin put her arm around Suzie's shoulders and pulled her close. When Suzie looked at her Tilly smiled. Tilly was surprised by Kaylin's actions. She so often stayed on the sidelines, waiting for permission.

Nathan knelt beside his sister. "You did it." Tilly reached out and touched the side of his face. She felt another surge of energy run through her, running from Nathan then back again. He smiled at her. She started to cry. The love she felt from him was so powerful it made her want to just let go and flow into the world around her.

"*We* did it." She said, ruffling his hair before dropping her hand.

They stood up and Matthew hugged her. Over his shoulder, she could see Nathan and Suzie exchange smiles which made her smile again. *We* did it.

"This is the perfect time for the balloon release," Nathan said. Tilly looked around and saw the dance had ended as the sky cleared, and the exhausted dancers had formed lines at the barbeques again. Her father was at the grill, but keeping an eye on Nathan.

"Let's go, guys." Nathan said, making a sweeping motion with his arm and headed to the podium. When he jumped up on it, the microphone was gone. "Don't forget about your message for the balloons," he yelled.

Suzie's father and Kaylin's sister walked through the crowd, handing out slips of paper and markers to replace the ones that had blown off the tables. Suzie's dad looked up at Nathan as he passed the podium. "Thank you," he said. "Tell her I love her."

"She can hear you," Nathan smiled and looked towards her. "She can hear you." Suzie's father winked, making him look just like Suzie in that moment. "She loves you too."

People lined up slowly, each with their slip of paper. They picked a balloon and tucked their message, wish, or name inside it, then moved over to the filling station.

"Don't let your balloons go until I give the signal!" Nathan yelled from the podium. He jumped down and ran over to the filling station. "Make a circle around the tarp." Nathan stood next to a tarp holding all the prefilled balloons. A man on each side was ready to release them.

"Thank you for coming," Nathan said. "We've all gone through a lot to get us here. I mean..." He seemed at a loss for words. He looked at Tilly. She smiled. "Today doesn't take away our pain or our loss; nothing ever will." He seemed to be finding what he needed to say. "I will always feel like a piece of me is missing, like someone came in and cut a hole in my heart where Tilly used to be." He looked around the circle. "But when I talk about her, that hole seems to get just a little bit smaller. I will talk about her every chance I get, because that's what helps keep her here with me." He placed a hand on his chest. "Tilly is still in my life." He looked at his dad. "And she will always be a part of me." He nodded to the men waiting for their cue. "I love you, Tilly!"

"I love you, too," she called out to him.

Then Nathan let go of his balloon and watched it become surrounded by so many others. They floated up, mingling, bouncing off one another, dancing on the gentle wind, a cloud of love.

"Because death doesn't have to kill the living," he whispered to himself watching the balloons become smaller and smaller as they rose into the sky.

CHAPTER 57

Tilly stood by her mother's hospital bed, looking at all the tubes attached to her, hearing the steady beep-beep-beep of a machine with blinking lights. She was waiting for her mother to wake up. Sorg was gone, so her mother should be waking up. Why wasn't she?

"Don't worry, Tilly. It might take a while," Nathan said, trying to comfort her.

"Tilly's here?" their father asked.

"Yeah, she's worried about Mom."

"Tell her I'm proud of her." His gaze searched the room for her. Tilly could see his love radiate from him like an aura, a glow around his body.

"She can hear you, Dad." Nathan rolled his eyes. Tilly was surprised by this. She smiled. Nathan was definitely becoming a teenager. "And she knows you love her. And she loves you."

They watched the red dot jump up and down across the beeping machine's screen.

Tilly went to her mother's bed. She slowly lifted her hands and placed them a foot above her mother's shoulders. She thought of what she had done at the park, but hesitated.

"It's okay, Tilly," Nathan whispered.

She let her hands drop slightly closer to her mother.

Nathan walked to the other side of the bed and faced her.

She lowered her hands to within a couple of inches above her mom. Then Tilly closed her eyes despite her fears. She envisioned energy flowing through her the way she had done in the park. She felt herself starting to cry. She was scared. Scared she couldn't help her mother, scared she might see something like she had with Sorg. Scared that despite everything she had done, her mother would still die.

"You can do it, Tilly." She heard Nathan say from across the bed.

Images played in her mind: camping trips, waterslide parks, Christmas mornings, shopping trips. She tried to smile but still felt tears.

"I love you, Mom," she told her. "You are the best mom anyone could ask for. I'm sorry if I ever disappointed you."

She felt her mother move. Tilly opened her eyes, but her mother's were still closed.

"You taught me how to be strong and how to be kind. You let me make my own mistakes and stood by me when I tried to fix them, and even when I couldn't." Tilly could see streams of her new-found energy leaving her fingers and soaking into her mother. Tilly's entire body started to tingle. She closed her eyes again. "I wanted to be just like you."

"Tilly…"

"I'm trying, Nathan."

"No, Tilly, look."

She opened her eyes and saw her mother looking right at her.

"Mom?"

"Tilly." Her mother started to cry.

Tilly started to drop her hands to reach out to her mother.

"Don't!" Nathan yelled.

She froze.

"Remember! You can't touch her!"

Tilly's father came towards the bed. Nathan stepped aside. While her father helped her mother sit, she wouldn't break eye contact with Tilly. Nathan propped up the pillows behind her.

"You can see me, Mom?" She was afraid to believe it. "Mom. You can hear me?"

"Yes, Tilly." Her mother had tears streaming down her face.

"But." The thought slammed her brain so hard she felt her knees buckle. She took a small step back trying to regain her balance. "If you can see me—"

"No Tilly." Nathan jumped in when he realized where Tilly was going with this. "She's alive. She's okay. We made her okay. *You* made her okay."

Tilly looked at Nathan then back to her mother. She felt her body start to shake. "She can see me?" She looked back at her mother. "You can see me. You're alive and you can see me." She struggled not to touch her. Instead, she reached out her hand, let it hang just above her mother's stomach. She watched as her mother slowly lifted her hand. She turned it towards Tilly's but didn't let it touch. Little sparks jumped back and forth between them. They tickled.

"I'm so proud of you," her mother said to her. "I love you."

"I love you too." Tilly felt like she could float like one of the stars on Nathan's lamp. "I love you, Mom," she repeated as her mother's eyes started to close. "Don't go."

"She won't be able to see you when she wakes up," Nathan told her.

"How do you know?" Her voice came out sharp, and she felt guilty.

"I just know." He looked at his mother. "Her energy feels different now. It's getting stronger, she's coming back." He looked at their father. "She'll be like Dad when she wakes up."

"But she will wake up, right?"

"Oh yeah."

"Tilly." Matthew's voice broke her thoughts. She turned.

Matthew and Kaylin stood shoulder to shoulder just behind Tilly. And *Joel* was next to Suzie! A woman stood resting her hand on Suzie's shoulder. They all looked like an over-exposed photo; they seemed to glow. It took a moment for Tilly to register what she was seeing.

"Joel!" Tilly shouted. "*Joel?*" She started to question herself. "You're here?" She looked at the others. "He's here! How are you here? I thought you were gone."

Joel's smile made his dark eyes seemed to sparkle.

273

"How are you here? Where did you go?"

"Whoa!" His voice had a chuckle woven within it. "One question at a time."

She decided not to wait for his answer; instead, she went over and hugged him before he knew what was happening. A spark snapped when they touched. Tilly ignored it and squeezed him tighter. She could feel the electricity running up and down her body. She welcomed it.

"I kind of got stuck," he said. "A little like right now." He chuckled again.

Tilly backed off. Alarmed.

"Kidding, Tilly." He pulled her back in for another hug to show her he was all right. "See?" he said as he let her go.

Tilly stepped back to give him space.

"When I tried to shove Coffey, get him off Nathan, I got stuck to him. I tried to break apart, but then it all went dark. I couldn't see any of you anymore."

Tilly tried to follow along, but he wasn't making any sense.

"I don't know where I went," he started again. "It was dark, and I tried to find you guys, but I couldn't. I didn't know how much time was going by since I saw you last. I just kept trying to think my way to you guys and hoped I'd end up with you."

"So, it was dark the whole time?" Tilly asked him. "And you don't know where you were?"

"I somehow got stuck to Sorg, I think."

Tilly sucked in her breath.

"I could feel her pain. I could kinda see her."

"Sorry."

"It was hard to see, and it kept changing, like a dream does. You know how something is happening and then suddenly it has changed, but it makes sense in your dream."

Tilly nodded even though she wasn't sure what he was saying.

"What I could see would blur sometimes or fade out." He paused for a minute. He took in a deep breath. "Sorg was so hurt and angry and in so much pain. Physical pain and emotional pain. I don't even think she *meant* to do all this—she was just in so much pain. She's a broken soul."

"Why? From what?" Tilly asked.

"People were so cruel to her. She's a monster because people made her a monster. She wants to be loved but she's so angry and hurt."

"How? Who did? What people?"

"I can't say what they did. I couldn't see it; I could only feel it. Hear it a bit." Joel must have seen the confusion on Tilly's face. "Like I said, it's like when you're in a dream. It's patches of stuff. And then, somehow, those patches began to show me the crowd in the park. And you guys' part in that."

"Do you know where Sorg is now? Is she gone? Did we kill her?" She cringed when she heard herself say that.

Joel chewed his lip for a moment. "I don't know where she went."

Tilly could see he was upset. "It's not your fault."

"No, no. It's not that." She watched him take a moment to put his thoughts together. "When you guys changed the mood of the crowd, she was angry at first. She wanted everyone to suffer."

"How do you know what we did?"

"Matthew and Suzie filled me in. But as I said, I also saw patches of what was happening through what was happening to Sorg." He looked at each of them. "She was so angry at first, but then as the crowd changed; she started to feel it. You weakened her but you also let her feel...."

Tilly wanted to ask but she forced herself to stay quiet.

"She could feel the love." It was Nathan who spoke this time. "She was able to feel the love we were creating."

"So, we didn't *kill* her? We didn't stop her? We didn't chase her away? She just decided to leave?" She realized her voice had a sense of being cheated in it, disappointment.

"We gave her some peace," Joel answered her. "I don't know if it will last forever, but we helped her feel love instead of hate. We helped her let go of her pain a little. And that's how I was able to break free and come back. That is what lifted the veil between where I was and where you guys were."

"But what if she comes back?"

"I don't think she'll be coming back, Tilly. I can't promise that, but I don't think she will."

"I agree with Joel," Nathan said.

"Why?" Tilly asked him.

"Because, look," he said and pointed to those standing beside Joel.

Tilly looked towards the small group. She finally took note of the woman standing next to Suzie.

"Suzie?"

"Yes." She nodded and looked at the woman. "This is my mom." The woman smiled at Tilly.

"The fact that I can see Suzie's mom and that she and Joel are here is a sign that Sorg's energy has changed. She can't block us anymore." Nathan said.

"Block us?" Tilly said.

"I finally know why I can't see... my imaginary friends anymore." He winked at his sister. "Sorg's energy was messing everything up, messing everyone's energy you could say. Now that she's gone, that energy is free to move around. And Joel and Suzie's mom are part of that." He smiled at the woman.

"That must be Sir Arthur," Kaylin said and pointed at the hospital bed.

Tilly turned to see a large, orange, striped tabby cat curled up at the foot of her mother's bed. She could hear him purring and saw the tiniest twitch of his whiskers.

"Like I said, I can now see my imaginary friends." Nathan smiled.

"I think it's time for us to go," Matthew said. "We seem to have finished what we were supposed to do." His smile was both sympathetic and excited. As he stepped forward, the others seemed to become unfocused, more transparent.

Tilly wanted to stay. Couldn't they take care of it themselves? She couldn't leave their family again. She didn't want to leave them. "Go where?"

"Heaven, if you still want to go."

ACKNOWLEDGMENTS

This debut novel was a significant undertaking, as anyone who has published knows. Many souls traveled with me during this experience and helped shape this story to where it is today. For them, I am forever grateful.

Thank you to my PEI Writes group, Patti L, Michelle H, Kirstin L, and Charity B, as well as Mark B, Tim R, Gilbert L from my weekly writing group, Josh S, Tyler H, and my husband Kim.

A special shout out and thank you to Patti L and Robin C for their support and sharing of their knowledge and insight, and a heartfelt thank you to Charity B for her contribution to the proofreading of this novel.

ABOUT THE AUTHOR

Born in Montreal, Kelly moved to Prince Edward Island as a teen and now calls this beautiful province home. She recently retired as a college instructor to spend more time with her family & friends, and pursue her creative interests in drawing, painting and continue working on her writing.

Share your Through the Haze photos with us

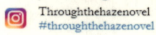
Throughthehazenovel
#throughthehazenovel

Kelly Kieran Sampson, Author

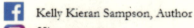
Kieransampson

Manufactured by Amazon.ca
Bolton, ON

39336419R00166